Praise for Stev

Advance Praise for

"*Pitch Dark* is a propulsive, layered
minds you of the terrible violence o.
the heart that must be called upon to endure. A reader can't hope
for more than to discover a writer possessed of both true talent
and true passion. Discover Steven Sidor."

—Michael Koryta, author of *The Cypress House*

"*Pitch Dark* is as relentlessly suspenseful as any crime novel
you've ever read, but at the same time it's as scary as the best
horror stories. Once you've met the walking nightmare who calls
himself the Pitch—and his devoted henchmen—you will never
forget them (try as you might). A harrowing, nonstop flight into
the very heart of darkness, *Pitch Dark* kept me up half the night—
and when I did go to bed, I left the lights on."

—Robert Masello, author of *The Medusa Amulet*

The Mirror's Edge

"Chicago native and resident Steven Sidor, author of the stellar
macabre thrillers *Skin River* and *Bone Factory*, has outdone himself with *The Mirror's Edge*, a supernatural-nuanced, soul-chilling
mystery.... Powered by a sublime sense of foreboding and an omi-
nous, phantasmagoric ambiance reminiscent of works by Aleister
Crowley and H. P. Lovecraft ... Comparable novels have been
mainstays on national bestseller lists (Scott Smith's *The Ruins*
and Joe Schreiber's *Chasing the Dead*, for example), but *The Mirror's Edge* blows them all away in terms of fright factor and over-
all quality of narrative. Crime fiction and horror fans alike will
find *The Mirror's Edge* a dark, disturbing gem."

—*Chicago Tribune*

"Bone-chilling ... Sidor is a master of the unsettling, and each
twist is more grisly and unexpected than the last. Readers won't

be able to resist staying up all night to finish this haunting tale."
—*Publishers Weekly*

"Compelling and chilling, *The Mirror's Edge* delivers everything a reader could want—strong characters, driving narrative, and the edge-of-your-seat suspense. Unconventional and challenging, yet engaging and very human, it is a wonderful novel from a talented writer."
—David Morrell, author of *The Shimmer*

Bone Factory

"Frank Miller's Sin City has nothing on Booth City. . . . This tale is a dark classic by an author with a long career ahead of him."
—*Rocky Mountain News*

"Sidor proved in his well-received first novel, *Skin River*, that he knows a thing or two about deviant human behavior. Now he delivers an equally laudable mystery about two homicide detectives, set in the fictional midwestern town of Booth City, that delves even deeper into the darker reaches of the criminal mind."
—*Publishers Weekly*

"It's a hard-boiled world, presented in a brisk, brutal shorthand as tough as its subject."
—*The Providence Journal*

"Sidor is a prince of darkness, steeped in the noir tradition and not giving an inch. That said, he is also bountifully talented."
—*Kirkus Reviews*

Skin River

"Take note, and you may see a star in the making."
—*Kirkus Reviews*

"A fast-paced crime debut. The salty prose and clever narration will keep readers hooked."
—*Publishers Weekly*

Also by Steven Sidor

The Mirror's Edge
Bone Factory
Skin River

PITCH DARK

STEVEN SIDOR

ST. MARTIN'S GRIFFIN ⚏ NEW YORK

PITCH DARK. Copyright © 2011 by Steven Sidor. All rights reserved. Printed in the United States of America. For information, address St. Martin's Press, 175 Fifth Avenue, New York, N.Y. 10010.

www.stmartins.com

Library of Congress Cataloging-in-Publication Data

Sidor, Steven.
    Pitch dark / Steven Sidor. — 1st ed.
        p. cm.
    ISBN 978-0-312-35414-5
    I. Title.
    PS3619.I36P57 2011
    813'.6—dc22
                            2010043574

First Edition: April 2011

10 9 8 7 6 5 4 3 2 1

For my father, Ronald Sidor,
taking the long road . . .

Acknowledgments

My deepest thanks to Matt Martz and Ann Collette for bringing this book out into the world and for helping me to keep the story tight and the words sharp.

Friends read my early drafts and offered moral support in the fragile stages. I especially want to thank Bob Tuszynski, Steve Neruda, Gary Heinz, Brian Padjen, Jamie Howard, and Ross Molho. Solid gold, each one.

Finally, this is a book about family, and mine is exceptional. My parents, Ron and Nancy, made it through a tough year. Hospital waiting rooms be damned. Lisa, Emma, and Quinn are the best part of any day, and of my life.

He that toucheth pitch shall be defiled therewith . . .
—Bible (Apocrypha); Ecclesiasticus 13:1

PITCH DARK

Prologue

The Rhodesian smuggler pawed at the blade sticking out of his back. It was an F-S fighting knife, nickel-plated—a nasty beauty. He was having a time with it. Dancing around and knocking over the furniture. A lamp here, a chair there. He fell on top of the trunk and died. That was one itch he'd never scratch.

Conner kicked him to the floor. He returned the dead man's gun, took the key from his pocket, and opened the trunk.

Well, he hadn't lied after all.

The stone box.

Conner lifted it, and placed it inside the army duffel he'd brought for just that purpose. He repacked his clothes around it and linked the hook closure.

"That wasn't so bad," he said.

The smuggler didn't argue.

"I'll need my knife back."

He did something the dead man couldn't do with two hands, and then he cleaned the blade on the sap's Savile Row suit. He put him in the trunk. Locked it. He'd drop the key down a

storm drain on his walk to the motel. He
pulled the window shades and set the furniture
upright.

He stuck his arms through the duffel straps
and lit a cigarette.

A curious Conner sat on the edge of his motel
bed. His newly acquired stone box lay propped
on one of its sides. The nature of the shape
made it appear a sharp and crooked thing,
offending to the eye: a double pyramid. The
surface gleamed evilly. He straddled the
foreign relic dug up years ago from the desert
and carted out on camelback. He wetted his
lips. Beneath the object's surface, figures were
trapped in strata resembling translucent black
ice. He detected Byzantine markings,
hieroglyphs, and odd spirals. Layers floated
under layers. So much depth it made him dizzy.
He traced his finger along six columns of
carvings, an alphabet of daggers. What was it
Belzoni had said?

"The mind muscle, for years contracted into a
knot, expands . . ."

The mad professor sure could spin tales. He
had the eyes for it. Wild, dreamy, arrogant
bughouse peepers and that Continental voice of
his, all saliva-doused explosives and
fricatives. Boy, he could sell it. Meaningless
drivel . . . but still.

How many people had died because of this
hunk of dry lava?

Conner counted sixteen he'd heard about or
witnessed himself.

Another hundred and fifty-four if he added all

hands lost aboard the *Kagachi Maru* when it sank, inexplicably, in calm nighttime seas a month ago. The stone box had been in the cargo hold; made it out unscathed according to a swordfisherman who scooped it up from an unoccupied life raft six days later.

And who, come to think of it, was also dead.

One seventy-one.

Conner's head hurt.

He was sweating.

He'd been smoking too much since his arrival. The place smelled like a match factory burned down. Conner opened the window and leaned out, hoping for a breeze. He swung his leg up on the sill and dangled his foot over the fire escape. Indian summer is what he guessed it had to be. Funny he hadn't noticed the heat this morning. Leaves flickered their reds and oranges at him. A rank coolness blew off the river. No sun up in the sky.

Sure was hot in his room though.

Steam floated up from the alley. They were frying the chow mein at a Chinese restaurant next door. He wasn't hungry, but could go for a drink. Maybe at that beer joint around the corner. Knock a few back, relax. Beer was the only thing the Krauts did right.

The walls were thin. He had slept just fine, but he could hear them now, voices murmuring below intelligibility but there nonetheless, like a pulsing beat that almost seemed to be coming not from the other rooms on his floor but from under the floor, under his bed it seemed. Under the stone.

A fluttering at the window.

He turned too slowly to see it. But he felt it . . . them . . . wings . . .

Down in the alley, long low shadows darted through the steam.

Dogs?

They were awfully big mutts, if that's what they were. More like wolves.

He shouldn't have taken the stone.

Those voices he'd heard were coming from inside it.

Conner didn't speak demon. Didn't want to learn, either. He sat there transfixed. Waiting, watching . . .

What were these things he'd brought on himself?

They couldn't be real. Yet somehow he knew that wasn't going to matter.

When they got to him, they'd be real enough.

The Winged Ones were back in view. Sleek, quick as spilled ink, and larger than any birds he'd seen before. Swooping over the rooftops. Cutting the dusk into parabolas. Getting closer.

And the wolves?

The wolves were climbing straight up the bricks . . .

(Excerpt from the story "A Chunk of Hell," by Max Caul, first published in *Interdimensional Magazine,* November 1950.)

CHAPTER 1

I'm driving on the dark side of the moon, Vera Coffey thought. She knew precisely where she was: pointed due north in northern Minnesota, at 3:01 A.M., early Christmas Eve morning. A hatcheting wind whistled as it worked over her red Camaro, trying to find a way inside. Vera felt safe for now. The Berlinetta's cranky heater was blowing warmth through the vents, lulling her as she rocketed on a cushion of steel-belted rubber and air.

Don't think about what you're running from, she told herself. Do that and you'll be just fine. She almost believed it was true.

Mostly she tried not to think at all.

The hum of the tires was hypnotic. Gray roadside monotony repeated while she tunneled ahead. Night sloped around her headlamps.

The radio didn't help. After the witching hour, following ten miles of steep and then steeper hills, signals were dropping off. Vera liked classic hard rock. Loud, wildman drums. Power chords. A singer who had some pipes and knew how to use them. Kick-your-ass-and-make-you-like-it music. Her choices were down to four FM stations. Judging from their playlists, the twenty-first century had never arrived. She punched a button. Black Sabbath. "Paranoid." *Finished with my woman 'cause she couldn't help me with my mind* . . . No, not tonight, Ozzy.

Vera turned off the radio.

This particular stretch of road appeared treeless, an experiment in desolation. Even the roadkill disappeared. You had a problem out here, you had it alone. Yet, every so often, a mailbox plastered with reflectors would tip into view. That must be how the scientists did their measurements.

Subject: Vera Lee Coffey

Age: 26

Marital status: Single

Subject has reached mailbox number 1457. She appears oriented to time and place. Exhaustion stage is near complete. Sense of reality likely jeopardized.

Sleep eminent.

How far until the next town? Hadn't she seen a sign a few miles ago?

Her face was drooping, melting wax. She prodded a fingertip into her cheek. The skin felt as if it would never go back to its original shape. She closed her eyes for a beat. Opened them again.

Nothing changed.

The same shadows encroached on the high beams. The unending tattoo of painted white lines passed on her left like code.

Her eyes closed.

Vera was not going to sleep. She promised. At most she would be taking a minibreather, a second or two of visual rest—that's all, before aiming once more through the windshield and pressing onward. A second or two . . .

Vera woke.

To the sharp spray of gravel hitting the passenger side, she woke.

She woke as the dashboard bucked. The car fell away. Like rope, the steering wheel turned through her grip. A mile marker spiked up green. Its vertical white numbers edged darkness and weeds. The numbers told her where she was crashing, where they would find her broken body in the morning.

Vera held on as her daddy's old '84 threatened to slam off-road.

The front bumper clipped the sign. Popped it over the way a skier pops flags going downhill. One headlight winked out. The road curved ahead.

The red coupe didn't.

Vera fought for control. She pulled until her shoulders hurt. The right half of the car dropped a few inches. Full-tilt crunch. Two wheels chewed rocks, two grabbed washboard asphalt. Vibrations kicked the chassis. Strapped in for the duration of the ride, she gritted her teeth as she pulled and pulled.

Bald tires skidded over the pebbly glass blacktop.

She had overcorrected.

180.

360.

Spin-out.

Vera heard herself draw in air, and say, "Shit."

Here was Death.

Death was a snow-packed guardrail and below, a shallow creek layered milky gray with ice. Reeds poked up their hollow stems. An opossum lifted his funneled face from the ditch and blinked at the sudden wall of light.

The moon above vanished as if a hand clutched it.

Vera saw none of those things. Her eyes viewed them. Lens to retina to optic nerve—her brain registered the data collected. Recognition would come later, a memory of landscape reeling across the windshield in black and white.

Vera saw only Death.

Her scuffed cowboy boot pumped the brake. Her daddy taught her that. He bought the "Starship Camaro" in '84, the year she was born. Daddy didn't know much about cars, even less about the raising of little motherless girls. In two years, the Berlinetta model would be discontinued. And although he tried his best to look after his daughter until the day he died, his advice was wrong. Antilock brakes don't need to be pumped.

Vera pressed the pedal up and down.

Up and down.

It shuddered under her toes.

Up, down, up, down.

The interior grew raucous. Frozen brush scraped the undercarriage. Pulverized snow mounds chuffed and blew apart, sending a burst of sparkly crystals drifting up over the hood.

The few remaining tire treads caught a strip of dry pavement. An astonished Vera steered to the middle of the road. She laughed. She didn't think she was a middle-of-the-road gal. The laughter wasn't really meant for her.

It was for Death.

After her second close encounter in the last twenty-four hours, she couldn't hold back the fear. Death had Vera on the run. She knew what to expect now. She had witnessed him up close. Death had shown his face to her in that West Side greystone back in Chicago. Six times over he did it.

Taunted her, saying, *Here I am.*

His forever grin made her sweat icicles.

Look at me, honey, I'm over here. Here too.

She wouldn't forget.

Now the reaper looked a helluva lot better in her rearview mirror. Fair's fair. Vera got her chance to laugh. No fool, she took it.

Safety arrived as fast as danger. Vera fingered the crucifix she wore on a chain around her neck. It had always been an accessory rather than a religious relic. She wasn't a believer. Silver looked good against her pale skin—that's all. Well, maybe more. Sometimes if stress ran high, or if threats surrounded her, then touching the cross was a way she calmed herself down, a superstition to ward off evil.

Can you believe in Evil without believing in Good?

On an ice-covered road in the middle of the night, Vera thought so.

She *knew* something evil was after her.

The car sped forward between the lines. No other cars passed. None followed. This road was well chosen for its loneliness.

Vera rolled her window down. She gulped cold air. She smelled a farm nearby. On her left, she watched barn doors slide open and the glow of a buttery light escaping. Cattle moved inside. A man came forward at a brisk pace. The farmer, it must be, in his red-checkered jacket, a bucket swinging in his—no hand—prosthetic hook. He waved to her.

Then Vera was past.

Fences divided the scenery. Ice buckled in the fields. Burning motor oil and wood smoke scented the wind. She licked her teeth. Her mouth tasted like Elmer's glue. Her left ear throbbed. Biting air poured into the front seat. Shivering, she cranked up her window. Maxed the heat with her thumb.

Thirteen hours straight through. Taking the blue state and county highways and staying a tick or two under the speed limit. She was nearing the border now but didn't want to cross it at night. That wouldn't be smart.

It might be suicidal.

Canada was for tomorrow.

Vera judged herself in no shape for scrutiny. She wasn't prepared to answer questions. She wouldn't cooperate.

Please open your trunk, miss.

She'd have to say, "No."

Then what?

Vera needed to get off this godforsaken highway. Her empty thermos clunked under the seat as she rounded each bend in the road. She couldn't afford to stop at a gas station for more coffee. Out here in Nowheresville, someone would remember her.

They'd say: *A stringy little thing, pale, hair like a blackbird mashed to her skull, blue-eyed. Couldn't keep her fingers out of her mouth.*

If someone showed them a picture: *That's her, oh yeah, I'm sure of it. So what'd she do? Must've been pretty bad. Did she murder somebody?*

Vera Coffey chewed her thumbnail, thinking about motels.

CHAPTER 2

The doctor stood at the entrance of the old house. Voices within whispered. He turned his back on them. Through an archway window, he aimed his two ebony eyes. A dead cornfield was filling with snow. They'd been fortunate to find shelter this good, this fast. Heat roared through the vent registers. A furnace burned somewhere under him. Snow slid off his boots and dissolved into puddles on the oak planks.

With the warmth, odors roused.

The house attached to a Wisconsin farm. Hills climbed away in three directions. A gravel road swirled into the fourth. Any traveler stopping here in error might conclude he or she was alone in the world. The view offered no relief from the claustrophobic sense of isolation. It wasn't so much lifelessness as a lack of humanity emanating from the place. If the road stopped without notice at a jumble of logs or a collapsed bridge, it wouldn't be a big surprise. *Cut off*—that was the feeling imparted. Land and hearth slumped together after so many years of neglect. Abandonment, when the time finally came, must have been a blessing.

Leaving ended the suffering.

Or put it on pause.

The sound of water *drip, drip, dripping* . . .

Busted windows; holes punched in the plaster. Leaf matter crunched underfoot. Spray-painted wallpaper: NOBODY'S HOME!!!

A pyramid of beer cans stood against one wall. Grimy floors. Fast-food wrappers. Condoms.

The heat smelled musty.

Dr. Horus Whiteside did not mind.

Someday I will have oceans of black and skies to match, he thought. It wasn't the first time he reveled in dreams. The future was his business. He built stark visions into reality. From beyond a locked door came the sound of the thief begging for his life. He had been at it for hours.

Now and again he screamed.

Horus cocked his head and listened for beating wings.

A flying creature had been sputtering around upstairs, rising and diving, venturing bravely down the staircase to the landing and back up again in a fury. The doctor finally caught a glimpse of the thing—like a glove fluttering in midair.

A house bat.

Then it was gone.

So their recent intrusion had not been unnoticed.

They had upset the creature's sanctuary dwelling among silences.

The silences they had broken.

Horus believed in destiny, and in destinations foretold. He didn't believe in maps. Not the kind other people used. He carried a numerical tapestry in his head. It scrolled by constantly. A secret GPS system guided his every move. Longitude and latitude might describe him as crossing the state line between northern Illinois and south central Wisconsin, an invisible barrier he had breached only hours ago.

His real territory was the borderland between worlds.

Illinois towns with legends of haunting, like Bull Valley and Grass Lake, operated under a cloud. Reason could never explain it. Horus knew the source of their unease. Recognizing the situation made him feel superior. Driving through, Horus saw the dead populating the streets. Souls snarled like hungry golden-eyed foxes caught in traps. They were everywhere. Bodies marched along. They sat on snow-covered frozen lawns or stood curbside at intersections. Some were following as close as shadows behind the living.

It was pitiful.

The dead were totally unaware of their condition.

Horus frowned at their predicament. He wanted to help set them free.

Death always held more fascination than life for him. Every time he killed someone his conviction was reconfirmed.

Death begat possibilities.

The dead gave his life meaning. He couldn't have survived without them.

Earlier today, his journey pushed up the asphalt river into southern Wisconsin. The land of Ed Gein and Jeffrey Dahmer. Ghosts flocked the heavens. They perched in treetops and swooped down the valleys. Horus fought the urge to acknowledge them. He had a full agenda of business to conduct.

The American Heartland.

What a poisoned crow's heart it was. Flyover country. Backwater USA—that's what urbanites from the East Coast and Los Angeles thought of it. Under the veneer of ordinariness, plain-spoken accents, and flannel shirts, a grave robber or cannibal could find a nice place to call home.

Horus liked to be underestimated, even ignored.

Today, he and his flock had needed a meetinghouse. Somewhere discreet so the thief's interrogation would not be interrupted. Time acted against them. The passing minutes and hours multiplied, popping and sticking, adding weight until Horus felt a tarry heaviness slowly encasing his body, bogging him down.

At an impasse, the pressure mounting behind his eyes, he had ordered his driver to pull the ambulance to the side of the highway. Passersby no doubt wondered at the sight of a vintage Cadillac from the mid-'70s, built like a hearse but painted shock white and topped with an enormous cherry light. They couldn't see the refurbished engine installed under the hood, or have known the degree of meticulous care given to details inside and out. The

Caddy was primitive by today's standards but it was fully supplied and everything was kept in working order. The back doors bore an emblem of a snake twirled around a staff: the rod of Asclepius, ancient symbol of medicine. Yet this retro medical transport remained on-call to only one institution—the good doctor himself.

The company name—Chiron Ambulance, a Private Health Service—was fictitious. The telephone number listed beneath the name: disconnected.

In the back of the ambulance, Horus sat, silent.

Beside him, strapped facedown to a gurney, a bundle of tan canvas whimpered. It was the thief, Chan. He mumbled wet words of contrition.

The doctor disregarded him.

Horus simply let the pressure from behind his eyes do its job. He couldn't make a vision happen. Force it and you lost. He was a receiver, a needle vibrating in space. He opened all channels and waited for the signal.

Tuned in, he listened.

Horus began describing an abandoned farm.

The thief, though he heard, didn't understand. At this point in his odyssey, comprehension would have been premature. He had other worries to occupy his mind. Primarily fear.

The ambulance driver, however, strained to catch every word. He spoke into his cell phone. Repeating to the others, who were speeding miles ahead now in their vehicles, what it was they should be looking for. They split in different directions. Some drove straight. Most searched for exit ramps.

Half an hour passed.

An hour.

The cell rang back. One of them found a farm.

"Ask them what they see, Pinroth," Horus said.

His loyal driver relayed the caller's observations. Horus stared at the thief's bound wrists peeking from under the canvas. Two purple hands opened and closed, as if they were squeezing invisible tennis balls. The caller was running low on details. Pinroth's eyes flashed in the rearview mirror.

In all matters, the flock sought the doctor's wisdom and guidance.

"Yes, it will do," said Horus.

Then they took the thief and forged ahead of the storm.

The first arrivals resorted to crowbarring the plywood nailed over the parlor window. Amazingly, the glass underneath remained intact. Other windows in the house shattered long ago. Winds came and went.

Looking out, Horus was oblivious to his reflection. Those seated behind him fixated on his strange eyewear. Metal goggles with black rubber eye guards and a leather strap sewn across the nose; an elastic band held them tight to his face. He never removed them except for sleeping. The doctor's skin was unlined, his age indeterminate. It was a mannequin's face, or no face at all, like something plastic peeled from a mold. At his throat he wore a velvet scarf. His tailored clothes underscored his angularity. Near the foot of the stairs, a mud-spattered overcoat hung on the banister. Around the room, the improvised lighting was dramatic. The doctor appeared to levitate inside a rippling antique windowpane.

Candlelight befitted this meeting. It was the season for burning tapers at windows. Uncommon stars beamed across the firmament. Prophecies were fulfilled. Wise men trekking from afar reached their objectives on nights like this. Prior to his arrival, the group attempted making a fire in the fireplace. Blockage in the chimney put a stop to that. The room clogged with smoke and its pungent odor greeted him when he swept open the door. His followers hushed the instant they heard him clopping on the front porch steps. They had no candles. An assortment of LED lanterns and opened laptops were stationed along the floor.

Horus Whiteside entered the unnatural blaze.

He believed he was not a man at all.

He was part of a larger whole that reached back for Eternity.

The Pitch.

Turning from the tall, now exposed, churchlike window, he addressed the others who eagerly leaned forward to receive their instruction. They were sitting on lawn furniture, sticky with spiderwebs, retrieved from the cellar.

His devoted believers: small in number, their fervor and willingness to please made all the difference. They were devoted. He hoped he had enough of them this time to get the job done.

He faced the gathering.

"Praise the darkness. My brothers and sisters, we must be thorough. We must be vicious in our quest. Tonight the thief has confessed that his girlfriend took the artifact and ran away."

Grumbles and cries of disbelief erupted.

He pointed to the window.

"I have sent a pair of finders into the wilderness. They seek her. She has stolen what belongs to us, what is rightfully ours to keep. We paid a price yet received nothing in return so we shall exact one. She will die. That is the penalty. Anyone helping her will die. That is the penalty. So it shall be."

"So it shall be," they answered.

Order played a crucial role in any plan of attack. Thrust and defend your flanks. Advance, always advance. Victory would come later. Those who survived the battle would enjoy the spoils.

One day he would reveal his true nature to them.

After he had the girl and what she possessed.

Soon.

Very soon.

For the moment, he dismissed his army with a wave of his hand.

They filed out into the storm. The lone figure of Pinroth would be waiting, warming the ambulance's interior, feeding gas to the big V-8 motor, and guarding the door until Horus summoned him.

Quiet now.

A beating of wings . . .

The sound of water dripping . . .

Weeping . . . the thief was weeping . . .

Horus spied a bent shape left behind on one of the sun loungers. He picked up the crowbar.

Stretching his arms forward, he noticed for the first time the dried stains on his shirt cuffs and the blood gummed under his fingernails: ten red sickle moons. The bar was heavy, cold, the iron black. He swung and heard the satisfactory slicing of air. Without warning, he smashed the parlor window. Glass showered him. He crouched and chose a shard from the floor.

Broken glass and an iron bar.

A perfect pairing.

He would introduce them to the thief.

CHAPTER 3

Wyatt Larkin stirred a gallon of paint with a broken yardstick. He'd always enjoyed the smell of paint. Pouring carefully, he contemplated the possibility of clean starts and second chances; it calmed him, the sight of this pigment suspended in liquid, thick and comforting as any homemade cake batter. He watched it lap the sides of the shallow aluminum pan. He put down the can, then tore the wrapper off a disposable roller, snapped it on its frame, and ran his palm over the soft, synthetic fuzz. A plastic drop cloth crackled under his shoes.

His reflection, opaque in the shrouded mirror, doubled his every movement. Man and his image. Together they reached upward.

Earlier, Wyatt had taken down the curtains and put them under one of the double beds. A bulb shone overhead, and at the window, a muted winter sun. He'd already finished taping. Over the years the wall color had soured to a varying tan, shaded darker near the ceiling—this being a smoking room. The fresh coat of paint appeared white until you looked at it more closely and saw a hint of the palest blue emerge.

His wife had picked it out.

Just like Opal, he realized, to choose something that wasn't quite what you thought it was at first glance.

Wyatt dipped his roller.

Cigarette smoke climbed Wyatt's cheek on his blind side and brushed over his eye patch. He shouldn't have been smoking. Coffin nails—he'd quit them once before. Then Opal started with her visions again. He needed something to take the edge off. He had the bathroom window propped with a screwdriver for ventilating the paint fumes. The smoke located the crack and quietly slipped out.

Wyatt wore a wool pullover. The sweater bagged below his lean, broad shoulders. Moths had eaten away most of the left elbow. It was his favorite sweater: a project from Opal's knitting experiment two winters back. She'd quit knitting. But Wyatt kept the sweater. When he'd risen hours ago—the clock radio telling him it was, believe it or not, 5 A.M. as he slapped down on the button before Opal stirred—he showered and shaved, his feet dancing on the frozen bathroom tiles, and he pushed his head up through the sweater's baggy neck, his arms swimming into the sleeves. He doubled them over at the wrists and scooted the rolls up his forearms. He was hoping his wife might notice her own handiwork. Maybe she'd even say something. She might show some recognition. If she did, that would be a good sign.

He hadn't seen many lately.

Despite everything, he told himself, *Keep trying*.

Opal didn't mention the sweater. She wasn't talkative. Not today. Less and less with each passing week if Wyatt stopped to think about it—something he didn't often do. He wasn't a person to dwell on the negative. Never had been. But his positivity bordered on denial. This woman was still his wife. True. He worried about her. Yes, constantly. Because . . . when Opal spoke, more often than not, a torrent of words flooded forth, as if she couldn't get them out of her mouth fast enough. The muscles in her neck bulged and her cheeks flushed. She spoke of a malignant strangeness lurking in the world. She had waking nightmares. Darkness, she said, crept through the streets and entered into people's hearts while they themselves were unaware of the changes taking place.

Demons lived among us.

She sought confirmation of these insights. A wife wants her husband to agree with her. Do you see what I see?

Wyatt didn't.

He wouldn't admit it to anyone, but Opal spooked him.

Her personality was unstable. She shifted into this gray zone where the otherworldly was possible. Apparently, the other world sought to destroy them.

The woman he loved began to disappear.

What was happening to her?

The doctors were no help. Wyatt was running out of hope.

And that realization terrified him.

Predawn, Wyatt headed downstairs. Out of the corner of his eye, Opal's fuzzy pink robe flashed in the door frame. He turned to tell her where he was going. Tiny, strong Opal. He remembered her nine months pregnant with their son, Adam, and eating every slice of pepperoni pizza in sight. Her weight never topped one-ten. Twenty years ago. Her sister, Ruby, nicknamed her Mighty Mouse when they were kids. The two lived their whole lives less than a mile apart. Ruby said Opal hadn't changed in forty-two years.

Not physically.

Opal's hair stood on end, crackling with static electricity. Penny-brown eyes, freckles, a frizzy auburn halo. A face Wyatt had fallen in love with.

His wife peered into the stairwell, her gaze passing right through him. Her hand flicked out and switched off the light, throwing Wyatt into darkness.

Her lips were moving.

Silently.

No words, only the shapes of words.

Mornings were hardest. When Opal's bad look would show up, her normal expressions altered. *She's wearing her rubber Halloween mask again,* Wyatt couldn't help thinking. Her whole head stuffed up inside, lost. Even her breathing sounded different: coarse, heavy, almost smothered.

Under the kitchen's fluorescent glare, he saw the mask in place.

He climbed back up the steps and kissed his wife on the cheek. He smoothed her hair, watching as the charged strands stuck to his fingers. The bad look always frightened him.

"Nobody's home," she said.

Is she reading my mind? Wyatt wondered.

"I'm here. You're not alone, babe."

She shook her head.

"Nobody's home," she repeated.

Wyatt took a deep breath.

Maybe the New Year would bring better days.

One week to go.

Opal sleepwalked to the sink. She grabbed a tea kettle. Lifted the faucet handle. Water shushed inside the pot. She yawned and glanced out the second-story window into the alleyway behind the motel. Wyatt followed her sightline. The sun hadn't risen. The edge of the horizon had started to go violet. Above it, the sky stretched out, unbroken, dark enough to detect stars. A floodlight shined down on a redwood privacy fence, a Dumpster encrusted with snow. Beyond the fence were yards, small houses, and the neighbors.

Opal grew up in one of those houses. Her sister still lived there with her husband and two daughters. If you stood on a chair, you'd spot their rooftop.

Small towns, Wyatt thought.

You'd figure that would mean safety, though it didn't.

Wyatt and Opal lived in an apartment above the motel office. Neighbors, once they had a look around inside, were shocked by the size of the place. It was bigger than many houses.

Living room, dining room, a full kitchen, and three bedrooms . . .

The den opened up to a bright bay window perfect for watching sunsets. After nightfall, the room diminished. But it deepened as well, around a pool table, matching La-Z-Boys, and a widescreen television. There was an electronic dart board. An old Pepsi vending machine hummed in the corner. The last button dispensed cans of Budweiser. The apartment's only bathroom had a whirl-pool tub and a sauna. Ceiling fans circulated air from room to room. Built-in bookshelves lined the walls. Paperbacks, mostly thrillers, jammed every slot. Wyatt and Opal often read through the evening, during winters especially, as the dark hours length-ened and business slowed.

People thought it was odd, the way the Larkins lived above an ever-changing set of strangers. The practice seemed unwholesome at its worst and at best, less comfy. After climbing a flight of car-peted stairs, visitors expected to be welcomed into the anonymity of another motel room.

The surprise on their faces never failed to make Opal beam.

Wyatt had done most of the work himself. He was handy with a hammer and saw. Drawing up plans gave him a creative out-let. Physical work burned off his anxieties; they were his fuel. He wanted their home to look like the picture he constantly redrew in his head. What he couldn't fix was the family living inside.

He couldn't repair a broken mind.

"You want two up and bacon?" Opal asked.

Wyatt shook his head.

"I've got to get started painting those rooms. I'll grab a dough-nut off the guest tray."

"Going to get fat eating all that sugar."

What a joke. The two of them together couldn't get wet in a thunderstorm. Ruby called them Mr. and Mrs. Beanpole.

"You'd love me fat," Wyatt said.

"I probably would," she said, smiling.

Wyatt was glad to recognize the real Opal. Mask off. Demons sent back to Hell where they belonged. Every time the woman he recognized returned, he worried it would be to say good-bye. His worry eased off, just a bit, when she smacked the seat of his jeans as he walked past.

CHAPTER 4

Wyatt opened the door at the bottom of the stairs and entered the motel office. He picked up the phone and checked his voice mail.

His son, Adam, should have called.

No messages.

Wyatt clicked on the weather radio and listened to the latest forecast. Nodding as the details streamed across. The baritone announcer read the same report he'd been reading for two days.

Big storm approaching, scheduled to arrive this afternoon. High winds. Heavy snowfall expected. The storm totals might break a Christmas record.

Be prepared. Stay off the roads.

The predawn hours used to be Wyatt's favorite: still dark out, the workday not quite fully engaged. After warmer weather arrived, he'd hear the birds chirping outside. They'd be his company. The front wall of the office had a glass door and a long window that reminded Wyatt of an aquarium. He'd sit behind the counter and watch the clouds swim by.

Not in winter.

In winter, he began the day alone. The sky was a hood that wouldn't lift for months. All useful light came from artificial sources. Reflections bounced back. Wyatt was the one inside the tank. He glided across the office, racking local attraction brochures in slots along the wall. He plugged in the Mr. Coffee. He tore open foil packets of fresh grounds and inhaled.

Hard to beat a hot cup of joe before you hit the road.

But Wyatt wasn't going anywhere.

He checked his computer screen. Ten rooms occupied last night. He'd make two pots, fill up a carafe, and start a decaf pot after that. Decaf drinkers had patience. The doughnuts were stored in a cooler, along with half-pints of milk, a few apples and oranges, and shots of cream to add to the coffee. Wyatt slid the pastry tray beside the front desk. He loosened the cling wrap but left it covering the doughnuts. He didn't eat any.

Instead, he pressed his ear to the door that led to the apartment. He heard nothing. He stepped over to the computer and wiggled his arm into a gap behind the retractable keyboard—his secret hiding place.

He fished them out.

American Spirit Ultra Lights. The crumple of the pack in his fingers gave him a pang of guilt. Quickly, he stowed them in his shirt and slipped into his jacket. He touched the outer shell pocket.

Yes, his lighter was there.

Wyatt went into the broom closet. He found the snow shovel and a bag of ice melt. His gloves and a Vikings stocking cap lay folded on a shelf. He put the cap on. The gloves were for below-zero days.

It was cold. But it was always cold this time of year. He'd lived with the cold his whole life. Like an old friend who comes around and stays too long, until you decided he never was a friend at all.

Wyatt pushed through the heavy glass door.

He tasted the storm like a steel drill bit on his tongue. Clouds sank to the rooftops. Tinsel glints in the streetlights: the first snowflakes were falling. The lot's surface was a jigsaw of cracks. Ice washed out the parking lanes. The highway beyond glistened. Summertime, he'd patch and fill in the potholes. Now he watched his step.

Rumble and the rush of an oncoming engine—Wyatt spun around to face it.

A snowplow drove past with its blade raised, throwing sand.

Wyatt waved to the driver. He recalled his years as a police officer, the early mornings he spent cruising along the grid of these same streets. Eyes and ears open for trouble.

The plow vanished around a corner.

The highway was quiet. Not another vehicle in sight.

Well, it's a holiday, Wyatt thought, and there's heavy weather coming.

Only one room was booked for tonight.

Walking around, the shovel in his hand, he assured himself that they'd make it through another year. As with most independents, the Larkins made only small profits. Enough to meet the bills, save a little, and spend even less for entertainment. Some years all they could manage was to pay bills. But they were cautious with money. Opal and Wyatt put back what they earned, improving the business or sprucing up their home. They took no vacations, spent nothing on luxuries. No, they came by what they had through sweat and dedication. They took good care of their property because they knew the cost. Knew they were fortunate, too. Sometimes hardworking people caught a nasty break, a streak of bad luck—or worse—and everything fell apart in the blink of an eye.

That had happened to the Larkins almost two decades ago. They'd never forget it. How could they?

Wyatt sprinkled ice melt on the concrete apron leading to the office.

A brand-new Super 8 went up on the edge of town last April. It was the first building anybody saw driving up the highway from the south. The parking lot held plenty of cars. What were you going to do? The chains had a right to exist. People who worked there needed jobs and had families just like his.

It wasn't a big family. Just the two of them since their son started college.

Today was Adam's first visit since leaving home.

Wyatt wondered if Opal remembered. He didn't mention it, because he didn't want her panicking if the blizzard arrived before their son did. Wyatt rolled down the top of the ice-melt bag. The keen wind smarted on his cheeks.

When he was a kid, he never dreamed he'd end up running a motel. Sounded boring and a little like failure. He wanted adventure, something better than the dull life he saw his parents living with their lumberyard shifts and union dues, football on the TV Sunday afternoon, then back at it for another week. His family didn't travel. He was an adult before he slept the night in a paid room. Back inside the cozy heated office, he was thinking it looked more like a cell.

Wyatt had been inside a few of those, too.

The weather radio announcer was talking at him again.

High winds. Drifting snow.

Whiteouts.

Stay off the roads.

Oh, and have a Merry Christmas.

CHAPTER 5

Wyatt shook a cigarette from the pack. He closed the door, heard his heart thumping against the background silence of an empty room. His painting supplies were on the dresser. He felt foolish hiding his smoking like a teenager. Told himself every night as he lay sleepless in bed: Tomorrow you quit. A whiff of betrayal followed each puff because Opal was so easy to fool. Prior to his relapse, he'd kicked the habit for almost two decades. He had every reason to.

After the shooting.

Wyatt had taken a bullet in his lung. A broken dagger of glass hung in his eye. That hadn't been the worst of it.

Opal. Opal, his pregnant wife, spread out and dying on the restaurant floor. He saw her blood. The blue and white waitress's uniform dyed red. Blood on her belly. A hole. Another wound creased her head.

God in Heaven, not Opal.

The shooting wiped out reality. Extreme violence plays tricks on the mind. Physical changes spur psychological alterations. You might experience the event like a movie projected in a dream. Feel yourself existing in and out of the picture. You semidetach, begin to float. Or maybe you freeze like any mammal caught under a claw on the forest floor. Laugh or whimper. Hold your breath and bite down on nothing. This was no movie. You weren't munching popcorn and sucking on a Coke in a theater. You were about to die.

Wyatt squatted between two booths.

He could reach out and touch his wife's leg.

He did. As he found his voice, he whispered her name. She wasn't responding. She lay in the open. He couldn't risk dragging her body through a slick of blood to bring her closer. He didn't want to draw the shooter's attention.

Bang. Bang. Bang. The guy wearing the fatigues made his way around the lunch counter. Shouts of agony accompanied him.

Screams. Voices pleaded for mercy and found none.

At first, Wyatt thought there were two of them. Two men with guns opening fire on the lunchtime diners. He'd seen them enter the restaurant together. He hadn't been paying any particular attention. They were a blur moving through the door as he glanced up. Two men walked in side by side. The taller one wore a black raincoat that swept the floor. He entered and turned. Wyatt saw his back. The other was dressed in full fatigues and a military cap with a squared bill, pulled low. He stayed put. The door closed behind them.

Wyatt didn't spot any weapons.

He didn't feel any quiver of fear snake up his spine.

He'd been too excited by his own news, stopping in to tell Opal the crib was finished. He even snapped a Polaroid of it. Crib in the foreground, his workbench behind, and sawdust scattered over the garage floor. Opal had been fretting. If the baby came early, and the crib wasn't ready, then what? Less than a month, she said. Babies don't follow calendars. So he brought the picture to show her he made the deadline. They would be prepared.

Opal was the first person shot. One second she was smiling and waving the photo around. Calling to the other waitresses working that day. Saying the word "beautiful." Tears bubbled in the corners of her eyes. The next second she fell to the floor at Wyatt's feet.

The shooters didn't say anything. There was a quick burst of activity once people realized what was happening. Then things settled down. And the killers began their work in earnest.

Wyatt resisted the urge to rush them.

The Pie Stop restaurant was shaped like a *U*. The kitchen was located in the middle. After the killers hit Opal with the opening volley of gunfire, they shifted to the other side of the restaurant, the opposite arm of the *U*.

From the sound of the reports, only one man was doing the shooting.

If there were two of them, the other might be providing cover. Watching and waiting to see if any heroes decided to show themselves.

Wyatt popped his head up over the edge of a bench.

Fatigues. A rifle barrel swinging from table to table. It looked like a Ruger Mini-14 Ranch Rifle. The magazine was pretty long. Wyatt guessed there might be twenty rounds in there, or more. A lot of killing.

The guy disappeared beyond the kitchen.

Loud pops.

Wyatt crabbed his way forward.

Brass cartridges littered the floor.

The tall man must have had the rifle under his raincoat. But now the guy wearing fatigues was using it.

Where was the tall man? Where was Raincoat?

Wyatt crawled over Opal. He wanted to stay there and shield her. But he couldn't do that.

The gunmen were his responsibility.

Wyatt knew he had to deal with this deadly situation quickly, decisively. He had to be smart, too. If he stood up and died, then he wasn't going to help anyone. He was here to defend the townspeople. Off-duty, but armed. He was dressed in jeans, a hooded sweatshirt, and a windbreaker. Yet everyone living in town knew Wyatt was a local cop.

The strangers weren't expecting him.

The holster was clipped in the small of his back. He drew his weapon.

Innocent people crouched on the floor of the Pie Stop, crying and quaking, trying to flatten their bodies against puddles of drying rainwater and spilled plates of food. Wyatt was their best chance. He couldn't return fire until he had a better idea of where the two killers were. In the pauses between shots, he heard the rain slashing at the sides of the building. The minute he started shooting back, everything would change. He needed that change to be for the better. He didn't want to risk making a bad shot, launching a ricochet, or nailing a bystander who had worked up the courage to break for the door.

Bang. Bang.

Bang. Bang. Bang. Bang. Bang.

No more time to think. He had to act.

He got an idea.

Wyatt stood in a crouch. He put a bead on the ceiling tiles around the U's bend. Aiming high. Following the reports of the rifle. Maybe he could flush out Raincoat. Maybe Fatigues would get nervous and dart around the corner. There was no sense in firing repeatedly until he had a clear target. His off-duty .38 held six rounds. He didn't want to be overeager and find himself reloading. Given the situation, reloading was a joke. Six shots and the game would end. He'd be dead or alive. Victim or hero. The Ruger had more mistakes in its clip than he did in his revolver's chambers. And the likelihood that Fatigues and Raincoat were carrying other weapons was high. Wyatt was outgunned. No question. But that didn't mean he was outsmarted.

He fired once.

A ceiling tile jumped its frame. Punched loose. It dangled, and then fell.

That did it.

Fatigues moved around the cash register. The glass case filled with chewing gum and breath mints. The chalkboard marked with the daily specials. The pie carousel twirling its array of sweet desserts. Wyatt saw khaki-clad shoulders. A head without a face, a hat tight above a patch of shaved skin. Fatigues was walking backward. Killing as he went. He knew trouble had surfaced. But he hadn't decided what position to take.

Wyatt aimed between his shoulder blades.

"Police! Put the gun down!"

Shoulders started to swivel. The rifle barrel came around.

Wyatt pulled the trigger.

He hit Fatigues high on the right side of his twisted torso. The bullet ripped into shoulder meat. The rifle dropped. Fatigues ducked. Blood dripped down the pie carousel. Wyatt heard the rifle stock clatter to the floor. A grunt of pain, then a curse.

Where was Raincoat?

Wyatt zigzagged, booth to booth. He made up ten feet. Twenty.

"Stay down! Everybody stay down! Police!"

Two family-sized tables separated Wyatt and the killer. The occupants of those tables scurried away. Wyatt peered through a forest of chair legs.

Fatigues lay on his back, fumbling with his belt. He was attempting to draw another weapon, an automatic handgun, but he couldn't slide it from his waistband. He suffered damage. The hand digging at his belt was trembling, awash with blood.

"Get your hands up! Hands up!"

The killer ignored him.

Wyatt shot him in the knee.

Fatigues rolled away.

Wyatt stood.

His eyes flicked. Left, right. From the front of the restaurant he had a clear view down both arms of the U.

No Raincoat.

Maybe Raincoat hadn't been with Fatigues at all. Spree shooters typically acted alone. A volcanic personality snapped and wanted revenge. They craved personal apocalypse. Maybe that's what happened here. Maybe Raincoat was just another unlucky person who picked the wrong place to eat lunch today.

Wyatt edged closer.

Fatigues lying facedown. His arms tucked under him.

"Get your hands up over your head or I will shoot you!"

The left arm came up. The right arm jerked. Bloodstains spread a crimson map on the killer's jacket. He moaned.

"I can't—"

"Turn over!"

Nothing.

Wyatt trained his weapon on the back of the guy's head.

He stuck the tip of his boot under the man's hipbone, and flipped the stranger over.

This man was no stranger.

Jesse Genz.

Jesse Genz, who gave Wyatt the chickenpox when they were in fifth grade together at Andrew Jackson Elementary. Jesse, who shot hoops with him under a summer moon. *Same time, same place, alright?*—the park on Moody Street, down by the river. Jesse would bring the ball. There were no houses down there, just an abundance of much-needed privacy the teenagers craved. They played one-on-one despite the swarms of mosquitoes that descended each night. They talked about girls in their class. They listened to the hypnotic swish-snap of the chain nets. And to each other's stories.

Jesse.

Who'd left town after the senior prom and joined the army. Who ran into bad times, got an early discharge, and lived, his family said, in sunny California. Rumor was he returned to town last month, though nobody ever saw him. Jesse's tan belied the messy March weather. His face had thinned. It shrunk to his skull. The flesh circling his eyes looked softly rotten. But the eyes were the same old Jesse. He smiled up at Wyatt.

"You ruined it, friend."

Before Wyatt could ask what he meant . . .

He felt a hard thump in the back. The hit shoved him forward. Clubbed him to his knees and stole his breath. He and Jesse were face-to-face.

"Uh-oh," Jesse said. Mockingly, the smile split his mouth wider.

Shot. Wyatt had been shot in the back.

The second man. Raincoat. Loose in the restaurant. Where was he?

Wyatt had no time to look.

There was a metal ring on Jesse's right hand—Jesse was spinning it, around and around. Only it wasn't really a ring at all. It was a grenade pin.

"Boom," Jesse said. He balled up his fist and snapped it open, his fingers rigid, shaky. Blood turned his teeth pink. He looked like a man without a sane thought in his head. Mad circuses frolicked behind those eyes.

He must've had the hand grenade hooked to his belt.

Wyatt didn't see the explosive. There hadn't been any time to search.

He dived for the only cover he could find—the pie carousel.

The bomb went off.

His body rode a wave of heat and noise.

Wyatt felt stinging all over his face.

He was deaf. He was blind. His baby was dead. His wife was dead.

He had one question for Jesse Genz. One he would never hear answered.

"Why?"

Wyatt had always hated hospitals. The smells, the human noise, the long aqua-colored hallways . . . now they had become a comfort zone for him. His wife and child were alive down one of those long hallways. Opal rested in a coma. The docs were hopeful. Her brain bleed had stopped. The swelling subsided. The emergency C-section went better than expected.

His *son* was hungry and crying. Wyatt held him through his breakfast bottle time, and then for a while after. A nurse returned the baby to the nursery.

Wyatt was alone and thinking.

A question bothered him.

He closed his good gray eye. He had a plastic shield and bandages taped to the other half of his face. Scabs furrowed his cheeks. They'd informed him about the extent of his injuries, how there was no saving his eye; enucleation was the medical term— removal of the eyeball. They cleaned the glass out. The socket had to heal; then in a few weeks, they'd take an impression. They would paint his prosthetic eye to match the good one. It would appear almost normal.

The question nagged.

He popped the morphine trigger looped around his bedrail. The painkiller quieted everything. The trees outside his hospital window went from bare branches to leafy green lushness as they waved at him. It seemed to happen slowly and quickly, like time-lapse photography. He could watch it all day.

The question didn't go away.

It dropped to a murmur.

On his discharge day, they gave Wyatt an eye patch.

Opal was conscious but weak. Her eyelids fluttered. She'd squeeze his hand if he squeezed first. And if he asked her a question, she'd whisper a word or two in response. Then she'd fade. She saved her energy for the baby. Soon they would be home with him. And she *would* recover. Everyone was so confident.

Wyatt sat with his family until it was time to go.

He was being discharged today.

An aide pushed his wheelchair to the exit. As soon as they reached the automatic doors, he stood on his feet and thanked her.

Outside again.

He'd never spent such a long period of time confined indoors.

Sweat cooled his skin.

He was surprised how big the hospital's parking area looked once he got out there. The rows of cars merged into an undulating metallic mass. Far away, the highway and its moving traffic trembled. It made him dizzy.

His depth perception was going to be screwed up. They told him it would take time to adjust. Remember, Wyatt, your vision is halved. On the sidewalk, first thing: He looked up to Opal's window. He shaded his eye from the glare. Was the world always this bright? He blinked until the involuntary tears stopped and he found the correct window.

Of course, no one was looking down.

He'd come back tomorrow.

It had rained recently. The spring air tasted of earth. It was good to feel the sun. He was a young man of twenty-three. He wasn't supposed to drive in his condition, but his car was still parked over at the Pie Stop. He walked away from the hospital.

The restaurant was closed. Blinds drawn. Police tape marked an X across the doors. He unlocked his car.

Got in.

The interior was stale. A burn flared inside his stitched chest. The bullet, they said, nicked a back rib, punctured his lung, and passed under his rib cage and cleanly through. With so much lead flying around, it was hard to tell when Jesse shot him. Wyatt insisted Jesse didn't shoot him.

It was the second man.

No, no, he was wrong. One gun. One gunman. The evidence said so. All the slugs they recovered matched either Jesse's rifle or Wyatt's revolver.

He was short of breath.

Hadn't smoked a cigarette in weeks.

He wanted one now. He found a Marlboro pack on the dash. Leaning to light one, he spotted himself in the rearview mirror. Welts flecked his face and throat where glass from the exploded carousel tore into him. They squirmed like pink worms as he sucked in smoke. He rolled down the window and tossed the cigarette. He didn't start the engine. Just sat there for a while, thinking about how much his life had changed since he last climbed from behind that wheel.

So who was Raincoat?

Where did he go? How come I'm the only one who saw him?
He sobbed.

Twenty years without answers.

Sometimes his missing eye ached. The socket became sensitive in cold weather. Typical morning along the Canadian border—the room was frigid. He'd already stripped the twin beds, put plastic over them, and wrapped an old beach towel around the wall-mounted television. Wyatt crushed out his cigarette in an ashtray balanced on the end of one bed. Green letters etched the glass.

RENDEZVOUS MOTEL

Under the ashes, two stylized ducks drifted in a pond. A third flew off.

He went to work on the wall.

CHAPTER 6

White haze washed over Opal Larkin's body. She sat in a wooden chair. Her legs spread apart. How long had she been sitting here? Staring down at the faux wood grain on the laminate floor, she attempted to follow a single dark line from wall to wall. It should have been easy. But she got mixed up somewhere along the way. Her focus shattered. Confused by a swirl, or tangling up in a knot. She returned to the wall again. Starting over.

The haze began pulsing like flashbulbs. Between the bursts of light her skin turned a luminous green; it reminded her of the glow-in-the-dark prizes you found in cereal boxes. Was there something wrong with the kitchen fixture?

Maybe the light had nothing to do with it.

The glow faded.

Vanished.

She'd been living in a haze.

I'm not crazy, she thought.

The sad truth was she didn't know anymore. Losing her mind was a real possibility. It wasn't Alzheimer's or a brain tumor.

It was a bullet.

As she thought the word "bullet," she tasted it on her tongue. The rounded nose of the slug, not much bigger than a Good & Plenty, rolled oily in her mouth.

The scent of blood exploded. Her nasal cavity plugged with blood.

Opal opened her lips, pressed them gently into her palm.

No bullet. No blood.

Yet, the thing tasted real.

You're a miracle, she reminded herself. Adam was a miracle, too. Born against the odds, finding life after that shooting gallery at the Pie Stop. All those poor people died for no reason. She'd almost been lost herself. She had no memories of the rampage, only knew what others told her. Wyatt was a hero. Jesse Genz had snapped and gone crazy. Maybe it was from something the army did to him? They didn't have anything to say about it. It was anybody's guess. People she'd lived around her whole life doing things she never expected. Shootouts in broad daylight. Thrill killings. Friends and neighbors, eating lunch one minute, turned into casualties the next.

Casualties.

Wasn't a random killer the epitome of casual? Flipping lives from on to off like light switches. Good night. Good night. You go dark. Go dark. Evil itself walked in the door that day. That day as it rained . . .

Tap. Tap. Tap.

Opal had good years. Many, in fact. All of Adam's childhood and the buying of this old roadside motel from the Houlihans, who'd owned the place for ages. They were nice enough people but not very business-minded. The motel was almost beyond salvage. Yet she and Wyatt did it. Working their butts off day after day, and actually loving it. Those were the great years, really, but they seemed like mirages. They trembled in the distance. She couldn't remember details. If she really tried and spent time on it, she'd dig a few up. Concentration yielded results. What lay ahead was more important.

Moods flowed through her; they changed her inside. She didn't like her temperament being so elastic. It freaked people out. She had her visions, too. Once or twice after the shooting, then not for years, and now they'd come back.

With a vengeance.

Since Adam left for college she'd had them almost every day. How could she deny it? They snatched her up and dropped her down and said, *Now listen*. They demanded attention. It was like the voice of God. Prophets had similar problems: anxiety, total loss of control, an invisible force taking over. She lived knowing self-control was an illusion. The awareness was the worst—the whole time feeling she was being used in an impersonal, tool-like way. And it could happen again at any second. No warning. She was powerless.

Opal had never been very churchy. She was a lapsed Catholic. There wasn't any special reason to believe God would talk to her. But, by God, these visions were terrible and strong.

She didn't really suspect God was behind it. The visions didn't feel holy. More like the opposite. It wasn't aliens, either. No little green men or skinny bald ones with giant liquid eyes. She wasn't stolen out of her bed at night and floated up to the mothership for a 3 A.M. probing.

Maybe these were seizures she'd been having. No one understood the human brain. Opal had learned that much from her neurologists. Those guys were quick to admit it. *We're operating in murky waters here, Opal,* they said. Mind, brain, soul—it's all there inside your skull. That and a bullet. Well, not a whole bullet but a fragment. Sucked up in the middle of her head like a droplet inside a sponge. They showed her an X-ray. There it was: a jagged white star. Her big gray brain surrounded it. The latest doctor thought she might be experiencing Moving Bullet Syndrome. The old fragment was traveling. Along the way, it was wiping out cells, erasing memories, and intermittently destroying her sense of reality. He compared her new films with ones taken the night after the shooting. Opal, Wyatt, and the doctor stood in front of a wall of lights, looking inside her head.

"Slight movement," the doc said, touching his thumbnail to the nova in her brain. "But it's been in there so long." Twenty years. He wasn't seeing any significant migration. Do doctors think it makes patients feel better when they admit their own bafflement? He didn't advise taking the fragment out. "Come back in six months. Call if you have any unusual problems."

She and Wyatt bundled up, climbed into their truck, and drove home.

What would she do without Wyatt?

He was her lifeline.

Since she'd started having these visions, he'd taken over more than his share of the duties at the motel. She saw the exhaustion in his face.

"Let's give it time," he told her. "The worst will likely pass."

It hadn't yet.

Mostly, Opal thought she might be crazy.

Tap. Tap. Tap.

What the hell was that?

It was too cold for rain, yet something was hitting the window panes. Pebbles?

Opal stepped over to the kitchen sink. She unlocked the window and tried lifting it. Iced in place, it wasn't budging.

Tap. Tap.

She tilted her head to the side. The roof? Snow melting through the shingles? Was there pattering up in the attic? There were no puddles on the floor, no stains on the ceiling. She shut her eyes to focus on the sound.

She heard the big storm blowing in, revving its engine. The Weather Channel predicted a snowy Armageddon. The gutters vibrated and buzzed. Bedroom shutters whistled. When the temperature really dropped during January or February, the motel's wooden frame cracked like a bullwhip in the middle of the night. Those were normal sounds to her.

She visualized her ears opening up; eardrums thumping like speakers.

What else did she hear?

There. Not the tapping, or the wind's effects, but a new sound. It wasn't coming from the roof, either, but from somewhere downstairs. And it wasn't rain falling or water dripping. It whined like a fan. No wait. Listen harder. It wasn't mechanical. A baby crying? Whimpering? Was that a dog?

The Larkins had cats. Three of them. The furry Musketeers.

But no dogs.

Guests traveling with dogs stayed in the motel's smoking rooms. The office and main strip doors opened to the highway. Thirty steps to the north, the building cornered hard left and a row of double rooms ran back to a patch of gravel where buses and boat trailers parked. They put the dog owners there because it was quieter. Wyatt was painting those rooms today.

He's smoking, too, she figured, and feeling guilty about it. Wearing that ugly sweater she'd made for him; she couldn't believe he even put it on to paint.

The whimper.

Stronger this time . . . then it trailed off. The pleading notes seeped back into the corners of the room. Wet and alive. Whatever it was, it was suffering.

Opal pulled her robe tighter, cinched her belt. She started down the steps to the office. *Tap.* Again the whimper followed, definitely growing louder on the ground-floor level. Why was she frightened all of a sudden? Scared to walk around inside the familiar surroundings of her home? Daylight hours. She wasn't going to find some thief rummaging in the office looking for a safe. They'd still be asleep, wouldn't they? A hellacious storm kicked up and people dove under their blankets. Wyatt was nearby. In twenty years, they'd never been robbed. Even drugged-out maniacs knew the real dough wasn't in mom-and-pop motels during the off-season. *Tap.* This was so stupid. *Tap. Tap.* She'd march right down there and open the door.

"Wyatt? Are you in the office?"

The doorknob felt hot. She pressed her palm to the door. Warm. She wouldn't say burning, but toasty like the side of the industrial dryer they used to launder the motel linens. If the air conditioner was switched off, then this door would get warm . . . in the summer. What was it they said about house fires? If a door is hot, then don't open it.

She opened it.

She found nothing out of order.

The office looked normal.

But she heard a dog crying, crying for real, from physical pain.

Opal could endure a lot, but she could not stand animal cruelty. Guest or no guest. She'd throw them out and call the cops. What was wrong with people these days? They tortured their own pets?

Opal tore through the office. She wasn't thinking about guests seeing her stomping outside in a robe and fluffy bunny slippers. She needed a key. She went behind the desk where the key hooks were screwed into a white panel board. She ran her fingers over the key tags. They swayed and clacked together. The smoking rooms: two keys were missing. Wyatt had one. The other belonged to a regular guest. She even knew his name: Max Caul.

He stayed with them every Christmas week since they bought the motel.

He was an odd guy, but she never would've pegged him for a sadist. He had an Irish setter with him. He'd been bringing her up north since she was a puppy. He took her for walks twice a day and fed her Swiss mushroom burgers from the local Hardee's. They spotted his battered Volkswagen Westfalia camper in the drive-thru at all hours. He loved that dog.

Max had no permanent address. Retired, he roamed the country, staying in campgrounds and motels, taking in the sights of America. "Choose your own adventure," he said. "I've chosen mine and never once regretted it."

Decades ago he'd made his living as a pulp writer. He'd been famous in his own peculiar way. He edited ten popular volumes of supernatural stories, *Weirder Than You Imagine*. Collectors paid hundreds of dollars for well-kept old copies. "Too bad they don't pay me," he joked. Now he considered himself a full-time cosmic adventurer. He never mentioned any family. "I'm a natural-born loner. Only two things I find myself needing are a good book and my dog."

Maybe there'd been an accident. Max had to be in his eighties. Always quiet and polite in an old-fashioned way that seemed to be disappearing from the world, he was easy to overlook. Yet he had the twinkliest, most mischievous eyes; they made Opal think of a six-year-old with a frog stuffed in his hip pocket. Max smoked little black cigarillos with plastic tips. Each morning when he left the motel, leash in hand, his dog trotting at his side, Opal would air out his room and fog it with freshener.

Had Max's number finally come up?

Was the dog keening over his body?

That could be.

Max was dead. Oh Lord, that was it. The dog was alerting them. What if he had a heart attack or a stroke? What if there was still a chance to save him?

She stormed out onto the motel's narrow sidewalk. She passed draped windows. Her slippers gliding on the melting ice, she turned and her feet nearly went out from under her. Cigarettes. She smelled them and the paint. The door ahead wasn't fully closed. She banged her fist on the door, not pausing, but shouting over her shoulder as she readied the next room's key.

"Wyatt, come on. There's an emergency. Something's happened to Max."

She knew it. A terrible tragedy had occurred, or worse, a crime. Perhaps there was time to stop it. Time to help.

The tapping sounded like a rainstorm. Maybe the sprinklers were on. The room would be damaged. A waterlogged rug never smells right again. They'd have to rip it out and replace it. How could she think so selfishly? If Max were dead, the smell would be the least of their problems.

She had her key in the lock.

She opened the door.

Oh, it didn't smell like rain. Or wet carpets. Or a dead thing. It smelled like blood.

The walls, the carpet, the beds and furniture—everything was drenched in blood . . . as if a person had exploded.

CHAPTER 7

Dead of winter. Vera understood what that meant now. It was like a bomb fell. Charcoal ruins, and everywhere you looked in the night, smoke rising from them.

She drove up to a gas station.

Better leave the engine running.

Her fingers gripped the door. She popped the latch and pushed. She hadn't even climbed out before the chill was on her.

She shut the door.

Shivering. That last breath forced ice down her throat.

She didn't want to leave her car.

Frost plagued the gas station's windows. She couldn't see anybody inside. Surgical lights shined. For the millionth time, she was second-guessing herself. One minute she wanted to press on and find a motel. Next minute she noticed her gas level dipping, needle approaching empty, and the thought of being stranded out here alone . . .

How far?

If only she had an idea how far it was until the next town. A burg that was sizable enough to merit its own gas, food, *and lodging*. She opened the console stowage compartment and rummaged through clutter. Forget GPS. No maps, either. She knew that already. Wishful thinking on her part, or maybe it was the first tingle of panic.

A shadow circulated behind the station's frosty glass front.

Okay, so some poor sucker was pulling the night shift. How long until he noticed the Camaro? If she didn't get out soon he'd start wondering. What's up? Why's she sitting there doing nothing? There wasn't exactly a line at the pumps.

Or even another car.

He probably *had* noticed her. Vera looked for the security camera.

The difference, Vera thought, between a late-night gas station and an early-morning motel was this: Those gas station clerks were buggy.

Wide-eyed and wired.

Be it speed, caffeine, or the slippery skin mag they just shoved under the counter; they had to make wakefulness their occupation. Maybe it was simply the fear of robbery.

Pulling into these lonely highway places gave her jitters.

There had to be a camera. She feared it. The concrete pad was lit up like a Hollywood premiere. She felt exposed. Strange eyes were watching her. They had to be. The sensation of two jelly orbs sliding against her skin.

She shuddered.

Keep going, girl. Stay in your car.

So damn cold out it seemed to be personal.

Listen to your gut. Apply your foot to the gas pedal.

Okay, good.

She turned back onto the dark highway.

Hell.

These red wool tights were not cutting it in the below-zero temps. She wiggled her ringed fingers under the heater vents. She tugged her skirt.

Why exactly was she wearing a skirt? She knew why. Chan liked it. He practically sniffed like a hound every time she entered a room. He had been the latest and most spectacular catastrophe. Three years wasted. It was over. She'd had her fill. Though there were aspects of Chan she'd miss.

One aspect in particular leapt to mind.

That image connected to another and another, links in a thick, unbroken chain. The chain ended on the bucket seat beside her. Her memories triggered a physical response. Her heartbeat accelerated. She got dewy. A belt of warmth cinched around her thighs. She glanced at her purse, where her .25 Bobcat slept.

Chan had given her the gun as a birthday present.

She knew the basics. He'd taken her to a range in the basement of this place where he bought his ammo; the air smelled like moldy blankets and fireworks. Chan getting off on the whole experience. He could turn anything into sex.

Load it like this here. Your palm goes . . . now put your other hand underneath. Snug. Feel it? Don't be afraid to grab on, she'll kick. Thumb the safety. Arms up. Get your finger inside. Point at what you hate. Squeeze.

She desperately needed a respite from this constant forward motion.

Early-morning motels were different than 'round-the-clock gas and doughnut peddlers.

If she put in a couple more hours of road time, it would pay off.

Find a place that would appreciate the business. No questions asked. An independent that didn't keep close tabs. Where they were glad to see you, whomever you were. Maybe the desk clerk would be sleep-deprived and already heading for dreamland.

You traded bills for a key and they forgot you.

At least she hoped so.

Dawn wiped the low edge of the horizon. Vera passed a pick-up, parked at the side of the road: a beater, an old Ford. Her headlights banked off the cab—the back window plastered with a decal— a furry buck-toothed mammal in a sweater leaning on a giant maroon *M*. A few miles later, she came upon a man walking, plastic gas can in his hand, thumb out. He looked eighteen, and in her estimation, like a straight-from-the-catalog All-American Jock. She had dated her share. Not that many years ago, but a different galaxy that was so far away.

What did she note? He was hatless, tall, stretching out the seams of his letterman jacket. The solid block of navy blue didn't fit this growing boy. He wore it unsnapped. His pants were wet to the knees. His hair stuck up and his ears stuck out. He wasn't ugly, though. Far from it.

What can a woman tell in her rearview mirror at fifty miles per hour?

Enough.

She pulled to the shoulder.

Vera, honey, don't you never ever pick up hitchhikers. Promise me.

Quiet now, Daddy.

This could work, she thought. Take the hitcher to a motel. Ask him to go to the office and pay. Nobody would see her. She didn't even have to step inside. Favor for a favor. Then she'd find a way to lose him.

Her window squealed, descending.

He broke into a jog, reaching the car before she could change her mind and drive away.

"You picked a great place to take a walk," Vera said.

"I only wish it was colder," he said. His breath clouded the air. He had red lips and rosy cheeks under a three-day stubble. Midwestern milk-fed, all the way.

"Hop in before you freeze to death."

"Thanks."

He yanked the door handle. Folded his body into the seat offered. He smelled like a Christmas tree. Vera saw pine needles stuck to his carpenter pants. He set the gas can between his drenched blue hi-tops. He closed the door. He wasn't talking. She hadn't expected that. Maybe he really was half frozen.

"You from around here?" she asked.

"Born and raised." He slicked a hand through his damp hair.

Nice hands, she noted. Vera was a sucker for strong, meaty hands, the kind where the veins and tendons showed under the skin. She liked watching them work, their machinery. Kung-fu grippers, she called them. It was a clue to the inner man. Chan had stellar hands. Her friends thought she was nuts.

"What's your name?"

"Adam Larkin." He reached out to shake.

She touched flesh as cold as any T-bone in the grocery store.

"I'm Vera Coffey, like the drink only more hyper."

She saw the corner of his mouth indent. A smile, at least. *God, make him not a creep. I'm over my limit of creeps forever.*

"I appreciate you stopping. It's a long walk home."

"No problem. If you don't mind me asking . . . how'd you get wet?"

"I jumped in the ditch."

"Why'd you . . ."

"A semi cut it close around a curve back there."

"That's awful."

"It could've ended up worse. I have a new sympathy for road-kill."

Vera shared her husky laughter with him. She tried hard not to fidget too much. She didn't want this guy thinking she was loopy. Giddy energy bubbled up inside her. The stress of the last few days, the long solitary drive . . . it began to hit home. She had to bite her tongue to keep from babbling. Face forward and drive, she told herself. Don't forget to look over at him, either. Show attention. Be careful not to crash the damn car.

"I've been driving all night," she said.

"Really?"

"My eyes are like—" she said, opening them wide. She made a *this big* circle with her thumb and finger.

"Where you coming from?" he asked.

"I . . . Iowa."

"I've got cousins in Iowa."

"It's not really a town where I live. I rent a room on a farm. I'm a boarder, you know?" Oh, God. How stupid did that lie sound? "I'm not in the barn or anything. It's a pretty little clapboard house with a big wrap-around porch, shady oak trees growing out front, and a vegetable garden. A creek runs through the backyard. There's a tire swing—"

"And a white picket fence?"

"You've been there?"

Vera's eyes flitted over to him. He gave her a big smile this time. He had white teeth and dimples. A lock of chestnut hair fell loose over his forehead. He looked about seventeen with that smile. But he wasn't seventeen. Underneath that pine scent, he smelled like a man. He crooked his knee and cupped it with one of those shovel hands. He hit the side of the red can with his shoe. She caught a whiff of gasoline. His eyes were smoky and deep enough she couldn't see their bottom with a quick glance.

Did he know she was lying?

His attention keyed on the road.

"I haven't really been anywhere . . . other than here," he said.

The Camaro raced past a signpost.

AMERICAN RAPIDS

POP.—

The town census number had been blasted away with shotgun pellets.

"I need to find a motel," she said.

The speed of his response startled her.

"I know a place," he said.

CHAPTER 8

The woman entered his motel room screaming.

Max Caul turned away from his reflection. Tendrils of steam twisted around him as hot water ran into the sink. She sounded close. He thought she might be standing right there, between the toilet and the curtained tub. But the space was empty. Had he left the TV on?

No.

The terror was too real.

The woman screamed again.

Max emerged, brandishing an orange Bic razor in his right hand. The room was smeared. He knew why. His other hand made a quick search of the dresser top for his eyeglasses. He stopped and touched his head. The round silver-edged lenses pushed up on his bald dome. He exhaled deeply through his nose as he lowered the frames.

He pivoted and saw Opal—one of the owners of the motel.

Saw her crumpling to the carpet.

Her husband, out of breath, appeared behind her in the doorway. The two of them gaped at Max. They both seemed shocked.

Max checked his state of undress: He wore corduroys, suspenders, and a flimsy grayed undershirt. His crooked, ivory toes protruded from holes in his socks. Half his face was lathered in mint shaving foam. Not ideal but it would have to suffice. "Is there a problem?" he asked.

"You're alive," Opal said.

Max laughed. "Yes, technically, that is true."

The dog materialized from between the double beds.

Her wet nose shined and her golden red tail wagged—the picture of excellent canine health. She ducked her head and nuzzled Opal's cheek.

"Ann-Margret. Annie girl, leave her alone." Max clasped the Irish setter's collar. She immediately sat back on her haunches and began licking his fingers.

Wyatt started apologizing.

"They're coming here," Opal said to Max. "It's too late."

"Excuse me? What?" Max bent and felt a familiar stabbing in his kidneys.

"The Pitch are coming for you. Leave now. The Pitch are coming."

Max nodded politely and frowned; his overgrown eyebrows twitching.

Wyatt helped his wife to her feet. "I'm really sorry about this, Max. Opal hasn't been feeling well. I think she's . . ." He was at a loss for words.

"Under the weather?" Max suggested.

Wyatt nodded. The lower muscles of his face clenched. He seemed to bite and chew on nothing. *He's teetering on the verge of panic,* Max observed to himself. This was not a panicking man. Something had him afraid.

"She's not been well," Wyatt said again.

Wyatt's eye patch made Max uneasy; the cancellation behind it couldn't be disguised. Max tried to focus on the remaining eye. It did no good. His mind supplied the image of a blinking red socket. Nausea rippled across his abdomen. He covered his mouth with his knuckles and expelled a tiny pocket of sour air.

Wyatt attempted to usher his wife from the room.

She wouldn't budge.

Arctic wind charged past them, invading the lodging. The three people huddled closer together for a moment. Opal reached out and snagged Max's bare wrist. Her grip was like pliers. Max became certain her purpose was to verify his corporeal existence; he patted her hand to reassure her.

She released him.

"I'm very sorry," Wyatt said as he led Opal into the bitter cold. Their steps crackled in retreat. A grating of ice particles showered them, blowing sharply into the room. Pinprick water beads formed on the old man's glasses.

"No problem," Max called out. "No problem at all. I hope she feels better later. Try some chamomile tea. Celestial Seasonings. Cup of tea and a nice long soak in a bubble bath can work wonders. I'm fine. Please think nothing of it."

Max closed the door. The automatic lock clicked. He engaged the deadbolt and carefully attached the length of chain.

He realized he was still clutching the disposable razor in his trembling fingers. He threw it in the corner. The shaving cream on his chin had started to sag and dribble into the notch of his throat.

From his pocket he withdrew a peg of chalk and began to draw symbols on the inside of the door. Hastily, he used the heel of his other hand to erase the symbols already sketched there from the night before.

Thank God they hadn't discovered his mild acts of defacement. He had no valid explanation to offer them. Usually he cleaned up with a damp paper towel whenever he left the room for longer than a few minutes. They had never caught him. His main symbol was a boxy labyrinth; around it he placed spirals. He recited the incantations. *Let my enemies be lost. May they find their pathways blocked. Let them wander in endless circles.*

Or circle around him like sharks.

He was old and he was dying. He knew that.

His blood flowered in the water. The scent of his wounds transmitted for all those capable of reception. *His enemies.*

They were out there, to be sure.

He went to the draped window and repeated the rituals. He didn't bother erasing his older markings this time. The drapery opened into the room like a huge wing. He worked feverishly over the fabric, slashing marks with his chalk stick. Yesterday's symbols were smudging, but soon the old and new together lay hidden in the folds of stiff material.

"At last." He sighed.

His protections hadn't failed. Thank goodness.

But a false breach was still a breach.

He was startled by what had happened: a woman bursting into his room and collapsing. Max sat on the bed. Ann-Margret jumped up and placed her soft rusty head against his thigh. He scratched her ears and she closed her eyes in bliss. He'd been startled, yes, but not entirely surprised. He had long suspected contact was eminent. But he hadn't foreseen it coming from the motel owners. An unexpected direction—it caught him off-guard.

He needed to be more alert in the future.

The ex-policeman, Wyatt, thought his wife had gone utterly hysterical, ranting and acting mad in public. Her husband was confused, embarrassed.

And wrong.

Opal didn't appear to understand the import of her visions.

Max wasn't about to explain. Not now. How could he? No one would believe him. He'd learned the hard way how reluctant people were to give up their assumptions about reality. He wasn't sure how much the woman already knew. Bits and pieces, likely, but she couldn't fit the puzzle together. She must have the gift. Funny, though. He'd been her acquaintance for years, and while he liked her and conversed with her easily, he had never detected she was psychic.

He hadn't planned on that.

Although, as he pondered, it occurred to him her talent could prove useful.

Go figure. The cosmos finds a route. Always does. It keeps on spinning. He hoped to keep Opal out of harm's way. He'd always gotten a warm apricot-hued vibe around her. Pleasant, quite strong. She harbored an old soul and a decent one at that. It would be a shame if she died.

But a greater excitement filled him.

To think the final process was in motion . . .

It gave him a delicious thrill. Like swallowing a smoking cold scoop of ice cream right off the top of the cone and feeling it slip-slide down his throat, burring up against his spine. He received the same chasing ice cream headache, too: a dull butter knife inserted behind his eyes at the temple and slanting upward at forty-five degrees.

The Pitch are coming.

Opal was dead on the money with that call.

In fact, he wouldn't be surprised if they were already here. The Pitch. Close at hand. Keeping to the shadows they loved so dearly. He shivered.

Dead on, indeed.

CHAPTER 9

Vera thought her tired eyes were playing tricks on her. Strangeness leapt across the highway after they passed the Super 8. Then she saw it again. On the gentle hilltop straight ahead: a red flickering lashed out in long erratic strands, daubing the pavement. The wind blew hard. She could feel it pushing down on the car, like it was trying to keep her away. A half-mile wide blade of snow guillotined the highway. The flickering disappeared. Whiteness. She turned her wipers on high and leaned closer to the windshield. The wiper arms shuddered, inch by squeaking inch, over the glass.

Her view cleared.

The red lashes were back, bouncing crazily off the snow mounds on either side of the freshly plowed four-lane road. They striped the countryside in crimson, growing more intense the farther she drove into town.

Red.

Red.

Red.

She eased her foot off the gas pedal.

Not slowing down too much. She didn't want to alarm her passenger. Merge a river of caffeine with anxiety and no sleep and you start to see funny things. As the Camaro steadily climbed the hill, her heart forced up against her sternum like a balled fist.

Police cars.

Two of them with their light bars swirling. There were no sirens. The silence was even worse, Vera thought. As if they'd been hiding in ambush.

Waiting for her to come up over the rise.

The two patrol cars were stopped, but their engines were running. One parked on the shoulder; its headlights frosting over Vera's skin. Goosebumps puckered on her arms. The second car swerved, drawing up perpendicular into a commercial driveway. She was forced to pass in-between. Under the amber haze of a business sign, she could make out the driver's silhouette, sitting behind the wheel, motionless.

The wind bellowed. It gave the illusion of gathering speed, as if the Camaro were being pulled into a vortex. The edge of town solidified. Vera looked at the cop car again. Her hands were wet. All her rings felt tight and itchy.

She slowed.

An insignia was printed on the cop car's door. Letters spelled out AMERICAN RAPIDS POLICE in a black rainbow above a blue-and-white waterfall.

The door opened.

In the distance, a third set of red lights bore down.

Was it a roadblock?

"Looks like something's happening up ahead," Adam said. His voice sounded soft, whispery. His gaze focused on the roadside.

It's a motel driveway, Vera realized. The spinning lights made her seasick.

Was this some sort of trap?

"Maybe there's an accident. You'd better slow down," he said.

"I hope that's not the place you're recommending I stay." She lifted her foot a millimeter. Already she felt like they were crawling. The cop with the open door hadn't come forward into the light. She could make out a shoulder, clad in inky blue leather, and the lunar curve of a man's jaw. Nothing else.

A radio squawked. The sound cut inside the sealed Camaro. Vera swore it patched right into her skull. Sonic fuzz followed a burst of harsh electrified voices. Vera couldn't discern the words. But they made her queasy. Her belly filled with a slow-dripping dread. Was she walking into a trap? Not knowing exactly what to do, she reconsidered every move she'd taken in the last twenty-four hours. Careful—she'd been so damn careful.

Yet apparently she wasn't being careful enough. Picking up a hitcher. Telling him her name. That was stupid. Okay. He was hers to deal with now. Or later. But the police were a bigger problem. She tried to calm herself and think logically. Could Chan have called them? Impossible. He hated the cops. And he had more to lose than she did, especially if the law got involved.

What about the people who hired Chan? The ones directly responsible for the slaughter at that house back in Illinois? You wouldn't find 911 on their speed dial. They'd be coming after her. That's for certain. But they wouldn't use the police. No, their approach would be stealthier. More lethal. And they'd do a lot worse to her before they killed her.

Those poor women in that house . . .

God, if she thought about them she'd definitely lose it.

Adam sat up. His back arched. He shifted his legs around and Vera caught another wave of gasoline fumes. It made her nauseated. Her mouth tasted like greasy rubber bands; the dread in her belly threatened to erupt.

Where was this guy leading her?

"Seriously, this isn't the place. Is it?" she asked.

He fixated on the scene.

Vera took the opportunity to slip her hand into her purse. Stroking the Bobcat's trigger, she said, "I don't know who you are, but—"

"Jesus, I wonder what's going on. Three squads, that's practically the whole town police force."

"What is this?"

"I'm not sure—"

"Tell me what you know!"

He looked over at her like she must be kidding . . . or crazy.

"Relax, okay. I'm riding along with you. What could I know?"

Vera had no comeback. As they passed the flashing police cars, she watched Adam's blood-lit face. He had a good point. Letting go of the Bobcat, she hoped he wouldn't notice her hand buried in her purse.

A tall cylindrical object loomed over the motel.

Vera gawked up at it. Near the top was a sharp protuberance jutting out toward the road. It looked like an awning. It was a beak. The snow parted and danced around the uniformly thick column, which stood inert along the windy roadside but craned forward like a bird hunting fish over a cold-running stream. They had to drive almost underneath it. Grotesque carvings were gouged into the trunk, stacked one on top of another. Masks and gargoyles. Frozen faces stolen from a nightmare.

"Is that a totem pole?" Vera asked.

"Behold the famous Totem Motor Lodge." Adam indicated a low, timber structure hunkering in a depression of land surrounded by sodium vapor lights. The yellowish stained accommodations recalled an outsized version of the liver-brown Lincoln Logs Vera played with as a child. An affront to their rustic charm, a large satellite dish roosted on the highest beams. Snowflakes obliterated it from their sight. The wooden tower in the foreground grew starker.

As they gathered speed, it, too, disappeared.

"That thing is spooky." Vera pressed the gas, felt her seatback respond with a comforting nudge. "What's it famous for anyway?"

"Nothing. It's only a gimmick."

"People are supposed to see that creepy pole and want to check in?"

"I didn't say it was a good gimmick."

Adam squeezed her shoulder and she jumped at the physical contact.

"Easy does it," he said, backing away. "Here's our turn."

CHAPTER 10

The Rendezvous Motel sounded pleasant enough. The parking lot exhibited a half-dozen snowcapped cars. A pickle-green neon sign glowed in the morning twilight, trimmed as the entire motel was, in multicolored Christmas lights: big, fat, old-fashioned bulbs—the kind Vera remembered from childhood. A plastic Santa sleigh, complete with reindeer, including Rudolph, warped in the wind but didn't dash away, cable-tied to the roof. Clean and presentable.

Homey and seemingly normal.

Like Adam here.

She stretched her arms, swinging her open palm close to him. He ducked.

"I wasn't going to hit you," she said.

"I didn't think so."

"Yes, you did." She resisted the urge to rub his scruff like he was her cat. Sleep deprivation made her this way; impulsive, horny, and slightly dangerous.

"Thanks for the lift," Adam said.

"There's somebody you can call? Gas your ride?" She smiled at him and ran a finger around the steering wheel.

"Yeah, I'm set. This is practically my home."

Vera peered into the vacant motel office. Wipers off. Snow caked to the windshield. She killed the motor.

"I was wondering if you could do something for me."

"I'm not sure what a guy with wet pants and no gas can do. But I'll try."

Vera twisted. Her short skirt rode up; her thighs flexed under her red woolen tights. She gave his knee a firm squeeze. "Go in there and get me a key."

His eyebrow kinked, amused.

"You've got a suspicious mind," she said. "I like that. Shows you're thinking. Men don't do that enough. Driving all night made me temporarily stupid." She dug into her purse. "Of course I'm paying for the room." She handed him a hundred-dollar bill. "Is that enough?"

He turned the bill over.

"Mr. Suspicious, I need a single for one night." She shooed him away.

He nodded. But he didn't go.

"I appreciate you doing this," she said. "The state I'm in . . . I don't feel like meeting new people."

Adam opened his door.

Climbed out.

He reached back inside, looking straight at her, his puzzlement evident. He snatched up the red can from the floor.

"Be back in a minute," he said.

He lingered. Searching for something telling in her face. A clue. He was trying to decide what she was up to.

Vera worried he might run. Steal all the money she had. He didn't seem the running type. Damn, she couldn't risk it.

"Know something? I don't want to be alone on Christmas Eve. That's too depressing. Come visit me. We'll party. You like tequila? Let's hang out tonight and see who comes down the chimney . . . if you're not busy . . ."

What she wanted most was a few hours of uninterrupted sleep.

She'd hit the pillow, shut her eyes, drift. She'd never fall asleep though. She could sense that now. Her tension ratcheted off the charts. Muscles twitched involuntarily under her skin. Out of the corner of her eye, the police lights were meandering over the grounds of the Totem Lodge. The night wasn't something she wanted to face.

Adam hadn't moved from the Camaro's bumper.

"Sounds interesting," he said.

"I thought so."

"Good people work here." He motioned to the office.

She still couldn't see anyone, anywhere.

"They'll treat you right," he added.

"I could use some right treatment."

"I'll get your key."

"I appreciate it, Adam."

"Always good to know," he said.

When he pushed off, she felt the Camaro rock. He walked through the sifting flakes. She watched ice crystals sugar his wavy hair. He looked good going away, even if he was too clean-cut for her taste. The red can brushed his leg with each step he took. Her last green bill flapped angrily in the wind. He'd look better coming back with a room key and her change. She leaned against the headrest, closed her eyes, and yawned. Sometimes the good boys turned out better than the bad ones. They surprised you, but the surprises didn't make you want to shoot them.

Or run away.

Movement—a growing blur at the edge of her vision. Someone approached the car. This stranger—had he been crouched behind the building when she pulled in? Her heart spiked. Who was it?

A man wearing a yellow hooded parka walking his dog—

It wasn't them.

Her body shuddered.

Not the Pitch.

She relaxed in tiny increments. Her hands trembled. She told herself it was the caffeine. It wasn't.

How would she know the Pitch if they came after her?

What did they look like?

The man spotted the Camaro. Saw her at the wheel. His hood turned toward the trunk. He stopped.

No, no, she thought. It wouldn't be an old man walking a dog. Though the way he stared didn't soothe her nerves. As if he could see through steel.

And if he could, what would he know of her cargo?

CHAPTER 11

Only Chan and the Pitch knew what she'd stolen. Yesterday, as she slipped out, finding her father's old Chevy parked beside a jungle of weeds, she became aware of the winter moon. She was leaving. Chan lay wrecked on the waterbed. Before their excursion he'd been jumpy, wired to the gills and grinning to himself. He'd taken something. Pills. She didn't know which ones. She could see the hard-on inside his jeans. He kept saying he wanted to go and see. "Come on, baby. Let's peek in on those funky bitches. See what the Pitch did to them."

Then he took her there.

To the witches' house.

And she saw the dead women.

It was a dreary afternoon, following a dreary morning. He'd been in the house once already, hours earlier, in the middle of the night, to conduct the theft. They say criminals return to the scenes of their crimes.

Chan brought his girlfriend with him.

They drove in circles. The Loop was due east; the Chicago skyline stacked in the distance. West Garfield Park—Vera saw the opaque zeppelin dome of the hundred-year-old conservatory rising above the rooftops. She'd never been there. Never seen the tropical hothouse blooms and palms. The park itself was barren, emptied of life. She wouldn't have stopped her car in this part of the city. Faces not like hers; a sense of trespass invaded her blood.

Vera watched the sun cannonball into the stripped trees.

Instant night.

They parked blocks away. And waited. Chan's plan was to walk shyly up on it. Scout it. Run if necessary.

She wondered if he'd wait for her to catch up.

Finally he said, "Let's do it."

They left the car.

Two- and three-story residences hemmed the boulevard. Shadow dwellings. Vera paid close attention to her surroundings. Wooden-plank back porches slapped onto cliffs of smudged brick. Through the alley, around the corner, Chan tugged her. Stone facades un-blinking like witnesses. Once they were grand. Now these subdi-vided homes became the shelter of last resort. This was living on the knifepoint. Those who tread here did not go lightly.

Or they did not go for long.

Fences—all varieties. Plywood closures snug at windows and doors; a prevalence of padlocks. Suspicion like a pall hung over-head. Whatever you were doing—this place, this hour, out of doors—was the devil's business or trying to escape it. The local graffiti artists were gifted. Shocks of shaped color injected into the bleakness.

Light traffic.

Telephone junction boxes expelled cable to nowhere.

A pair of scissors lay dropped on the sidewalk like a warning. Glass, sampling the spectrum, decorated the gutters.

Here it was.

Rough-hewn and crooked as a tombstone.

The house. All the lights were out.

Chan slipped into a gangway between residences. He motioned for her to follow and keep her head down. Vera saw a shadow dart behind Chan.

"Was that a rat?"

"I didn't see anything. Hold my light for a minute."

They went in through a basement window. Chan mentored Vera in lawbreaking. Keep your hands in your pockets. Don't touch anything. Walk where I walk. Ears open. Listen to the house. There may be others inside.

There was no one.

No one alive.

"Holy fuck," Chan said.

Eight women. Vera knew when Chan had last been inside the house, they were asleep. The rooms were redolent of Nag Champa, patchouli, and a pot of curried rice cooked and eaten for dinner. He said he'd stumbled upon marijuana plants in a closet growing under egg yolk orangey lights. Another door revealed a workbench, a mounted mini-vise, and small drawers of beads, chains, and spooled wire. The witches made jewelry they sold online. He peeked into the bedrooms. They shared their beds, lying together in pairs, lovers asleep under warm, homemade quilts. He had listened for their slow regular breaths.

Now they were naked on the floor.

Six white women. The other two might've been Latinas; their skin was darker. None of the women looked dark under the flashlight beam. Their blood shined red black. It wasn't theirs anymore. It had left them and gone wandering.

Gone wild.

Chan and Vera surveyed the carnage.

The smell . . . she couldn't stop gagging.

"Let's get out of here," she said.

"Crazy for them to live in this neighborhood," he said, tying a bandana around his nose and mouth. "They stood out. The Pitch knew they bought this house. They knew every move these hippie skanks made. Followed them cross-country from Corvallis. That's in Oregon."

"I know where Corvallis is," Vera said.

It was hard to believe what she was seeing was real.

Chan couldn't stop talking. "These motherfuckers got a thing for the eyes. It's their symbology or whatever. They go for the peepers. Get a load of what they did to this señorita before they tore her throat out . . ."

Vera threw up on a wall.

Hot bitter tang coated her lips. She stumbled. She rested her forehead against a door frame to keep from falling over. The dizziness resolved into an internal sloshing. The bottom of her alligator boot stuck to the floor. She peeled it up and wiped it on a bathroom rug without looking down. She wanted water. Her hip bumped a sink. She turtled her hand into her sleeve and twisted the cold tap. But she couldn't bring herself to drink. She turned it off.

"What the fuck? I told you not to touch anything."

"I want to leave."

"Shit, babe, I know. This is heavy-duty. What am I doing bringing you here?"

"I don't know."

His look cut to the outer room. "I had to see it. Curiosity killed the asshole. I had to know what they did. I knew it would be fucked up. But talk about overkill . . ."

He lifted his bandana and kissed the top of her head.

"Okay, you saw it. Now can we please—?"

"Shhh . . . shhh. You hear something?"

Chan clicked the flashlight off.

Wind blowing—the moan made her neck hairs dance.

Scratching.

He gripped her in the darkness. His hand snaked under her jacket. He was sweating. Breathing through his mouth. Electrical current flowed through his wet fingertips. He was kneading her breast. She felt a tug on the zipper of her jeans. The noises coming from him were feral.

"You sick fuck, get off me." She pushed him into the dark.

He laughed.

If something happens, he'll leave me here. With the other girls.

"Follow me," he whispered.

She did.

They made it back to the car. Before Vera could shut her door, Chan was leaving rubber on the pavement. Plunging off his high, paranoia kicked in. He rattled on and on. Pausing just long enough to draw another smoke-laced breath. He kept switching lanes, tailgating every bumper ahead of them. His look said he was punched out, a black-eyed terror. Full-body exhaustion sandbagged him. Then came the silence; his mouth tight as a suture. He couldn't hold eye contact.

"What're we going to do?" she asked.

"That's murder 666-style back there, babe. We've ventured deep into the black. I messed up big time. I'm dealing with psycho murdering devil worshippers, okay? Fuck me! After I get paid, I got to disappear for a while."

"You're disappearing?"

"You and me, I mean."

Vera had to wonder. Chan the bad boy. Always playing angles and seeming to win more than lose. One step up on the competition. She'd first met him more than three years ago, in a Bridgeport bar with a shamrock on the door. She was downing cinnamon shots with a couple of roommates who'd just bought cruise tickets to Puerto Vallarta. The three girlfriends had talked for weeks about going down Mexico way.

Toes in the sand. Swim-up bars. A fruity drink with an umbrella and a name you couldn't remember. Maybe a hook-up to match.

When the time came, Vera didn't have the cash.

She'd started a new job. Office admin for a company that sold plastic coffee lids and stirrers. No vacation days accrued on her paycheck until Christmas. That, plus she was switching apartments. Trading her spot in their sixth-floor triple for a cheaper, garden level studio closer to the El train.

She was deeply bummed and trying not to show it.

A supercell ripped across the South Side that night. Thunder rolled. The lights flickered, drawing a chorus of oohs and ahhs. In walked Chan. Wearing his bike leathers and soaked to the bone. He was drowned-rat cute. Mirrored aviators pushed up into his slicked hair. He had a quick toothy smile and, when he shucked off his jacket, Vera could see through his T-shirt: a hard stomach ribbed like a desert road. He walked up, pulled out a wad of cash, and ordered a whiskey shooter. His eyes were large, acid green. He looked right at Vera.

"Where you been hiding?"

Lightning struck a transformer down the block.

The bar went dark.

It was a thrilling game. Over the next forty months she learned about how he made his bankroll. Home invasions. He was good. He had the tools, the skills, the guts. He had future plans. He wouldn't call himself small-time, not with the cash he pulled down. He stole from rich assholes. They had insurance, right? He shunned violence. Said it was impractical. Classless.

Bars and clubs. Vera guessed they spent more hours in them than the people who worked there. She didn't work anymore. Chan forbid it. He kept her in finery, he said. She made new friends. Chan's friends. Or she sat alone while Chan did business. He set his goals high. He mixed with a heavier and heavier crowd. Times were good. She wouldn't deny the excitement she felt in the beginning—and later, too. When he scored, it was Christmas on steroids. She didn't think about danger as anything real. It gave off energy. You'd catch a buzz. The aphrodisiac effect never failed. Chan *always* wanted her, in every permutation conceivable. She wanted him, too. It was animal. They tore into each other. They made each other raw. This was the most fun she'd ever had with a man. Her eyes were open wide to the fact it wasn't love and it wasn't going to turn into love. Three years together, knowing one another's secrets and fears, maybe that was all you could hope for.

Sharing imperfect lives.

One night, when he told her about how two of Chicago's finest walked inches from his nose, shining their Maglites as he recoiled inside an air vent, she tasted the dust and metal. Her stomach twisted for him.

And when Chan came home with a pit-bull bite—blood saturating the leg of his jeans—his belt in his mouth to keep from screaming . . .

She knew she needed to get away.

But she didn't.

Chan hit a dry spell and money got tight. Police stopped by their apartment and questioned him about a Gold Coast condo job he had nothing to do with. His name was floating around. There always seemed to be a patrol on their street or behind them when they were driving. Vera had trouble talking to acquaintances without lying. Everything felt like a setup.

It was like the lights in the bar had finally snapped on.

She didn't like what she saw.

Chan told her about this special assignment. A freaky group needed him to steal something for them. They couldn't do it themselves. It wasn't the danger involved that bugged them, it was freak rules. They were a kind of sect and another sect took their stuff. They wanted it back. He didn't ask too many questions. Because it looked like easy money. A decent chunk of coin to bounce them out of this rut. Vera thought it sounded too weird. She didn't like the name the group called themselves, either.

The Pitch.

Back inside their apartment, their security felt weak. Chan cracked the seal on a bottle of Old No. 7. Drank. The bottleneck clinked against his skull rings. She watched his whiskered throat move in jerks. The stolen item sat on the kitchen table. He came up for air. His face sweated rivets.

"Put that thing in the closet. I can't look at it," he said. He rubbed the bottle against his flushed cheeks.

He went into the bedroom. Taking the bottle with him but not taking Vera. He shut the door. Her heart tripped when she heard the lock turn.

"Tired," he said.

Vera jiggled the knob. "Let me in, Chan."

"I can't do that."

"What do you mean?"

She'd never seen Chan scared. She felt like a lost kid. If she had a mom, then she would've called her to cry. Chan talked to her through the door. It sounded like he'd fallen down a mine shaft. He needed to rest up before he turned the item over to the Pitch.

"Tonight, you hear me? Midnight I'm supposed to see them. I've about had it with these fucking Satanists!" He swore at himself. He laughed without joy. Hollow thumps as he banged his head into the wall.

Then he realized she must still be listening.

"I'm gonna be okay, babe. We're okay. The creature features want to meet me at midnight. So be it. I have to be prepared. Sleep a little bit first. Clear my mind. Now you go away. Let me do this thing like a man."

He wasn't sleeping. She smelled his Marlboros under the door.

The item.

It was a box. That was what Vera decided. Though it looked a whole lot stranger. The shape was not cubic. Instead, it was two pyramids with their bottoms melded together. She couldn't locate any seam.

If it opened, she didn't know how to open it. But it must.

Why would anyone want a box that didn't open?

She sat beside the box with her feet on the kitchen table. With the pointy toe of her boot, not really thinking about what she was doing but just doing it, she gave the box a little push. Eyeing it dreamily as it slid.

She sat up.

This didn't make sense.

She rubbed her fingertip on a mark she found on the table.

A scorch mark. She pushed the oddly shaped box out of the way.

There underneath—three dark brown burns on the butcher's block . . . an outline in the shape of a triangle.

The wood was grilled.

What the hell?

Chan owned an old Zippo lighter. A flip-top. It had an oily metal touch. He liked to play with it. Flip and shut it again. When he got bored. Flip. Shut. Open a flame and hold it to things. See how they reacted. That must've been it. Vera nodded as she envisioned him doing it—the hot lighter pinched between his fingers, the flame licking at the box.

Though Vera hadn't actually seen him do it.

He told her the Pitch treasured this item. To them it was sacred. Why risk spoiling it because you were bored?

She felt a sudden terrible conviction that they should not, could not, give this thing, this box, whatever it was—they couldn't simply hand it to those killers.

She knocked.

"Chan, open this door right now. Let me in, or I'm walking. I'm walking and taking that thing with me. Maybe I'll throw it in Lake Michigan. That's exactly what I'll do. You can freeze your balls off diving for it."

No way was he sleeping. He'd heard every word.

This was a test. Chan's game of chicken. Well, he'd always underestimated her. She had more guts in her pinky than he did in his whole damned body. Then something occurred to her. She knew the bait that might lure him out of his hiding place.

"I'll take the Pitch's precious box and give it to my Aunt Helene up in Manitoba. She's a nun. She'll know how to destroy it."

Chan wasn't answering. She didn't smell any smoke by the door.

As she stood there, sniffing, the door jerked open. Chan's shirtless torso canted into the light. Greasy jeans snagged off his pelvis. The bedroom lurked behind him. His tongue traced sandpapery lips.

"You wouldn't," he said.

"Try me."

Arms loose, he hooked his elbows over her shoulders. He pulled her close and kissed her. His devilish mouth tasted sour from the whisky and too many cigarettes. She hated what he stirred inside her. How easy she made it for him. An old wind-up doll ready for play whenever he cranked her key. He bent his knees like a boxer and cornered her until her backside slid up the doorpost. Her hips unstuck. She swiveled like he'd squirted her joints with WD-40.

He pushed.

She pushed back.

He growled his satisfaction.

"Don't cross me ever," he said, backing up to take her measure.

"I might."

"And you might get more than you expected."

"Never from you."

He hit her.

The slap landed a heartbeat quicker than her surprise. The sting crawled on her skin like a thing alive. She tried to rub it away.

He slammed the door.

She was caught outside, staring groggily at unpainted pine-wood.

He'd actually *hit* her.

Bastard.

Shame on me, she thought.

She went to the hall closet and collected everything of hers that wasn't locked in the room with Chan. She lifted the box from the table. It was heavy, like the dumbbells Chan scattered around the perimeter of their king-size waterbed. The box's surface was metallic. She was sure it glinted in certain light, though at this moment, with no sun sketching her situation, she thought it resembled stone. She wrapped the box in her leather jacket. She didn't want it to touch her skin. Through her jacket she wondered how it would feel. It felt like nothing but pure weight.

She made her way out.

No cries of remorse from behind the bedroom door.

Downstairs.

Into the night, under the moon.

She placed the box inside her trunk. Where was she really going?

She didn't know.

Aunt Helene would be an old woman by now. Her mother's elder sister, a Grey Nun of Montreal, lived and worked with the poor in Winnipeg. They'd taken the train up to Manitoba one summer, Vera and her mom, to visit Helene at the convent. The trip was a blur. Vera remembered birch trees. The train rocketing through vertical trunks—the repetition hypnotized and exhilarated her. A memory so keen she once shared it with Chan. She told him about the lakes surrounded by high lichen-carpeted cliffs. A wolf stepped out onto a ledge, nose to the wind. She alone saw it. The woods seemed cold even in July. Places formed by ice, its mark imprinted on their souls.

Aunt Helene might be dead for all Vera knew. They had written to each other weekly for years after her mother died of cancer. Aunt Helene's words and prayers had helped her in ways Daddy couldn't. There was comfort in the idea of her—a petite woman, dressed plainly, kneeling at her bedside and praying—out there talking to God and the angels on little Vera's behalf, if she believed her. And she had no reason not to. Helene did nothing but show her kindness. One Christmas, Aunt Helene mailed her a silver cross on a chain, informing her that the relic had been dipped into a font of holy water at St. Peter's Basilica in Rome.

It was blessed.

Vera touched the cross around her neck.

She had warm fuzzy recollections. But in high school, she stopped replying to Helene's letters. Her aunt had become as real as Santa Claus. Vera was too old for Santa. She had more important things to do, like live her life.

Now she didn't have anywhere else to run.

North was as good a direction as any.

Away from here. From Chan. From the Pitch.

She didn't even know exactly why the box—the *artifact* as

Chan said they called it—why the artifact was so important to them. Meriting elaborate plans, money, and sacrifices . . .

A cause for extreme violence.

The Pitch feared it.

She knew as much. That was why they hired Chan to steal it for them. They told him they couldn't enter the greystone as long as the women were in possession of the artifact. It wasn't permitted. That's why they needed an outsider to steal it for them.

They may not obey society's rules, but they had a rulebook of their own.

They killed to possess the artifact.

They killed *after* they had it. Going for the women when Chan called to say he had the box. He'd boosted it. He didn't know the Pitch's ultimate designs.

The women at the house—those hippie witches—were their victims. The ones she knew about. Chan said the Pitch told him this struggle had been going on for ages. They were in a war. The Pitch needed allies. There were benefits. They had resources, influence. They would pay cash.

So the box, stone, whatever it was—it had to be worth money.

Vera's life philosophy didn't contain a lot of absolutes. A few. Example: You don't murder people in cold blood.

And you don't slap your girlfriend.

She had to keep the box away from the Pitch.

Chan would give it to them. He owed them.

Now she took it and left.

Would they hurt him?

They had killed and were ready to kill again. She felt it in her blood. They were chasing her. She felt that, too. Their pursuit made it hard to breathe.

All these hours on the road, she'd pushed a question from her mind.

Chan heard her leave the apartment. The cheap apartment was too small not to hear. He was probably watching her from the bedroom window as she climbed into the Camaro and drove away.

He didn't stop her.

Why not?

Maybe he didn't stop her because she was going to be his excuse, his private escape tunnel; he could tell the Pitch she ran off with their artifact. He'd get out of the midnight meeting. Wash his dirty hands of the whole affair.

Chan would bail out.

He'd put them on her trail instead.

The man tugged at the leash and spoke to the dog. Vera saw the frigid air make clouds of his words. Turning his body, but not his stare, he urged the dog to return. They went away. Disappearing behind the brick wall from where they had come. Around the corner, out of sight.

She kept a lookout. Her heart revved. He's just a guy. An old guy from the way he's shuffling. Out for his morning stroll. He's harmless. He's an old curious guy, that's all. He sees an attractive girl. She surprised him. What was she worrying about? She needed to chill. As soon as Adam got back with the key, she'd try for some sleep. Remember sleep? Sleep was good. Sleep worked wonders. Maybe later Adam would stop by. A few beers and, who knows, an early gift? Wrap him with a bow? Hang a star on his tree. Stop giggling. That's nervous energy. He's not going to hurt you. Neither is the old guy. He has a cute dog. Could a really bad guy have a cute dog? I mean she had every right to be terrified but not of these two. . . .

A dark oval peered at her from the bricks.

The hooded man studied her.

Taking her in and taking her apart. *Like I'm being swallowed,* she thought. She gulped. Chewed up. Devoured. She almost blacked out.

The old man. Something about him was . . . wrong.

Adam clicked her room key against the window.

She jumped.

The blackout feeling fled. Adam pulled open her door, asking if she was okay. Being gentle because he saw she wasn't fooling around. He was a good guy. She knew it. Looking back, her eyes sifted through the arabesques of snow.

No old man.

CHAPTER 12

Wyatt took Opal upstairs and settled her in bed. Returning to the office, he wrote a note for any customers who might wander in, saying he'd be back at the desk in fifteen minutes. He taped it to the front counter. Fifteen minutes would be long enough for what he needed to do. He put on his jacket, crossed the highway, and started walking along the gravel shoulder. Wind swirled snowflakes around him. He was intending on checking out those flashing lights at the Totem Lodge. He also wanted to get away from the motel for a while. Opal barging into Mr. Caul's room. Wyatt was embarrassed, and angry. Her damned visions. She was going to drive away the few regular guests they had, acting hysterical like that. He lit a cigarette and trudged ahead through the falling snow.

The Totem Lodge was Henry Genz's place.

Like everyone else in American Rapids, Henry had been horrified by the Pie Stop shooting. He took a special interest in the Larkins' recovery. When he discovered they were considering buying the Rendezvous Motel, he encouraged them, going so far as to open his books and tutor the young couple in the pitfalls of the hospitality business. He was a decade and a half older than his brother, Jesse. A devout man, Henry viewed his support as atonement for the suffering wrought by his brother's unspeakable crimes. Over the years, he'd become one of Wyatt and Opal's closest and most loyal friends.

As Opal climbed into bed, she pointed to the window.

"Go help him," she said.

Wyatt looked out and saw the lights at Henry's. There was too much snow to tell what kind of vehicles—police, fire, or ambulance—they were.

"It's across the street, Wyatt . . . that dog I heard."

He put an extra blanket on her, tucking it around her slim shoulders.

"Don't be silly. You didn't hear anything. I know *I* didn't."

"The Pitch are coming. Henry needs our help."

"Stop talking like that. You sound . . . you'll feel better if you rest."

"Promise me you'll go check it out."

"Jesus Christ! Opal, you've got to quit this—"

"Promise me?"

He sighed. "I'll go and check it out."

She stared at him.

"I promise."

He stepped onto the Totem's sidewalk.

One of the policemen tipped his head in Wyatt's direction.

"Hey there, Wyatt."

"Bill."

Bill Eppers was five years older than Adam. He liked to stop in and talk to Wyatt about police work. It was hero-worshipping from the get-go, plain and simple, and Wyatt hadn't liked it. He did nothing to encourage the conversation. But he wouldn't be rude to a fellow lawman. Their talks evolved into a kind of informal mentorship.

"Bit of a situation over here this morning," Eppers said.

"What's up?"

"We got a call from Henry. He thought he might have a prowler snooping around outside. Says he heard nothing, but his dog was antsy. The pooch kept looking out the window and growling."

At the mention of a dog Wyatt's eyebrows arched.

"Did he see anybody?"

"Nope, but he let the dog out just in case."

"Sheba? That old girl wouldn't chase a squirrel dipped in Jif."

"Henry says all he wanted to do was scare them off the property."

Opal had been right about the dog, yet a doubting man might be willing to write it off as coincidental. Weird coincidence though. He couldn't decide if he would tell her when he got home.

Thick, silver dollar snowflakes cascaded down. Eppers moved aside to let Wyatt stand under the canopy overhanging the office drive-up. From his new vantage point Wyatt saw a clutch of officers near the rear of the lot. At their feet was a blue tarpaulin, its color a bright flag tossed against the concrete.

Eppers said, "Henry found her there. Somebody chopped off her head with an ax, or a damn big knife. Henry's steamed. The collar and tags were laid out on top of the body. The head is missing. We're looking for it."

Wyatt was stunned.

"Killed her in the parking lot?"

"Guess so. I can't imagine they hauled the dog off, removed the head, and then brought the carcass back. When she didn't respond to Henry's whistle, he followed her outside. It was only a couple of minutes at most. We picked up a bloody towel from those bushes." Eppers pointed to a side entrance. "A rock was wedged under the door, propping it open."

"You think he went into the lodge?"

"We're searching. It might be a guest who put the rock there. Might be a guest killed the dog. Henry said he didn't argue with anybody, nothing like that. This thing happened fast. Somebody was outside, waiting. And whoever it was already had the weapon. They didn't think twice about using it, either."

"Why take the head?"

"That doesn't figure. Prowlers, junkies, or whatnot, those types aren't going to stick around and hack up your pets. They'll run."

Wyatt thought about the dog lying under that tarp. It was more than Opal's uncanny prediction bothering him. He remembered Sheba's brown rheumy eyes, gray whiskered muzzle, and the arthritic roll of her narrow, furry hips as she came over to greet him when he visited; a soft lick tickling against his knuckles while he and Henry sipped Cokes on an August evening.

"What kind of person does a thing like that?" he wondered, not realizing he spoke the words out loud until Eppers responded.

"Somebody who doesn't like dogs, I suppose."

Behind them, the glass doors swung outward. Henry stood there unshaven. He looked at both men and said, "You'd better come with me."

Eppers went in and Wyatt followed.

"A young lady," Henry said. "She's pretty upset."

Inside Henry's office, the woman sat, exhaling the ragged breaths of someone who'd been crying. Henry had gone into his linen chest for the Hudson's Bay point blanket wrapped around her shoulders. She trembled. He asked her if she wanted coffee. She said no thanks. He put a cup beside her anyway. She smiled at him. She had on a flannel nightgown, printed festively, with vertical rows of dancing candy canes. Bare feet tucked away under the chair. Her hands were dimpled, small as a child's. She pulled tissues, one after another, from a Kleenex box that had mountain scenes pictured on the sides.

Eppers sat on the corner of a rustic log desk.

Wyatt stayed back.

Henry said, "This is Christine Lucy. She's from Milwaukee. She booked a fireplace suite with us for two nights. Her husband is returning from a business trip, up in Thunder Bay. They're meeting here for the holiday. He's due in a couple of hours. They were planning on going to a restaurant for breakfast, then hanging around the lodge, building a nice fire, relaxing . . . is that right, ma'am?"

Christine Lucy nodded.

"She had intruders in her room," Henry added.

"You tell us the rest," Eppers said, edging closer.

That brought tears from Mrs. Lucy.

Wyatt said, "Take your time. And remember you're safe now."

She drew in a deep breath and began.

"There were two of them. Like brothers. Similar, I mean . . . they didn't resemble each other . . . I didn't get a real good look at their faces. The way they acted—I'd call it brotherly. They had this light. A white, white light. Not a flashlight but more like a spotlight. I had to shut my eyes it was so bright. My door was locked when I went to sleep. I never heard them break in. I woke up. They were on either side of me. Looming. Maybe it was because I'd been asleep, but at first I thought they were animals. They shined the light in my face. Only one brother talked. The other had a huge knife. The one said, 'She's awake.' His partner poked the knife into me. I felt it." She touched her stomach. "The light got closer. After a minute, he said, 'It isn't her.' He told me to keep quiet. Asked did I ever see a deer field dressed? Yes, I have. That would be me if I moved. He said I better not watch them go. I didn't want to, but I closed my eyes. I don't know when they left. They were silent. I was thinking that and I started to sing the song to myself in my head, *Silent Night, Holy Night*. I didn't want to think about what might happen to me . . . it wasn't until I noticed the police lights on the ceiling . . . I decided to come out."

She touched her stomach again.

"What's that in your hair?" Eppers asked.

"Pardon me?"

Christine blew her nose. She turned her head around so the men had a better view. The hair was matted into tangles of red.

"Looks like blood," Eppers said. He didn't touch her.

"What do you mean?" she asked, her voice rising.

Awkwardly, she dabbed at the sticky wetness with her Kleenex. She took one look at the tissue, jumped up from her seat, threw the Kleenex down on the carpet, staring at it in disbelief. Then her expression changed. Her eyes widened as if something unspeakable were climbing up through a hatch in the floor.

Christine Lucy started screaming.

Henry, wary of smudging fingerprints, turned a master key in the door of Christine Lucy's presumably unoccupied suite.

The lock clicked.

He paced off one, two, dramatically tiptoed steps, giving Patrolman Eppers the opening he needed to take over.

"Stand back," Eppers said.

After they determined that Christine Lucy had no wounds, Wyatt urged Eppers to inform his superiors about their gruesome discovery. The senior officers were milling in the parking lot. Another guest might, indeed, be hurt. The possibility existed that the pair of dark intruders had never left the lodge. They might've hidden themselves. Under a bed? Inside a shower stall? Christine admitted she hadn't seen them go. She clearly recalled releasing her door's deadbolt in her rush to escape. They couldn't have gone out that way. Wyatt advised caution and numbers. Bill wanted a quick look-see. A first crack at finding glory, too, Wyatt suspected. He let it pass. This wasn't his business, not anymore. He was a motel manager. A citizen. That's all.

He moved aside as Bill unsnapped his sidearm holster.

Bill Eppers took a deep breath.

And he pushed open the door.

Heat blasted.

A choking smell. Black curls of acrid smoke crashed softly against the ceiling. Glad for the onrush of oxygen, burning furniture crackled in the gloom. Smoke alarms, throughout the lodge, wailed.

Eppers shouted, "Fire!"

He reached for his gun, realized the futility. He let the door slam shut.

Henry ran for an extinguisher hooked to a recess in the wall. "Why, those monsters!" He yanked the door handle and shouldered his way past Eppers toward the consuming flames.

Wyatt followed with a hand on Henry's back, ready to pull him away from hazards unseen. Fire engulfed the queen-sized bed. The mattress bared a mass of twisted blackened springs. A hole gaped in the center of the bedspread. Tentacles of orange flame darted out of the hole and thrashed about the room.

Gasoline fumes lingered.

Wyatt noticed a star shape radiating on the carpet under the bed's edge.

An incendiary device. Set to a timer. Blown.

Henry discharged the extinguisher.

Wyatt grabbed the nozzle from his friend's hand and guided it downward.

The fire shrank.

It was then that Wyatt saw the wall. First he thought the surface of the varnished logs had sustained smoke damage in the blaze. But it was only one wall, above the bed, that was discolored. The lines were graphic, man-made.

Like a cave painting.

Primitive and yet filled with meaning.

A hieroglyph.

In blood.

After the fire truck pulled away, and the last patrol car swung out of the lot, Wyatt started his walk back to the Rendezvous. It wasn't the story of the dark brothers that scared him the most. Neither was it the firebomb left under the bed, nor even the pitiful sight of Sheba's severed head sneering from atop the pillows, displayed beside the spot where Christine once laid in fear; Sheba's tongue stretched out in an act of desecration as lewd as it was monstrous.

It was the image.

Drawn crudely in dog's blood above the bed. Unblinking, solitary. An arched brow with two strange lines—a tear and a lash—scrolled underneath.

An ancient all-seeing eye.

CHAPTER 13

Impatient and alone, Horus Whiteside paced inside his trailer. He owned a half dozen of these no-frills, single-wide, mobile homes. They were scattered on private semiremote lands across the Upper Midwest. Though the units varied somewhat in their exteriors, all appeared shabby and seemingly uninhabited. Dented, weather-beaten siding was standard. A bit of rust never hurt, either. They lacked outward decoration. No flags or flowerpots. No chimes or garden gnomes peeping from the weeds. Not a single piece of visible evidence indicated homeowner pride or a neighborly invitation.

The message was crystal.

If you should be in the vicinity, you'd find no welcome here. The location of the trailers discouraged chance encounters, being situated as they were, on narrow hidden plots amid the thickest overgrowth available. Debris often lay strewn around their perimeters, but never enough to draw undue attention. Yet it was important that each trailer remain accessible by road throughout the year.

The ambulance needed to make it up to the door.

Inside they were virtually identical. A cubicle curtain, the kind used for privacy in hospitals, ran on a *U*-shaped track and partitioned off the entryway from the rest of the interior. Viewed from outside the opened door, curious eyes would discover aqua fabric hanging ceiling to floor.

Steel grilles secured the windows. Roller blinds and interior plastic sheeting kept out the sunlight and dust. Potential burglars would encounter a painful, though nonlethal shock if they attempted to breach any window or the door. Whiteside didn't want to kill anyone accidentally. Bodies drew questions and worse—cops. If someone wanted to steal from the trailers badly enough to defeat the security, then he'd let them. And if any burglar ever did get inside, the shock of what he saw might very well send him away empty-handed.

The trailers were freestanding ICU patient rooms.

They wouldn't have lived up to the minimum requirements of any hospital in the United States. But they didn't have to. Many doctors elsewhere on the globe would have marveled at the array of monitors, pumps, intravenous lines, tubing, and catheters. A laptop-sized electrocardiograph sat on a shelf. A red crash cart with its defibrillator and drawers of life-resurrecting drugs stood in the corner. Chief among the expensive equipment was a refurbished Bird Products medical ventilator. Everything ran off batteries or a generator secreted in a concrete bunker underneath the mobile home.

The room contained two standard hospital beds.

Horus paced between them.

His acolyte was late. Late again. Late, late, late. Horus checked his pocket watch. His energies started to disperse. It was so exhausting being an innovator. But what really aggravated him was Time. Time spent. Time wasted. Horus didn't have much time left to work the kinks out of his plan. He needed to make some real progress. He desperately needed to find the girl and the artifact.

The stone.

He tried not to perseverate on its loss.

If only he had more help. But good help was always hard to find. His pool of potential recruits was infinitesimally small compared to what most executives of similar caliber and ambition had at their disposal. He reflected for a moment. Really, he could not think of anyone alive he regarded as his equal.

Life's lonely at the top, he told himself. Lonely at the beginning.

And at the end, too.

Time.

The stone.

Missing for so long. Then a magnificent reemergence. His hard work and talents were paying off after all these years. The Tartarus Stone. Gaspar Romero's legendary discovery: a double-pyramid onyx, unearthed near the mythical site of the Garden of Eden. Romero the Blasphemer, a heroic man who rebelled ferociously against God and His Church—he burned at the stake, martyred in the fight to restore the dark gods. The stone, in the keep of his murderers, was lost. But now it was found. Verified. And carefully the Pitch had watched those who guarded it. They chose a strategy. They commissioned the theft. They executed their adversaries. Only to be undermined by a young woman acting out of spite in a lover's quarrel. To imagine the artifact in her illegitimate, ignorant, reckless care . . .

They'd been so close. He could almost feel the impossibly brilliant weight of its ancient geometry in his hands.

Now it vanished again.

Perhaps forever . . . but, no, he would have the Stone.

Not someday, but soon.

The curtain shrieked as he ripped it aside. He flung open the door and peered into a bracing wind. Trees surrounding the trailer scratched against its sides. Their empty limbs clacked and shivered.

Where was Pinroth?

Horus didn't own a cell phone. Not in his own name. He'd never carry around a bit of machinery like that in his pocket. He worried it would be used to track him down. The government had ways. The public thought the government, although bureaucratic, was at its core about realism. Oh sure, there were crooks holding office, they'd freely admit. Maybe most of them were dirty. But they were businessmen and businesswomen. Goddamn lawyers, every last one. They understood how things worked at the deepest levels. They cut corners and read bottom lines. Yet certainly those who were smart enough or crafty enough to land the choicest jobs in Washington believed in rationality, scientific methods, and order. Perhaps their only difference was they began life privileged, or they had been schooled to be more ruthless than plain folks busy eking out existences in the suburbs. That wasn't the worst thing in the world. Was it? Having the big shots running the show—savvy operators who utilized computer logic and the latest information, who had at their fingertips the best cutting-edge technology money could buy, eager to serve their selfish purposes, yes, but also, indirectly, to protect ordinary citizens from harm and keep them happy enough not to care?

Horus knew better.

The shadow people in the government paid to see the occult at work. Firsthand experience taught him that eggheads in the intelligence community and square jaws at the Pentagon liked nothing better than a little old-fashioned hocus-pocus. They turned over a roomful of personnel for a demonstration of the Whiteside method; over the course of a long weekend, a conference table of men bore witness to unprecedented feats of mind control: mass mesmerism, rapid inductions, and confusion techniques. After a few odd-sounding conversations, soldiers would emerge as fearless automatons, capable of anything the doctor ordered. He weaponized brains! The subconscious was clay in the hands of the dark gods and their servants. At the end, the generals clapped. Whether it was remote viewing or brainwashing, MK-ULTRA or UFOs—it was all the same.

If you invented a secret weapon, a new toy, their wallet opened.

The government was a child.

And like children, they grew tired of their toys. They said they were broken or claimed they were never very good. They called them garbage.

So Horus took his toys and went away.

It was essential to keep moving. Sharks had the right idea.

Horus stomped his feet. The space heater radiated warmth at his back, but with the door open he needed to stay in motion. Being stationary got those witches killed in Chicago. It wouldn't get Horus. That's why he bought the trailers. No one, except for Pinroth, knew all their locations.

Horus tucked his chin deep inside his overcoat.

He scanned the white void. The lane before him had no light poles, no signage. A soft bend dropped off to the right into invisibility. Five miles beyond came the turnoff from the county highway, a frontage road. In good weather, it was easy to miss. Blink and the brief interruption in the landscape melted away. He made a visor of his hand and gazed at what served as the yard—a level strip of snow-covered gravel bordered by stumps of varying diameters; a burn barrel and the carcass of a John Deere tractor emerged in chalky monochromatic relief.

Remorseless day lurked above.

A sandstorm of gritty snow ate at the periphery of his vision. White sky devouring white ground until nothing was left but a dull milky blindness.

His shoulders sagged in disappointment.

He closed the door.

He was growing weak. He hadn't slept at all through the night. His muscles stiffened. Blood beat in his temples. Against the door, he slid to his haunches and then sat on the floor massaging his sore legs.

From a nightstand between the beds, a Tiffany desk lamp cast a fan of honeyed light into the trailer. The stained glass harkened back to a more mysterious age. Earlier, Horus had turned on the lifesaving equipment; testing it to be sure he was prepared for anything that might happen. Fishy gray monitor screens and LEDs glowed in the shadows. Nocturnal gem eyes. Over the years, Horus learned to find comfort in them.

Built into the nightstand was a bookshelf.

Hardcover volumes lined it.

From his seat on the trailer floor, Horus could decipher the titles embossed on their spines. It wasn't necessary, because he knew them by heart. He'd read them over and over again. He'd committed entire passages of their contents to memory. They were great books. The best he'd ever read.

He loved them.

In his mind he turned pages. He stopped.

A curious Conner sat on the edge of his motel bed. His newly acquired stone box lay propped on one of its sides. The nature of the shape made it appear a sharp and crooked thing, offending to the eye—a double pyramid. The surface gleamed evilly. He straddled the foreign relic dug up years ago from the desert and carted out on camelback. He wetted his lips. Beneath its surface, figures were trapped in strata resembling translucent black ice. He detected Byzantine markings, hieroglyphs, and odd spirals. Layers floated under layers. So much depth it made him dizzy. He traced his finger along six columns of carvings, an alphabet of daggers. What was it Belzoni had said?

"The mind muscle, for years contracted into a knot, expands . . ."

The lines came from a story written by Maxwell Caul. The story, "A Chunk of Hell," was published in a short-lived pulp magazine, *Interdimensional,* in the winter of 1950, and had been reprinted a dozen times. Horus thought Caul's best work came before he started writing scripts for television, certainly before the late '60s when he got his hands, and mind, on psychedelic drugs. It wasn't only the drugs. Caul lacked courage. He'd seen what few men had. Seen and understood it, too. Yet fear kept him from exploring further. Fear turned him into a shade. And a liar. Max, oh Max, where did you go wrong?

The good news was the finders had spotted Caul in American Rapids as expected.

The bad news? They hadn't found the girl or the stone.

Not yet.

As with many instances concerning the whereabouts of the stone, Horus found his visions were useless. The stone threw off high quantities of residual energy. He couldn't cut through the static. But it would only fit if the girl and the stone ended up with Caul, who spent every Christmas writing in that motel in American Rapids. That much was guaranteed. The rest was a hunch. So Horus had sent his finders to see if the girl would find Caul.

Or vice versa.

Then the Pitch would have them both.

Knock, knock.

"Doctor? It's me."

"Yes, I'm coming." How quickly situations changed. Minutes ago he'd been consumed by worry. Now he felt relief. He stood and the headrush broke over him like an ocean wave. He leaned against the door until the spinning subsided. All would be well soon. Pinroth was here. The ambulance had arrived. They would get to work. Tonight was a new opportunity. It almost made him cheerful.

"What kept you, Pinroth?"

"The storm, Doctor . . . these country roads are bad. And the patient wasn't at ease. I stopped and administered more sedatives."

"You don't decide such things!"

"He was asking . . ."

"I don't care. Your job is to do what I tell you."

"Yes, Doctor."

Horus removed his overcoat and rolled up his shirtsleeves. He was late for his transfusion. Pinroth, blank-faced, watched him from the open door.

"Shall we begin then?"

"As you say, I'll start unloading."

"Wonderful."

CHAPTER 14

Three doors down. She was so close Max could hardly contain his excitement. The young woman backed into the parking spot outside her room. She exited the little sports coupe. Into the trunk she went for a backpack, a red suitcase, and a bulky leather jacket. Max couldn't help but wonder, what else? *What else?* The snow interfered. His angle was bad. Yet he practically danced a jig.

Calm yourself, he thought.

Stop wringing your hands like an anxious old maid.

The young woman swept her gaze side to side, clearly on the lookout.

She's looking for me . . . because I scared her.

He'd gotten back into his room without her seeing him enter. He chained the door. Shucked free from his Canada Goose parka. Pulled off his winter galoshes. Disengaged the dog's leash. Chalk in hand he quickly drew an outsized spiral on the door. He pressed his nose to the window, rearranging the drape in an attempt to conceal his body. He'd spent far too long staring at her in the car. First Opal intruding on his morning shave, and then . . . could it really be the stone? Driven to his doorstep? He was awestruck. He couldn't tear himself away. The young woman hadn't seen his face, not most of it. His yellow parka—she'd remember that. She'd seen his dog, too.

Ann-Margret lay in a warm cove underneath the desk, her nose between her paws. She was watching him. Wherever he moved, her lashes twitched and the big brown eyes followed.

"I'm not going anywhere, Annie. Don't worry."

He'd been talking to his dog for years now, nothing inherently unusual in that; but since his wife's death a decade ago, Max had been having, well, daily, one-way, human-level discussions with Ann-Margret. He knew loneliness to be the cause. It didn't embarrass him anymore. The feelings of sadness had gone away, too. Comfort replaced them. Max had always been a talker. His wife said on more than one occasion over the course of their fifty-year marriage that he was better suited as a monologist than a conversationalist. She'd been correct, of course. The decade of her absence was ample proof. Dear Gertrude rested in peace back at their family plot outside of Pomona. Max went on talking. Only his audience changed from a patient spouse to an adoring Irish setter.

Max flicked his fingers. The drape fell into place. He could wait.

"I don't think the girl's heading out soon. Not with the storm. She looked tired. She's scared of us . . . the poor thing. I'll bet she's crawling into bed right now. Pulling the covers up over her head and wishing her problems would go away. They won't. Not if she is who I think she is. Not if she has the stone. Her problems, I'm afraid, are far from over. Bound to get worse. Much worse."

Max looked down at the dog.

Her expression seemed to say, "Go on. I can't wait to hear more."

"Let's make a little popcorn first. Would you like some popcorn?"

Ann-Margret cocked her head to one side. Tail wagging.

Max pried the lid off a plastic storage container. He kept an assortment of these snap-top bins inside his motor home. They were handy for a traveling man constantly on the move. He'd labeled them for convenience. This container was SALTY. He sorted through the thirst-inducing packets of teriyaki beef jerky, Slim Jims, cheddar cheese pretzels, and sour cream and onion potato chips until he found the Pop Secret Movie Theater Butter popcorn. He removed a single bag and tossed it in the microwave that came with the motel room. While the microwave hummed, he dug his hand wrist-deep into a wheeled Coleman cooler and extracted a soda. He wiped ice chips off the bottle. This brand was his favorite: Mountain Dew Code Red. It didn't really taste like something a person should be drinking. But he was addicted. If he went a few hours without gulping the cherry concoction, he got a pounding headache. Caffeine wasn't going to hurt him at this stage of his life.

Nothing was.

An alert sounded in the corner of the room, indicating he had incoming e-mail. He opened his MacBook. It was a Christmas e-card from his daughter, Janette, living in Saigon, out on the Asian Pacific Rim where she'd taught English for twenty years. He opened the card. Santa Claus surfing in a red one-piece. Catching a big wave and shooting the tube on a peppermint surfboard. Dick Dale's rapid-fire rendition of "Misirlou" played in the background. Janette had about as much reverence for Western holiday traditions as Max did. He laughed and tilted the screen so Ann-Margret could see. He punched up the volume.

The dog wasn't interested.

Here was another postmodern update Max appreciated. He loved his laptop. Take it anywhere. Charge up and go. Only connect! Sure, he had a fondness for his classic Olympia SM9. He'd written so many stories on it, novels and scripts banged out in cheap, interchangeable, California rentals. The words looked great though. Crisp and clean. Every time he hit the keys he felt a masterpiece was possible. Typewriters had solidity to them. Heft. If need be, you could throw an SM9 across the room and kill someone. Laptops never achieved that. They weren't built to last forever. They took you out for a fast ride on the here-and-now information superhighway. And that's what Max wanted.

He wanted to be like that Santa: knees relaxed, his hand leaving a trail of bubbles in a Technicolor blue wave, a sack of goodies slung over his shoulder.

He didn't want to think about what would happen after the wave flattened and his board skidded up a gritty gray shoreline. The sun going down on him, replaced by a chill, then frigid night.

The microwave dinged.

"Chow time!"

A puff of steam leaked from the torn bag. It would've made Pavlov proud: the way Ann-Margret had been conditioned, gravitating over to him, salivating.

Max dropped a handful of fluffy goodness into her bowl.

"You don't want to eat too much," Max said, crunching. "It'll make your tummy hurt." His gut pained him every hour of every day. The pills didn't do much except induce compulsory sleep. Screwing with his brain's chemistry had given up its charm. In his halcyon days, he tripped along on a fluid elastic road to tomorrow. Altering reality was reality. Comical terrors. Terrifying comedies. Where everything was, if not possible, then at least imaginable.

A looking-glass world.

The darkest corner showed him more than he could bear.

He got out alive.

Max didn't have flashbacks. He had memories. What he experienced changed him. He didn't want the drugs. He had to keep his guard up. The stories he wrote failed to thrill him the way they used to. They scared him instead. Part of him desired to burn the pages, to torch every scrap of paper he'd ever published or written upon. All his outlines and notes, character sketches and misfires. He'd lost control once. *Strangers are livelier than fiction.* That's what a fellow writer assured him over zombies at Kelbo's tiki bar. His compatriot lifted his hurricane glass and toasted, "To strangers!" He meant strange women. Fiction and life were both managing to be passing strange . . . especially when one sunny day you opened your door and found a *stranger* who appeared to have stepped out of fiction. He demanded things from you. Took your life's work more seriously than you did, more than you ever could've dreamed. Those were only words, you said. Words written to make money. They came back to haunt you. Bind you as tightly as a curse. Because he hunted you down. You went ahead and invited him in. A stupid, drunken, rash mistake.

Only later, afterward, you became a cautious man.

A vigilant lookout.

Looking for Horus Whiteside to show up again.

The Pitch.

"I'm the Pitch," he had said, offering his hand.

You shook it. Because you were friendly, open-minded, ready to laugh at weirdness that swam across your ken. He confessed to being a fan. Your blinds were pulled. Your wife and daughter traveled out East, visiting relatives. You were batching it. Working on a teleplay. Sci-fi, insect space invaders, not your usual cup of tea. The pay for the job was better than above average. You hadn't ventured forth in days. No shower, no shave. The doorbell rang. Sunlight clobbered you. Maybe he wanted an autograph? You offered to sign his satchel of well-thumbed books. He said he'd like that. But he didn't go. It was a sizzler of an afternoon in Los Angeles. Remember the rippling air? Sweet smoky haze drifted over the redwood fence—a neighbor barbecuing shrimp and pineapple kebabs. It occurred to you: You were famished. Hours spent working through a liter of Bacardi Dark and a bag of Acapulco Gold; food had been an afterthought. You sipped tremulously from the slick, beaded glass in your hand. Limes and cola, the golden undercurrent of liquor. You'd eat later. He, the self-proclaimed Pitch, patient as a wax preacher man, was waiting on your doorstep in his black suit, and not sweating a drop. Come in, you said. Thinking this was the fastest way to get rid of him. Anxious to return to your air-conditioned cocoon. Why not let him share a beer or a joint with his literary hero? He could tell his friends at home. You needed a break. After he went away, you'd get back to the script you'd been working on. Knock it out.

You were wrong.

"Tell me about the Stone," he said. "You've actually seen it?"

Returning with more ice, sitting in your orange Barcalounger, you added a splash of rum. Your eyes were adjusting to the umber room.

"What?"

He was on the edge of the couch with his satchel of autographed books.

"The Octahedron. Gaspar Romero's onyx. He was the first to identify the relic correctly as the Tartarus Stone. Logic dictates that you have met Romero at least once. Given the quality of your descriptions I'd say it's likely the two of you conversed on multiple occasions. I'd be fascinated to hear about your encounters."

"You're kidding, right? Did Ross send you over here? Stefano, that's who'd pull a stunt like this. Was it Stefano? I love that guy."

The look on the visitor's face said he wasn't joking.

Who was this goofball on your couch? The leather cushions sighed as you sank deeper into the recliner. You crossed your arms. It was no use hiding the suspicion creeping over you. Who was he?

The jet-clad man held up his palm as if to halt any concern. "Listen, I understand the need to fictionalize your reports. To conceal details from the general public's view." He smirked conspiratorially. "Events necessitate a degree of obfuscation. Or shall we say a screening process? For the sake of protecting the Stone and its secrets, only select clues are revealed. People panic when they don't understand what's happening to them. Don't you agree? News on this massive a scale must be diluted. Informed readers"—he tapped himself on the temple—"see through the fog. You did what you had to do . . ."

"What'd you say you called yourself? Pitchfork?"

"The Pitch."

"You weren't born with that name."

"Horus Whiteside. I've metamorphosed since then. My spirit guides led me to the Pitch. I enjoyed a total shift of consciousness.

Thus my name changed. I have become obedient servant to the venerable celestial movers who—"

"You're serious, aren't you?"

"Unequivocally. Your stories are the prophecies I've sought for years. These parables of the dark gods divulge the rules of the stone. Correct? I am here to learn. Teach me, Mr. Caul. Even under torture, I will keep the secrets."

Torture? Mr. Caul? Jesus H. Christ. You had to put a stop to this now, before it got out of hand. "Call me Max, okay?"

"Alright, Max."

"You won't bend under torture, huh?"

"Never."

"That's good to hear." You walked to the nearest bookcase. At eye level, on two shelves, was every word you'd ever had published in English. "You're talking about my stories. I wrote the Rick Conner supernatural adventure series. Several of those pieces dealt with mysterious occult artifacts. The Tartarus Stone? Rick first heard the legend on a riverboat excursion into the Amazon. He met the Italian professor, Bel . . . Bellini . . ."

"Belzoni."

"Right, Professor Belzoni. And Belzoni captivated him with a tale of an ancient stone that pointed the way to Hell. A shrewd unscrupulous graverobber named Gaspar Romero excavated an oddly carved chunk of onyx in Persia. It was a kind of compass. In the right hands, with the right amount of incantation, and so on . . . the rock spun and showed you the location of the damned."

"The fallen angels—"

"—who after their rebellion God had cast into the pit, the infernal regions, Gehenna . . . call the place whatever suits you."

The plots came back to you in a rush. But you didn't want to indulge Horus any more than you had to in order to get him out of your life.

"Tartarus suits me," he said.

"Then Tartarus it is. Truth be told, it's the stuff of mythology, religious lore. It's fiction. A long time ago, men made it up. I embellished on their work. I created it from here." Now it was your turn to tap your head.

"I've read other books. Sources that confirm your—"

"Stop right there. I did research. You were able to find the same information. That proves it was out there. Get it? I read the same occult publications you did. Then I came home. I sat in that chair over there and on that typewriter I wrote some stories."

"You're lying."

"I'm telling the truth." You raised three fingers and with your other hand you covered your heart. "Scout's honor. It's bullshit, Horus. Pulp fodder. Total. Utter. Complete bullshit." You laughed nervously.

"Is the Stone here in the house?"

The chill you felt had nothing to do with the air-conditioning.

"It's time for you to leave." You moved for the door.

"No, wait."

"Can't barge in here when I've got a script to write—"

"I'm sorry. Please. Could you do me a favor before I go?"

You turned to see what he wanted.

He was crouching beside his satchel. The top of the bag stretched open and his hands were in there with the books. It was a deep bag.

"I have a gift," he said.

Senses distorted. The booze and the grass. Your reaction time slowed. He had the knife out of his satchel before you realized what was happening. Nylon cords, like a nest of wild blue snakes, slithered from the bag as he kicked it over when he lunged. You looked. He punched you. In the stomach. The rum was rocketing back out the way it came. You bent. He kneed you in the face. Broke your nose. A starlike flash. The knife butt driven downward, two-handed, into the bones of your neck. You woke as he finished tying your legs together. Vomit-soaked. Blind panicked. Unable to thrash.

He was unpacking his satchel.

The pincers and the branding iron with the funny Egyptian eye shape twisted on its end. He kept you a prisoner of your house for three days. Carrying out his personal version of the Inquisition.

Together, page by page, sentence by sentence, you went through every word you ever wrote. Him: asking questions. You: thinking and answering. Eventually just answering. Saying anything you could to stop him. There was nothing. Horus Whiteside. The Pitch. Hovering over you, searching for places on your body he hadn't tried. Touching you indelicately with his tools.

Your wife saved you. She called the police when you didn't answer the phone for days. She thought you might've hurt yourself drinking. You might be lying on the floor bleeding to death. And you were.

Just not the way she thought.

Max set down his bag of popcorn. He slid a hard plastic case from under the bed. He unlocked it.

"That gal's going to need our help, Annie girl. We had better be prepared."

He put the contents on his nightstand.

Stainless Ruger GP100 .357 Magnum, with a four-inch barrel. Loaded with semi-jacketed hollow points. Two HKS speedloaders set to go. A wheelgun, plain and simple. Sometimes the old ways were the best. He'd learned that during his years of study after the attack. His obsession grew slowly at first, then uncontrollably, like the cancer now feeding on his liver. He didn't have much time left; a few more months, maybe a year. The pain would become intolerable. He wasn't planning on languishing in a hospital bed. He picked up the pistol and spun the wheel. He held it at arm's length, sighting down the barrel.

He had to know if the Stone was real.

After his wife died, he took his files on the Stone and the Pitch and left home for good. He crisscrossed the country, searching, following every lead. He'd found the witches in Corvallis, and he watched them. Did he think Whiteside would show up? Did he want revenge after four decades? Max toyed with the chalk stick in his pocket. Protection only went so far. If the Pitch sent his emissaries, or better, if he came through that motel doorway himself . . .

Max would aim to ventilate.

CHAPTER 15

"You'd better watch out, you'd better not cry. You'd better not pout, I'm telling you why . . ." Springsteen's version of the classic holiday tune was running through Adam's brain as he helped himself to a cup of Rendezvous coffee. The office was empty. Across the highway cops were crawling over the Totem Lodge. A few miles farther out, snow buried his truck. He hadn't quite thawed yet. Oh yeah, and an older woman—probably crazy, but definitely smoking hot—had picked him up off the side of the road and invited him for drinks and, he was fairly certain, a chandelier-shaking romp in her room at his parents' motel. Huh.

He read the note taped to the counter. Dad wasn't here.

That *was* strange.

Christmas.

Weird was better than bad.

Bad was what he'd been expecting since he drove away from his dorm.

He'd learned a new word in English Lit the other day: "confluence." It meant the flowing together of two or more streams, a juncture point. That's definitely what had happened to him. A confluence of bad.

Adam had been popular in high school. He made Honor Roll. He lettered in basketball, hockey, and baseball. He knew, and liked, almost everyone from his graduating class. Bethany Davis, his not-too-serious girlfriend, messed around with him all through senior year and the summer with no drama. They exchanged e-mails from college. She won a full-ride swimming scholarship to the University of Arizona. She loved it. The school was awesome. Sun!!! Yay!!! She'd met so many new people. Even a new guy. Wasn't college the coolest?

In his case . . . not so much.

Adam's grades nosedived. Classes were huge. His roommates sucked. Everything happened around him, not to him; big campus anonymity came as a culture shock. He wasted days alone, camped in a beanbag chair, drinking 3.2 beer and watching ESPN Classic. He was bored and let down. He didn't know what he wanted to do or who he wanted to be. His whole life he'd waited to get away from home, but he hadn't figured out what to do once he got there. Inside his backpack, under the seat of his truck, was a piece of paper that said he was failing half his classes. His academic scholarship was in serious danger. Lose it, and the cost of college would be too high. He could never make up the difference.

He'd be back here in American Rapids.

Look at a weather map, any day of the year, there's a good chance American Rapids, Minnesota, would be in the running for the coldest temperature, the lowest low, in the contiguous forty-eight. Sane people didn't live here. They passed through on the way to somewhere else. They'd buy gasoline and a bag of Doritos; stock up on fudge, fleece, and rubber tomahawks; flush a toilet and check their hair in the mirror; eat some fast food, guzzle some coffee, and put ole AmRap in the rearview as quick as possible.

Highway living.

Folks stopped here for a little satellite TV and forty winks.

Towns like this: They're where a person's from and, usually, what they left behind. Adam wanted to escape. Hanging out around these same six blocks looking for entertainment—the Snowy Owl Tap on one end and Darby's All-Star Diner holding down the fort on the other—you didn't need to ask why.

Nothing ever happened in American Rapids.

And nothing ever would.

The door to upstairs was locked. Adam used his key.

Bruce, Chuck, and Jean Claude huddled on the stairs, staring at him.

"Hey, guys. What're you doing here? Only time you three are in the same room is when I pop a can of Chicken of the Sea."

The cats whirled around his legs, purring. He picked up Jean Claude, the runt, and the most affectionate of the littermates. As he'd been doing since he was a kid, Adam put Jean Claude up on his shoulders. *Sniff, sniff.* The purring magnified in his ear. A furry black-and-white cheek brushed against his.

"Hello!" Adam called out, "Anybody here run a motel?"

He took the stairs two at a time, careful not to jostle his rider or stomp any tails. Reaching the top step, he was surprised by the silence. He heard the clock on the wall ticking. The wind was speeding up like an overdue trucker. Nets of white flakes masked the windows. The heat kicked on. Warm air blew and the curtains swayed. He had the immediate sensation no one was home. Yet he didn't feel quite alone, either. Without knowing why, he clenched his hands into fists. The cat's muscles grew rigid, stiffening. Tendons flexed. Claws dug into Adam's neck. Jean Claude sprung from his perch. He shot to the bottom of the stairwell where he joined his two brothers. They fled out the door.

"Goddamn, that hurt. Crazy cats," he mumbled, rubbing his neck.

He tried to ignore it, but he noticed something, too. An odd charge of electricity filled the air. He was afraid to touch metal. The carpet crackled underfoot. Living room. Kitchen. The bathroom and den.

All dark.

The sight of his parents' bedroom door shut in the daytime was about as bizarre as the roof suddenly lifting off the top of the house. Snow falling in his face wouldn't have been any more peculiar. Or more unsettling.

"Mom? Dad?"

He rapped his knuckles against the wood.

"You two aren't in bed? Miss the alarm clock this morning?"

What about the note downstairs?

They hadn't missed the alarm.

He grabbed the doorknob. It sparked. He felt a tiny jab of pain enter his thumb. He opened the door and went inside.

CHAPTER 16

Opal had left her body. She knew on one level of her consciousness that she was in her bed at home. That someone, Adam,
knocked on her door. She heard him call to her. She wanted to respond. She tried to speak but could not. She hovered somewhere
between waking and sleep. This wasn't a dream. It reminded her
of the days she spent in the hospital after the Pie Stop shooting;
wandering through a hall of mirrors that her doctors called a coma.
She tried to sit up.

Fear overcame her as she realized she could not move.

She was paralyzed.

She pushed again.

In the next instant, she was out, standing up, and looking at
herself lying in the bed. She'd slipped free from her body. But not
completely: A long smoky rope anchored her to her physical self
in the bed. As she moved away, the cord stretched. No vision had
been this powerful; no hallucination, if that's what they were, this
lucid. Fascination took over from fear. She was warm, comfortable, and safe. Her mind was keen. Her senses dialed in, acute
and attuned.

She was naked, too.

Her spirit skin looked very pale. Ginger hairs tufted between
her legs.

She sensed Wyatt. Saw him in stark relief as he trudged along the side of the road on his return from the Totem Lodge. He didn't know she was watching.

She wanted to go to him.

He walked on.

She was no longer in her bedroom. She had the slightest notion of passing through the bedroom. But she encountered no resistance. She glided into another place. Fast, very fast. The sensation of a distance being crossed.

Whiteness surrounded her.

Whiteness? White? Whiteside? Yes, that was the word flashing bold in her brain. What was it? A name? She'd never heard of anywhere around American Rapids called Whiteside. Though she had the distinct impression that was where she was heading. The vision pulled her to Whiteside.

Where was Whiteside?

Through a bleach fog she traveled. Before her, abruptly, was a doorway. She recognized the paint, the color and the surrounding frame, the bricks on either side. It was one of the Rendezvous room doors, but it had no number. Her ears popped as she opened it. Snow-covered hills came into view. Evergreens. She smelled their perfume. Leaning past the threshold, she gazed side to side.

It resembles Minnesota, she thought. She didn't recognize any landmarks.

A rural area.

Forest. White brilliance of ice and snow. The northern country held beautifully in the deathgrip of winter. She'd traveled miles from her bed in no time. But this place wasn't the other side of the world. It felt familiar, close-by.

Opal entered. Glided—she couldn't call this walking—toward a dense copse of trees. Jagged branches reached for her. She wove through them.

The trees parted.

She saw a dilapidated trailer.

And an ambulance that looked like it had driven straight out of the 1970s.

Was this a memory?

Did her vision show her the past?

She melted through the side of the trailer as easily as she had the wall of her house. Her feet touched the floor. Suddenly, she could feel her weight again.

She was naked in the trailer . . . but this was a hospital room.

The antiseptic smells of rubbing alcohol and bandages. Quietness filled with anticipation. Someone had taken great efforts to build a two-bed hospital room inside the trailer. She looked around for a gown or something to cover herself. Because before her were a pair of men—one a patient, and the other she guessed was a medical attendant or male nurse. He wore a white lab coat. The nurse inserted an IV needle into the patient's arm. She could see the legs of a third person under the sheet tucked into the foot of the second bed.

The nurse partially blocked her view.

Whoever occupied that second bed was large.

Opal kept an arm shielding her bare breasts. She attempted to maneuver around a cart to conceal the lower half of her body. The cart was too near the wall. Using her free hand, she pushed it forward to make more space. The cart's wheel caught on an unused IV pole. The pole came crashing to the floor. The nurse spun around, raising his hands in a defensive posture. The male patient turned his head right at her. Nowhere to hide. She scrambled to think of what she could possibly say to explain her presence.

She didn't need to say a word.

The nurse came up to Opal. He was taller than Wyatt, six-four at least. His breath tickled her. He gazed over the crown of her head. She was about to say something when he turned away.

He bent and set the pole back on its pronged feet. His eyes narrowed. He looked around at the baseboard behind her, and then scanned underneath the cart. Frowning, he slid the cart against the wall and went back to his patient.

He couldn't see her!

The nurse leaned over the bed, checking the needle in the man's arm. He taped it. He put the ends of his stethoscope in his ears and listened to the patient's heart. Checked his blood pressure. Satisfied with his readings, he pressed a button on the bedrail. The head of the bed lowered to a prone position.

Opal had a clear view of the other bed and its occupant.

Something was wrong.

Blurred.

Like Vaseline smeared on a pane of glass.

She saw the bed and the apparatus framing it. The taut sheet at the foot of the bed was clear to her as well. But midway up the mattress, her vision failed. She had a sense of shape. Of mounting size, immensity. And movement: a vague undulation, a squirming beneath the sheet. As if a great deal of pain afflicted the person reclined there.

Or was it someone struggling against restraints?

Opal smelled an awful odor.

Like low tide. Dead fish on a sundrenched windless day. Rot.

She covered her nose and mouth with her hands. She stifled a cough.

The odor worsened: roadkill, backed-up toilets, sulfurous spoiled eggs.

Her eyes watered; an almost chemical burning scoured her throat. Viscid, greasy film condensed out of the air, coating her skin. She rubbed two fingers together—it felt like handling a used garbage bag.

She couldn't take any more. She stepped toward the blue privacy curtain that separated the interior from the trailer's door.

The blur moved with her.

How could that be?

She stepped back.

Left, then right. Never taking her sight off the ill-defined bed.

The blur slid along like a movable screen; always maintaining a barrier between her line of vision and the second bed's occupant.

"What are you afraid of?"

Opal jumped.

The occupant, a third man, had spoken to her.

He whispered in a voice very old. Something impeded his speech. The words were not fully formed. Perhaps he'd suffered a stroke, or had no teeth. He might be wearing an oxygen mask.

Opal considered the possibility that her hearing, like her vision, might also be impaired. Either way, she didn't respond to his question. She couldn't. Her words died before they left her lips. Briefly, she wondered if she'd heard him correctly. Perhaps he was talking to the first patient and not . . .

"I asked you a question, Opal Larkin. What are you afraid of?"

He could see her.

He knew who she was.

How could he penetrate the optical mantle when she couldn't?

"Wondering how I can see you? And you can't see me?"

He read her thoughts.

While she contemplated this new form of nakedness, a battery of sounds assaulted her ears. First, gases erupted. She didn't laugh. Next, huge quantities of something dry and grainy—*was that sand?*—audibly slipped off the bedside and piled onto the floor.

"See, I've had lots and lots of practice," he wheezed. His throat crackled and he moaned with pleasure. "And you . . . have a lovely body."

Opal reached for the curtain. But it was too far away. She didn't want to turn around. Didn't want to look away from the bed, either. She backed up.

The scene remained as it had been: a hospital room with two beds, two patients, and a nurse. The blur floated over the second patient's features like a pixilated balloon. No further form emerged.

The nurse tended to his business. He crossed Opal's field of vision. His figure continued to be in perfect focus. The blur emerged from either side of his body as he stepped in front of it. He tore the sterile packaging of a fresh IV needle; tossed the empty wrapper on the sheet. He thrust his arms into the blur. His lab coat sleeves transformed into milky bars of white.

White. *White.*

The sounds continued. They repeated, following their exact sequence and duration, as if they were being played on a loop. The questions replayed as well.

"What are you afraid of?"

"I asked you a question, Opal Larkin. What are you afraid of?"

"Wondering how I can see you? And you can't see me?"

"See, I've had lots and lots of practice. And you . . . have a lovely body."

Opal stood her ground. She waited for the cycle to begin again.

"What are you afraid of?"

"Are you Whiteside?" she asked.

The noises stopped.

Silence.

The tableau changed. A leap of seconds into the future—now the nurse stood with his spine rigid, shoulders pressed flush to a wall. He held a black German pistol. The first patient, who she noticed wore dark goggles, stood beside his nurse, leaning on his shoulder for support. There was a problem. The patient with the goggles had ripped the needle from his arm. Blood dripped on the floor, staining his gown. It trailed over to where he slouched, pooling at his feet. Both men's gazes ricocheted back and forth inside the trailer. They were pallid, breathing open-mouthed, sweating. Expressions of fright contorted their faces.

The blur had disappeared.

Fled, it seemed.

The other patient lay entirely under his sheet.

Opal had been wrong about his size. He wasn't fat. In fact, the body outlined under the sheet appeared well formed and athletic. Opal watched and counted to sixty. Her confidence was building with each second. The body's chest did not rise and fall. To be sure, she counted off another minute.

Not a stir.

The confrontation was a victory.

Whoever Whiteside was, calling him out had been sufficient

enough to scare him off. Even in the psychic world, bullies were all talk.

Opal never let herself be bullied.

She'd rather take her chances, stand her ground, and fight.

The body didn't scare her.

She was glad she'd spoken up. She relaxed. None of these visionary experiences were really real. Were they? She could use them as a type of exercise. To improve herself, and the lives of those around her. If the bullet in her brain gave her these experiences, then why waste them? Her visions might lead her in more positive, self-affirming directions. They gave her inner strength. A depth of understanding denied most of humanity. She should feel proud to have them. They were part of a special talent. She'd never shied away from being a unique individual. She wouldn't do it now.

The body.

She couldn't help her curiosity. She needed to see him. The sense of an impending threat had passed. No vision had ever hurt her. Not physically, not permanently. The intensity of a moment ago dissipated. The evil old man's voyeuristic advantage over her was gone. Opal felt the safety and warmth she'd experienced earlier. She saw the cord that attached to her body, threaded securely through the trailer's outer shell.

She went to the bed.

She grabbed a top corner of the sheet and pulled it back.

No.

Opal's knees buckled.

It was her son. It was Adam. He was gaunt. The life drained out of him. His flesh was waxy and cold when she touched his cheek. His eyes fixed on an approaching terror only he could see. Jaws locked open, howling silently.

Adam was dead.

Opal fell backward into oblivion.

CHAPTER 17

Vera ran the shower until the small bathroom packed wall to wall with thick billows of steam. She closed the door, locked it. Stripped, then stepped over the edge of the tub, and eased under the showerhead. With wet hands, she tore the wrapper off a bar of soap and lathered up. The hot water pulsed, cascading down her back. For the first time since yesterday evening some part of her wasn't in danger of frostbite. Warmth enveloped her instead. Muscles lost their tension, unkinked. Circulation returned. Layers of road-trip grime washed down the drain. She split the corner of a complimentary shampoo packet, squirting pearly pink gel into her palm. A scent of fresh strawberries filled the misty room. It was too sweet, clearly artificial, yet so much of an improvement over the combo of stale coffee and dried nervous sweat that accompanied her from Chicago. She sighed and closed her eyes. Leisurely, thoroughly, she washed her hair.

Where was she going from here?

The more she thought about Aunt Helene, the less she wanted to involve the peaceful geriatric nun in this violent mess. And what would she tell her? That her thief of a boyfriend stole a relic box from a group of lesbian witches? He planned to hand it over to murderous Satanists? Vera had a hard time wrapping her mind around that herself. Yet she saw the mutilated bodies. Damn it, Chan! How could he be so stupid!

Tomorrow she'd figure it out.

Maybe she'd end up burying the thing out in the woods.

Couldn't do that—the ground was hard as concrete.

Minnesota was the land of ten thousand lakes. Well, she'd find a really deep one, drill a hole in the ice, and drop the stone into the abyss. Send it sinking to a cold watery grave. Good riddance. The Pitch could search all they wanted and never have a chance of finding it down there. Of course, they'd find her first. They'd force her to tell them what she did with their little treasure.

What if it was worth money?

A lot of money.

She hadn't given that thought really serious consideration before. Though now it seemed almost obvious. This stone/relic/box was old . . . old as rock, in fact. Maybe it was an archaeological treasure, like those prehistoric spheres scattered all over Costa Rica; she had seen a program about them on the History Channel. She might sell it to a dealer in antiquities, or even a museum.

It sounded far-fetched, but who knew?

This spooky Pitch business had to be an elaborate charade: a cover story designed to ensure Chan would steal the stone for cash; thinking it was only important to a select group of believers, he'd make no attempt to run off looking for higher bidders. Whoever hired Chan knew the stone box's value.

Maybe it wasn't a box at all.

Chan never said it was a box. He kept calling it "the artifact" or "the item." In any case, Vera had come up with her own theory— a puzzle box with treasure locked inside. How else did you account for bloodshed over an ugly pointy rock?

Madness. It made no sense.

Unless . . . the rock was something rare.

The thing itself had to be the treasure, not anything it contained. Could it be a giant gemstone? Or maybe it was precious metal? Silver, gold . . . platinum? To an amateur's gaze, a chunk of unearthed raw metal would be hidden in plain sight. Add a can of spray paint. You might even fool an expert.

Scratch a stone and uncover a fortune.

Vera would take a closer look after she dried off.

She rinsed the shampoo from her hair. Eager now, she hurried to make her inspection. She had a Swiss Army knife in her purse. That would do the trick. If not, she could drive to the local hardware store and buy a hammer and chisel, a can of paint remover, too. By the end of the night, she'd know what she had on her hands; even if it meant reducing the stone to a small pile of rubble. Blinking water droplets out of her eyes, she turned off the shower and reached for her towel.

She dried her face.

Water gurgled in the pipes.

She lowered the towel.

The bathroom was dark.

Had the lights burned out? It happened every day in households spanning the globe. So it must happen in motels, too—probably more because people often kept the lights on in their motel rooms. There were two shining when she went in to take her shower: one connected to the exhaust fan and a fluorescent tube above the vanity mirror. Two bulbs don't flicker out simultaneously. She leaned over to the wall switches and toggled them. Nothing happened.

A fuse.

That was it.

The motel had Christmas decorations—those strands of primary colors attached to green wires, running front to back on their property. There must have been an overload. They blew a fuse. She'd call the office immediately. Ask if they could correct the problem or move her to another room.

Quickly, she dried off in the dark.

She detected a strip of felt gray half-light at the bottom of the door.

Vera had the oddest sensation of time passage, hours missed: an intuition that when she ventured beyond the door, it would no longer be daylight but a persistent, irrevocable night.

She went out.

The motel room was dim. Yet she was glad to see it brighter than the closed bathroom. Clearly, it was late morning outside, though a bleak December rendition of it. The curtains hadn't been drawn fully. An armchair blocked the way, snagging the drapery. Shadows played on the walls. She had left the table lamp on and now that was off, too. The face of the digital clock read blank.

Fuse.

She picked up her room phone.

Dead silence.

This phone had a cord. It was an old-fashioned landline and not subject to the electrical circuitry of the motel. Part, or the whole, of the town must have suffered an outage. The storm winds felled power lines. Telephone lines, too.

At least she had heat.

Funny, but the room was stifling. Even naked she felt uncomfortably warm. Her spine dampened with a dew of sweat and her cheeks flushed tight.

The only heater she saw, it was also the AC unit, was mounted into the wall at the back end of the room. She lifted the trapdoor on the facade and started punching buttons . . . but this thing worked on electricity, too. She put her hand over the vents. Air didn't blow.

She smelled cigarettes.

Not cigarettes.

Matches.

She put her nose over the vent. The smell wasn't coming from there. She turned and walked over to the armchair, then the bed. To the closet and bathroom, her orbit brought her back again.

The smell was strongest by the armchair.

As if, while she was showering, a person had sat there in the dark, striking matches one after another, then blowing them out.

Obviously, no one was sitting in the chair. Her bundled leather jacket rested in a lump on the seat. Inside was the stone.

She remembered the scorch marks she'd discovered on the kitchen table before leaving home.

But Chan had done that with his lighter. How else . . . ?

Despite the heat, she slipped into a pair of jeans and a black knit sweater. She didn't bother with underwear or socks. She tugged her boots on and grabbed the room key off the top of the television. There was something she wanted to see. She propped the door open with the armchair so the room would cool.

Out on the narrow sidewalk, the cold shocked her, nearly driving her backward into her boiling murky accommodations. Snow was falling in earnest, slanted left to right, obliterating any views far from the motel. Flakes swarmed the air. Already the lot needed plowing; her Camaro was entombed in white powder. The spotlight above her car surged star-bright. She had to turn away . . . so icily bright . . . then she heard it explode with a glassy pop.

Brittle fragments rained on her car's hood.

Vera stood at the center of an encircling darkness.

An overhang shielded the sidewalk. The downspouts were frozen solid. Floes thrust out of them like pale paws. Icicles elongated before her eyes and frosty snow tongues licked over the roof's edges.

That's where the Christmas lights are, she thought.

I want to see them.

She braved a blast of Arctic wind and, clutching her arms to her chest, staggered forward and planted her two boots firmly in a drift alongside the curb. She faced the motel, looking for evidence of the lights. She had no difficulty picking them out. The childlike meanders of stapled wire and colors were obvious. Their gaudy flavors leaked like snow cones into the surrounding ice.

Only the lights strung above her door were unlit.

Unnerved, she stumbled closer. Her boots skated on slick icy crust. She caught her balance, reached up on her tiptoes, and jiggled the strand of bulbs. A couple of staples pulled loose and fell.

No flickers.

No lights.

Cell phone in her grip, she waited for a satellite link. She'd tell the office.

"C'mon," she said, shivering.

A journey around the perimeter of the motel to the office was unthinkable. She'd end up snowblind. The cold proved too much for her. She wedged into the doorway. One side of her face going numb while the other half baked. The storm whooped. Ice pebbles chattered along the walkway. No linkup. The satellite tumbled in the heavens beyond her reach. She didn't even know the number to the office. It would be labeled on her room's telephone, of course. She stared into her room, afraid for no reason she could name, when a voice beside her spoke.

"*Deep into that darkness peering, long I stood there wondering, fearing/Doubting, dreaming dreams no mortal ever dared to dream before . . .*"

"Excuse me?"

It was the old man. No dog this time, no yellow coat. But she knew it was him. He wore a long wool cardigan frayed at the elbows and covered in rusty dog hairs. A thin cigar fumed between his fingers. He smiled.

"Here I am acting silly, reciting Poe. My name's Max Caul. I'm staying right down the row from you."

"In a nonsmoking room?" she asked, and pointed to the cigar.

"No, no. I enjoy the brisk air. Having a problem?"

"My electricity's out."

"How odd," he said. "Mine's working fine."

"And there's a strange smell in the room . . ."

His eyes widened, the wrinkled lids unpeeling. "Sulfur, would you say? Matchsticks?"

She pulled back slightly. "How'd you guess?"

He shook his head, shrugged, and dragged on the cigar. The orange crumb of ash reddened. "Would you like to come into my room? You could ring the office. I'm sure they'll fix whatever's wrong."

What were her options?

Fear, freeze, or acquiesce. Up close the old man seemed terribly thin despite wearing a sweater. His hands shook with a mild palsy. When he toked his cigar his eyes pinched with the effort. He was feeble. She'd only be in his room for a minute, long enough to warm up and call the office, and if he was a dirty old man and tried anything, she was confident she could handle him.

She acquiesced.

CHAPTER 18

The police left the Totem. Wyatt walked home alone. Two men were waiting for him in the Rendezvous lobby. He didn't have to ask who they were. He knew. The dark brothers—the pair who beheaded a dog, terrorized a sleeping woman, and set fire to Henry's place. One was drinking coffee and punching keys on the computer behind the counter. His partner acted as lookout. His raven stare smoked two holes through the glass door. Striding in a driving snow, Wyatt sensed them before he saw them: *sharp, hunting eyes.*

His first thought was Opal. Had he locked the apartment door? Was she asleep upstairs, or had they already paid his wife a visit?

He craned his neck for a glimpse at the bedroom window.

A rectangle of gray framed in white lace.

He could decipher nothing. The brother behind the desk stood and spoke to the lookout. Wyatt saw his lips moving, sneers knifed across two faces in a single stroke. He had no weapon on him. In the motel safe, yes.

But the safe was under the desk. Behind a combination lock.

No turning back. They tracked him coming up the apron. He could make a dash for it. The ice made running a gamble. And Opal—he had to protect her. His best bet was to jump into the mix. Stay coolheaded. If they had guns, well, he'd be finding out about that soon enough . . .

"Weather fit for neither man nor beast," he said.

A strap of sleigh bells tinkled, shaken by the swinging door.

The men answered with silence.

"You fellas need a room?"

He flicked snow off his shoulders, stomped his boots, and hung his jacket on an antler protruding from the wall. Moving slowly. Drawing in a deep breath, letting it go, then another, before he turned around again. His ears keen for the squeak of boots, the rustle of cloth.

He poured a cup of coffee.

Sipped it.

If they wanted to keep quiet, he could do that. The quiet helped him to think. Reality was he had only the one eye. He knew it. They did, too. In a fight the disadvantage would quickly progress from unlucky to deadly.

Adaptation, he told himself. Be smarter.

The brother behind the desk appeared to be the brains of the duo. Wyatt watched him. That left the other on his blindside, behind his eye patch. Wyatt caught pieces of him with a quick head rotation. Using reflections in the glass to flesh out what he was missing from a straight-on view. A slab of meat stacked on two legs. Prison denims head-to-toe; a yard coat with a dirty lamb's wool collar; hands hidden in his pockets. Wyatt wasn't too thrilled with the position he'd drawn. But he'd make do. The Brains would show a sign. If his counterpart engaged, there'd be a signal, a flinch.

Something. Anything.

Anything at all . . .

Wyatt would go for broke. Try for a knockdown shot with the edge of his hand. Throat, jaw. Kick out the guy's kneecap. Deliver him pain. He didn't want to get trapped behind the counter with both of them still able-bodied. He'd have no space. They would close on him.

He leaned over the counter.

A role reversal: the intruder was standing where Wyatt usually did. Daring him to mention it with his body language—the provocation would give them an excuse to cut to the action. Action was their forte. He was sure. These weren't a couple of negotiators or clever strategists.

They didn't know what he knew. Didn't know he'd been to the Totem Lodge and seen their handiwork. He'd use their ignorance. Keep them guessing. Make them relax in the catbird seat.

They were a couple of swaggering bad dudes. Maybe killers.

He would kill without hesitation to save his family.

They didn't know that, either.

They might learn.

"We're looking for our sister," Brains said. "That's her car, we think." A gloved finger jabbed in the direction of the Camaro's parking spot around the building.

"Let's switch places. I'll look her up."

Brains rounded the counter. Suspicions playing inside his skull, his brow bunched, shoulders tensed. A gamey smell wafted out from under his clothes. But he came forward. Thinking he had control of the situation.

He passed close.

If the knife's coming, this is when he'll do it . . .

"What's your sister's name?" Wyatt asked. He slid to the desk.

"I looked on the computer already. Didn't see it. She's a real joker though. Likes to play games, use aliases. But if there's a single woman here, that's her."

Tapping keys . . .

"I have quite a few single guests . . ."

"You're not listening. We see her car. So that's her room, right?"

"Which room's that?"

"Round the corner . . ."

"The only person booked there is a gentleman."

The desk phone rang.

"Give me a key for the damn room out there or I'll—"

"Hold that thought a sec . . ."

Wyatt answered the phone, "Front desk. How can I help you?"

The brothers exchanged glances of frustration.

"Yes, sir . . . I see, a problem with the electricity. I'm checking in a couple of guests, but as soon as I'm finished, I'll take a look. Sure thing. Be there in a minute." Wyatt thumbed the connection. He spoke into the dead receiver. "Sir, let me look in my toolbox here and see if I have a spare fuse." He reached for the safe under the desk and began spinning the combination.

"What are you doing?" Brains asked.

Wyatt didn't respond. He had one more number to go. His hands were sweating. His back ached from shoveling. Inside the safe he'd find a Glock 27, loaded with 40-caliber rounds, facing butt-out in a carpeted slot.

Brains tore the phone from his grip.

The dial tone rang out.

"Take him," Brains said.

And his brother lurched over the counter.

Two hundred and twenty fast-moving pounds dropped into Wyatt's lap. The office chair crashed out from under Wyatt. He had the safe open.

A gloved hand—a steel blade flicked into view.

He lost it behind his eye patch.

He reached into the safe. His fingertips slipped off the gun butt. He tumbled backward and slammed into a file cabinet. His head hit metal.

The top drawer popped, catching his attacker flush on the forehead.

It didn't knock him out.

He sat on Wyatt's chest, straddling him, stunned, blinking. His brow creased with a red welt. The serrated knife in his hand suspended midthrust.

Wyatt punched him in the throat.

Then he bucked him. He tried to seize the knife hand at the wrist.

Missed it.

The big man rolled, choking, crawling. Wyatt shot a leg forward.

Plowed his heel in the man's crotch. A muffled scream and the guy curled up, fetal.

Wyatt didn't see Brains's fist zeroing in.

He went black.

When he came around, he was lying on his belly. The brothers were dragging him out from under the desk. Cursing him. The one he kicked was whimpering and making other sounds, too. Lunatic yelps. Grunts. Wyatt saw his eye patch on the floor. Blood—he guessed it was his—smeared a desk leg. His lip was fat. And the left side of his face had gone completely numb.

He stretched for the open safe.

Too far away.

He planted his hands on the floor and tried to stop the dragging.

He couldn't.

"You start opening him up. He'll tell us where the girl is."

A grunt.

"Then he's yours."

A squeal of pure glee . . .

Wyatt heard a door opening. No jingle bells this time.

It was the apartment door.

"No, Opal! Go back!"

"Dad? What the hell . . . ?"

"Adam?"

Wyatt twisted to warn his son. But it was too late. Adam shoved the brothers. Wyatt felt a jerk as they collided into each other and let go of his legs. Adam was strong, agile, but his main leverage had been surprise. The brothers were quick to violence. Unlimited in their use of force. They didn't think about consequences. Didn't worry what they were destroying.

The sound of blows landing, muscle and bone smacked together at speed.

Wyatt wanted to join his son in the fight.

But he knew his best option.

He scrambled for the safe.

Pulled the Glock. Spun. Aimed.

Three bodies massed together. His son between the denim-clad siblings—the scrum pushed past the counter and spilled into the lobby.

Wyatt lunged after them.

Adam had a headlock on Brains whose face contorted as he attempted to pry loose, his lank greasy hair hanging over a mask of fury.

The knife on the carpet . . .

The brothers dived for it.

Brains throwing elbows into Adam's rib cage. Breaking free. Seeing Wyatt's gun. Panic replacing his wild anger.

Wyatt's finger feathered the trigger. Wanting a little more separation.

Air between his boy and the attackers . . .

Adam leaping to his feet, not knowing he also crossed into the line of fire.

Wyatt holding back. Maybe the hardest thing he'd ever done.

"He's got a gun! Go! Let's go!"

The brothers hit the door running low into a blizzard.

Adam started after them until his father put a hand on his shoulder.

"Don't," Wyatt said.

Adrenaline shook them.

Wyatt glanced down.

They had the presence of mind to take their knife.

At that, he trembled.

CHAPTER 19

Henry Genz carried his leather-bound King James Bible to the fire-damaged room, where he opened it at random, feeling the Lord would guide him to the passage most appropriate to his current situation. The tang of loitering smoke offended his nostrils. He'd prepared an egg salad sandwich but was too exhausted to take a single bite. He left the plate on the windowsill and sat there in the oyster light emitting from the window. His gaze returned to the ruined bed; the black star scorched in the carpet. The Egyptian eye—he couldn't stand to look at it, but neither could he look away.

Resting the book across his knees, he parted the covers, allowing the crinkly pages to fall of their own accord. The wind under the eaves played strange flutes. Its song wormed inside his head. Unconsciously, he hummed along.

The firemen's hoses had soaked the carpet. Henry could smell the wet subflooring underneath. His shoes squished. The damp air saturated his bones, as if to crumble them from within. He rubbed his neck. But the pain only tightened. The Word—he'd find his balm there.

Poor dead Sheba, his best companion. He hoped she hadn't suffered much. To think of her last minutes fanned his anger . . .

Leaning over the page, licking his lips, he began to read aloud. *"And the man in whom the evil spirit was leaped on them, and overcame them, and prevailed against them, so that they fled out of that house naked and wounded—*"

"How are you, Henry?" a voice asked.

Henry thought he might be hearing the Devil himself. So soft came the utterance. Yet, familiar to his ears. When he lifted his gaze, the speaker was standing before him like a living inkblot. Black lenses dancing with refracted colors. Hands folded, though not in prayer.

"You," Henry said.

"Long time. Have you read anything good lately?"

Whiteside slipped the Bible from Henry's lap.

"Give me that!"

"Certainly," Whiteside said.

The doctor handed the volume over. He'd kept his finger tucked between the pages, saving Henry's place, and now re-opened them to newspaper clippings.

Henry looked. His face paled. He was cold-sweating, shouting.

"What have you done?"

"Why, *I've* done nothing. Don't you enjoy reading about yourself in the newspaper?"

The front-page photos. Broken glass littered the ground. Gaping holes where the windows had blown out in the explosion. In the background shadows, blood and prone bodies. The Pie Stop. Lower on the page were the grinning headshots of the victims. And set apart, above and left, the portrait of a soldier.

Henry's brother, Jesse.

"This is my favorite," Whiteside said. He tapped a headline.

MISSING SHOOTER? COP CLAIMS SECOND GUNMAN

Henry tried to say something, instead his throat constricted.

"Glad I can still leave you speechless. Let's talk facts, Henry. Fact is I need a place to stay. I like it here. Always have. I need a base of operations. I've decided the Totem Lodge is perfect."

"Get out."

"That isn't going to happen."

"I won't . . . help you hurt anyone else."

Henry's doughy face stayed low and focused on the carpet.

"Are you afraid of me?"

Henry gazed up. He was confused.

"How can you look younger than before? After twenty years?"

"You're the one who gets older, Henry. I never change."

A small pistol appeared in Whiteside's hand. Maybe it had been there all along. It was an antique. The kind gamblers hid up their sleeves on riverboats in days gone by. A derringer, that's what they're called, Henry thought. He concentrated on the word. He didn't want to fall apart. To cower in front of this evil man. He knew his weakness though. The pistol waved. Henry stared down the tiny double barrels—a child's fingers could plug them. Decorative metalwork etched the tarnished silver: petals and curlicues. The grip was inlaid ivory, a surface networked with pits and fractures, like two sides of a dead moon. Whiteside touched the pistol under Henry's chin, and used it to raise him up.

"When you look for your soul, what is it you find?" Whiteside asked.

The derringer probed Henry's Adam's apple.

Henry opened his mouth.

Whiteside pushed the pistol in.

"God's not here. Is He, Henry?"

That voice was like poison dripping in his ears.

The pistol eased out.

"I . . . I don't know," Henry said.

"Let me assure you because I *do* know. I've looked for the good in people. I've looked for the godliness in them. And what I've found is holes. Emptiness. Voids within voids. I sense foulness. Life degenerates as the universe winds down. I think that's what I smell. The rot. We are a rotten species. When I was a boy, I experienced my first vision. I'd fallen off the roof of a shed where my parents kept rakes and other tools. I hit my head on the ground. Lost consciousness, the doctors would say. But I say different. I was awake. It was after supper. Dusk. I lay there staring at the first, faint evening stars. I tried to make them move. I was a child.

I did not understand moving stars was outside the boundary of my powers. I just tried it. And I failed. I tried again. A bird hopped over to my shadowy place in the grass and cocked its head."

"A bird?" Henry asked, in amazement.

"*Hello there,* I thought with my childish mind. I felt my thought penetrate the bird's consciousness, like a straight pin thumbed into a sponge. *Hello, little one.* The bird skipped and skittered around me, never taking her eyes off me. I knew that she was a female. Using the pins I pushed in, I drew things out. This bird lived in a heating duct on top of the yellow house next door. Her nest was fashioned of lint, string, and twigs. It was a warm spot. Safe and dark. The opening onto the outside world, the dangerous world where I lived, was small. The duct resembled a long metallic box. I knew something about living in a box. My mind was a box. I was climbing out. Suddenly I saw through the bird's feathers and skin. A thimbleful of blood circulated round and round inside her body. She'd eaten that morning—seeds left on a white plate with bacon suet and a scoop of crunchy peanut butter. I tasted the peanuts on her breath. I tried to make her blood stop."

The black lenses flashed red like playing cards shuffled in a dealer's hands.

"What happened to the bird?"

"My mother found me. I couldn't move. Couldn't even call out to my own mother. She picked me up in her arms. I was bleeding from my scalp. As she carried me into the house, I lifted my head and saw a dead sparrow on the grass."

Henry went deeper into the blackness. A man spirals down a well.

"I learned something that day, Henry. So in the future I could be a teacher to others. Like Jesse. Like you." The voice was a hand propelling him forward.

Whiteside put the pistol away.

"Come, Henry. Lie on the bed."

Henry stood and walked across the wet carpet. He did not

want to, but he could not stop himself. His body responded, like muscle memory. And he had real memories, too, of the first time he met Whiteside at his parents' farmhouse.

"*He's done it to me before,*" *Jesse said.* "*Like I told you ... about that weekend at Fort Riley? He did a bunch of us. We felt indestructible, like gods.*

"*Now you feel like shit. Wanting to kill yourself. You ever think he did that to you, too? Put that awfulness inside you, so he could take you back whenever he wanted?*"

Jesse shook his head.

"*He says I'll feel that way again. He'll make it permanent. Whiteside can do anything he says he can. I'll ask him if he'll do it to you, too ...*"

Henry lay down on the soaking-wet bed. He smelled the burned mattress. Bare springs dug into his spine. He looked at the ceiling.

"*Explain to me how he's doing it?*"

"*I don't completely understand it, Hen. But he puts you in a trance. It doesn't hurt or anything. It's peaceful.*"

"*He hypnotizes you?*"

"*Sure, you could call it that, but there's more to it. It has to do with the words. There's a special way he says them ... look, he's a conduit for something bigger than you and me, that's what it is, bigger and older than all of us.*"

"*Black magic?*"

"*Black magic, white magic ... oh, who gives a damn? I'm telling you it's the best I ever felt in my life. I wrote him a letter and told him so. And now he's here in American Rapids visiting me. That's special. Don't you want to feel what I felt? So much power inside ...*"

He and Jesse reclined on two couches in the dimness of the parlor. Whiteside sat between them on a kitchen chair, just talking to them, slowly, his words forming a rhythm, telling them he could make them better than other men, stronger, fearless. They would be godlike warriors when he finished.

"Take deep breaths, Henry. You remember this part. Don't you?"

"Yes."

"See the mind muscle. It is contracted into a knot."

"I see it." Henry's energy drained away. He sank into the bed.

"We will loosen the knot together. Can you do it?"

"Yes." His willpower followed the energy flowing out of him.

"Let's begin. Imagine dilation. Releasing the knot to open the mind . . ."

A man spirals down a well. And every time he hits the bottom, a new bottom replaces it further into the depth of slick tubular walls. The dizziness is too much for the man. As he's falling, he closes his eyes. He remembers falling down this well before. He remembers and he sleeps. A man spirals down . . .

Henry climbed the stepladder and removed the false ceiling tiles above his office. He poked his head up into the hole. The raincoat was right there. Inside a dusty Kmart bag bound with duct tape. All those years ago, he'd thrown away the pistol. The one he used to cover Jesse during the attack inside the restaurant. The one he shot Wyatt with in the back. Later, he wired the trigger guard to a cinderblock and heaved it into the Rainy River. Lights from the girders of the International Bridge leading to Canada sparkled on the water. He heard a loud splash. A chain of bubbles surfaced in the shadows. Then only shadows.

He snatched the raincoat from its secret hiding place. He turned inside the attic hole. Careful not to lose his footing on the ladder, he peered into the unlit space. Where was it?

There.

A pump shotgun, chopped down to a wicked handgrip.

And a full box of shells.

He grabbed them and climbed down.

Whiteside had left the lodge. Henry wasn't sure where he went. He only knew that he would return. Henry had given him the keys to the place after all. He'd told the current guests that the morning fire had damaged the sprinkler system and they would need to check out immediately. It wasn't safe to stay. That much was true. The least Henry could offer was to save a few from death.

For others he would be the executioner.

There was nothing he could do about it.

He loaded the shotgun.

Then he tore through the Kmart bag and unrolled the old raincoat.

He put it on.

He'd gained weight over the last two decades. The coat wouldn't button. It fit snugly around his shoulders. He left it hanging open. Coattails spread at his sides. Slack wings. Whiteside once told him the coat would render him invisible.

He was stuffing away extra shells when he felt a small hard object deep in the raincoat's right pocket. No bigger than a fisherman's lead sinker. He retrieved the object and rolled it between his fingers.

He'd almost forgotten.

The forgetting was a kind of gift from Whiteside, too. Only it wasn't really forgetting. More like a temporary amnesia. The horrors of the past lingered off-stage. Henry was aware of them. Occasionally he caught glimpses in the corner of his eye. When the purpose suited him, Whiteside ushered the horrors out, front and center. He threw a hot spotlight on them. *See?* He insisted Henry look. *The worst things that happen never go away. Never retreat. They were here the whole time. Waiting for you, Henry. Sleeping inside you like a disease.*

Henry rummaged around a desk drawer until he found a felt-tip marker.

The task at hand was difficult. A constant struggle of will. Requiring total concentration. Whiteside had programmed him for a mission. Search and destroy. Any deviation was pure hell. His body came alive with pain. Whiteside had put triggers in his brain. Pain or pleasure. It was up to Henry to decide.

After he had finished with the marker, he was sweating. The

sensation of a blowtorch licked up and down his back. Nails pounded into his insteps. The skin on his belly shredded to ribbons. His muscles seized. Teeth gritted. He dropped the uncapped marker on the floor. He surrendered completely to the commanding voice of Whiteside.

The pain washed away.

Soothing relief replaced it.

Henry became a cool blue . . . killing machine.

He ripped the cord from the office blinds. He tied a sling and hung the loaded shotgun out of sight underneath his arm.

Tears fled down his cheeks. The last of what was human in Henry was saying good-bye. Saying good-bye to the world he lived in, the goodness he had done here. The beauty he'd known. He bid farewell to himself, too.

As he walked out the door, he noticed a firefighter's ax sealed inside an emergency case in the lobby. Blood was dripping from the blade. He knew it wasn't real. The blood wasn't there. Not yet. But it would be soon.

He didn't cry anymore.

The feeling part of him had been locked away forever.

The ax was no longer a tool for breaking down doors and rescuing people. Only a weapon appeared before him, with a wedge of blade and a pointed pick head. Using a miniature hammer on a chain, he shattered the glass.

Blood ran down the yellow fiberglass handle.

He hefted it.

The pleasure triggers clicked furiously.

A smile broke.

Yes, tonight was going to be a lot of fun.

CHAPTER 20

Something was wrong. Max didn't want to alarm the young woman any more than necessary. She already seemed to be on edge. He turned from the window and let the curtain fall back into place.

Two men running into a blizzard.

He'd watched them go.

The second man slipped, fell. The first man never broke stride. Never looked back. Zigzagging. Then the fallen man launched himself off again from a three-point stance. Something elongated in his hand. A gun? Or a knife? All Max saw was a clawing blur. The men crossed the highway. A truck waited. A dirty purple plume of exhaust reared upward and the wind obliterated it. A scarlet, dragon-eyed flash of brake lights. Max's hearing wasn't so acute, but it sounded like an engine growling south.

Wyatt hadn't come to check on the electrical peculiarities. He hadn't called back, either. Max rang the office twice and received no answer.

Definitely not good.

Max's inquisitiveness was getting the better of him, too. He wanted to search the woman's luggage. He wanted to see if the stone was there, to feel its presence. The possibility he might actually encounter it after all these years . . .

"I could go take a look inside your room," he said.

She stared at him. Silent.

"Maybe I could figure out what's awry."

"I don't think so," she said.

"You'd be surprised. I'm fairly handy. That's a by-product of traveling as much as I do. You learn how to fix things. Minor glitches."

"I have a feeling it's not minor."

I'll bet you do, Max thought. When he'd seen her exit her room in a rush—the puzzled frown, her jacket left behind—he hid his revolver under the mattress and hurried out. Lighting a cigar on his way through the door, he'd have a plausible excuse for being there on the sidewalk during this icebox of a day.

"Annie likes you," he said.

The Irish setter had cornered their visitor and now she flopped on her back and exposed a taut pink belly for scratching. The woman, who told him her name was Vera, squatted down and obliged. The rub of skin through silky hair crackled with the winter static and seemed to comfort them both.

"She sure is a happy dog," Vera said.

"We take care of each other. I think I have the easier part of the job." Max unpacked a box of liver treats and passed them to Vera for doling out.

The setter executed what appeared to be an impossible physical move, flipping over and spinning around in a swirl of russet fur. She gobbled the snacks and licked Vera's hands clean of crumbs.

"Good to have a companion on a road trip," Vera said.

"You aren't going it alone this Christmas Eve?"

"Yes . . . well, no, not actually. I have a friend stopping by later."

"What brings you up north?"

"I'm visiting an aunt in Winnipeg."

"But not in time for the holiday?"

"No, I hadn't planned on any storms. This one slowed me down. I'm not going to make it."

"Ah, that's a shame."

"How about you?"

"This is my whole family, Ann-Margret and me. We bop around the country. Stay as long as we care to, leave when we like. Vagabonds. We make it a habit to spend every Christmas week in American Rapids. For sentimental reasons. I'll be working, too."

"What do you do?"

"I write horror stories."

Vera laughed. "Remind me to tell you my horror story sometime."

"I'd love to hear it." Max meant those words. He wondered if he could get her talking. He'd temporarily lost contact with the stone's whereabouts after the coven left Corvallis. He wavered when it came to approaching the women. He thought it might be best to watch them for a while. Frankly, he didn't even know for certain if they had the stone. There was no rush. He had time. Wrong, of course, on both counts. He'd been stuck in the Good Samaritan Regional Medical Center when they decamped. The pain in his gut attacked relentlessly. It started in his lower back, below the ribs, igniting like a fuse along his spine then blazing outward at his shoulders. Crucified on an invisible cross of fire, he'd stumbled into the emergency room, holding tight to Annie's leash as he collapsed across a row of waiting-room chairs. By the time he got out, the women were gone.

He discovered they'd relocated to the Midwest. Tracked them as far as Chicago. But then, nothing. He bribed a real estate agent for the listings the group had been looking at—family dwellings on the South and West sides. When Max drove to those first addresses, he was surprised. The houses were large enough that the whole coven could live together, as they had on the commune in Oregon. But the neighbors would certainly notice their presence: a clan of women, mostly white, wearing long handmade dresses, up all hours of the night, living together with no men and no children. Work wouldn't bring them into contact with anyone in the community, either. They ran an online Wiccan store. Sold candles, herbal spell mixes, oils, and Druidic jewelry. The whole operation could be moved at a day's notice with a U-Haul. After reading about the murders, he realized he had their final address in his pocket. Second to the last on his list, but by then the Pitch had gotten to them.

"What are those drawings?" Vera asked.

"Sorry?"

Vera pointed over his shoulder.

He'd forgotten to erase his symbols on the door. The damned curtain, too. He felt the chalk residue on his fingertips. Saw a smear of white powder on his sleeve. The pulse in his neck hammered. A ripple of nausea passed through him.

"I must have neglected to . . ."

He fumbled with the buttons of his sweater. One pulled loose and he closed it in his sweating palm. "At my age, a man sometimes finds himself doing strange things." He offered a weak, unconvincing smile. "Inexplicable acts."

Vera reassessed him. He could almost see the calculations floating in the air above her head. She'd had her guard up, dropped it, and now she was chastising herself for making that mistake. Old men can be liars, too. They can be crafty, dangerous, and above all else, patient. Weren't old men the most diabolical on earth? This young woman needed to look no further than her current predicament for an example. A well-ripened Horus Whiteside pursued her with a vengeance. He was more ancient even than Max. But she couldn't possibly know that. Could she?

If she did know more than she was letting on, then the signs on the door would have sent her warning sirens screaming. She wouldn't be wasting time posing questions to him. What he saw looked like innocent confusion. Maybe with a touch of paranoia added. She couldn't be that good of an actress. No, she still stumbled blessedly in the dark. At least, he hoped that was the case.

"I'm going back to my room," she said.

The labyrinth he'd slashed in ivory chalk under the peephole—she stood up and marched straight for it.

"Allow me to apologize for my . . . artwork. It's a kind of therapy," he said.

- 137 -

"Thanks for letting me use your phone. I need to get moving."

He stepped in front of her. "I have an obsessive compulsive disorder, you see. These harmless drawings make me feel safe in unfamiliar places."

Her voice cut to a whisper. "Please let me go."

How could he stop her? He wouldn't dare lay a hand on her. And she was young, strong, a fraction of his age and about the same weight. He could see her muscular thighs through her jeans. He wasn't so decrepit he didn't notice a handsome athletic woman. Color flamed in her cheeks. His mouth opened and closed. He could think of no verbal way of making her stay. He moved aside.

She left.

Ann-Margret whimpered.

"Easy, girl, it's okay. You wouldn't think a writer would be at a loss for words. What was I going to do? Pull a gun on her?"

Through the walls he heard the dull thump of a door closing. He went to the window. With two fingers he opened a slit in the curtain.

Vera, jacket on, hands thrust into the pockets, shoulders hunched. She walked quickly past. She rounded the corner. Heading for the office. Would she tell Wyatt and Opal about his chalk symbols?

Max lifted the edge of the mattress with his knee. He slid out the Ruger, tucked it into his waistband. He went into the bathroom and wet the end of a towel. He wiped the door and curtains. He was drying them when someone knocked. Rapid, loud knocks. The sound made him jump. Ann-Margret barked sharply and backpedaled between the beds.

Max rested his palm on the Ruger's grip.

A voice, Vera's, called out, "Max, open up. It's Vera. Max?"

He tugged his sweater forward to conceal the revolver.

Turned the deadbolt.

The cold wind hardly had a chance to invade the room. Only a few granular snowflakes were able to sneak past the jamb before

Vera rushed in and slammed the door behind her. She rested her back against it, closed her eyes, and sighed.

"What is it?" he asked.

"You're not going to believe this."

"Tell me."

"I was going to the office. When I got about ten steps away, I saw a tall man coming out . . ."

"Did he say something?"

She shook her head.

"I'm afraid I don't understand why—"

"He was carrying an ax."

CHAPTER 21

"They live above," Max said. He pointed to the extra level over the motel. The hood of his parka muffled his words. Vera looked up into a furious whiteness, icy pecks on her cheeks. Her eyes were tearing from sheer cold. He was talking about the owners. Their apartment had its main entrance through the motel office, but Max said there was a wooden staircase that angled down the back of the building, like a fire escape. If the office wasn't safe, they could go up the stairs, ring the bell, if there was one, and see if anyone was hurt.

Or dead, Vera thought.

It was the witch house in Chicago all over again.

She didn't want to think what an ax could do to a human body.

"Oh, damn it." Max had reached the stairs. They were clogged with snow and ice. The steps were buried. Only the red painted pickets of the staircase were visible. At the top of the stairs was a storm door, and behind that, a wooden door with a frosty window. Both were shut tight. Snow drifted as high as the handles.

"I can make it up," she said.

"Are you sure?"

"Only one way to find out."

Vera plunged her boots into the knee-deep snow and began to climb. She could feel the hard ice underneath the layer of fresh powder, its surface sleek as steel. The soles of her boots were leather and treadless. She gripped the rail with her bare hands. She was climbing sideways, with her butt braced against the siding of the outer wall. After three steps, her skin stung. She looked up. Another twenty steps at least. The wind thrust under her jacket. She tucked her chin and concentrated on the next step.

Then another.

The staircase swayed beneath her weight. *Me plus all this snow,* she thought. She could see she wasn't imagining it. The structure pulled away from the building a few inches and slammed back again. She watched the gap open and close as she shifted her balance. Her bottom smacked the wall. It felt like walking across an old rickety bridge. *Step.* Only this bridge angled upward. *Step.* A toboggan chute, that's what it reminded her of. *Step.* She heard Max calling up to her and turned to catch what he was saying.

"You're doing great!" He waved her on.

She lifted a hand from the rail to wave back. Her ankle bent as her boot glided frictionless under the drift. Body rushing forward. *No.* Grab something. The railing knocked the breath out of her. A horrible sensation of toppling head over heels into the alleyway—she reeled back and hit the wall. Hard. Stars as her skull made contact. The staircase swayed. She pitched forward again. Staying low. Her face mashed into freezing darkness. On her knees, she immediately sensed wetness seeping through her jeans. The cold felt much worse. Snow filled her eye sockets, her mouth. Lifting her head, it was hard to tell the snow from the air. A sudden panic of suffocation overtook her. Grit in her mouth. Burning cold wedged between her teeth. She tried spitting. Blinded. Ice pressed on her eyelids. She scratched the whiteness away. Her face and fingers were numb. She might be mauling herself without feeling it. But when she blinked, the world came back to her.

Grayer. Dimmed.

To her left, open space.

To her right, the motel wall towered.

She was still on the stairs at least.

She had hit her nose. Dark marbles of blood dotted the snow.

No pain, though. Not yet. She wasn't warm enough for pain. She widened her stance and continued to walk.

Step after step.

At last, the door. No bell.

She made a fist and knocked.

It sounded quiet in the storm.

She knocked, louder this time.

Her hands, red as crabs, poked out of her sleeves.

She kicked at the snow mounded against the storm door. She'd kick the door in if she had to. She wasn't going back down the way she'd come. With the heel of her hand she pounded on the storm door's glass.

"Anybody in there?" she yelled.

The wind was so loud she didn't hear the inner door open. Her gaze aimed at the foot of the storm door—the target of her kicks.

She didn't see the face appear behind the glass.

When she did look up, she saw herself—her reflection—bending. The door bulged out at her. Ice broke around it. Dropping like scales. The metal door swinging at her, and a man behind it, reaching for her—

She tried stepping back. Her boots flew out. The railing hit her and, having no choice but momentum, she teetered backward. She was falling.

Max shouted.

Arms groped for her.

Rough hands squeezing, gripping, hauled her in.

As the door sprang shut behind her, her confusion compounded and she heard Max's voice cut off as if he'd been unplugged.

CHAPTER 22

"You okay?"

"What're *you* doing here?" she asked.

Vera was in his arms. Her cheeks shined bright and wet, and the collar of her jacket spilled clumps of snow. He had two handfuls of her sweater. Her muscles were tensed. His knuckles brushed her naked ribs. She shivered. He had grabbed her hard. Grabbed her and dragged her inside this narrow little room filled with brooms, mops, and bottles of household cleaners. To one side were an industrial washer and dryer. Bleach, ammonia, and powdered soaps stocked the shelves opposite. Cotton rags lay folded in neat rectangular piles. Boxes of garbage-can liners were split open and sprouting slicks of black and white plastic. The cloudy domes of lightbulbs protruded from their cardboard sleeves. Feather dusters hung swaying from hooks in the ceiling. It smelled like a hospital, a bus station, a public washroom. A motel.

"I live here," Adam said.

"I don't understand—"

"Sure you do. Think a minute. You're only missing one piece. My parents own this motel. I grew up here. I was on my way home for Christmas break when I ran out of gas. You picked me up and brought me right to the door."

"This is your home?"

"Nice, isn't it?"

"Are you going to let go of me?"

"First tell me why you were kicking in our back door."

"I thought something bad might've happened."

"Like what?"

"Like somebody got hurt or killed."

"What makes you say that?" he asked, the exasperation leaking into his voice, a sharpness he hadn't intended.

"I saw a guy downstairs, leaving the office."

"You mean two guys. Those guys who came in here with a knife?"

"A knife?" She squinted at him. Shook her head. "Not a knife."

"Trust me. I saw it up close. They had a knife."

"But the guy I saw had an ax. And he was alone."

Adam released her. She didn't look like she was lying. She looked worried. About what was going to happen to her? Or was she concerned about him, too? As if her brain had kicked into overdrive but still she couldn't figure things out. Part of her was ready to punch him in the mouth. He accepted that. Maybe she had a reason to be angry, though he'd just saved her from a bone-shattering fall. Windblown and pink-cheeked, something about her intrigued him. Intimidated him as well, but that was the key to it. Up close, inches apart, she was hard to take your eyes off—it wasn't cookie-cutter cuteness like the sorority sisters he'd seen on campus. This strange woman crawling up his back steps was a unique female variant of the species. He hadn't met her kind before. He wondered which of them was more afraid.

"Your nose is bleeding."

"I fell on the steps. I'll be fine. Did you see the ax guy?"

"No. I saw the knife guys. I wrestled with them actually. Come into the kitchen and I'll get you some ice for your nose." He opened a passage through the shelving. There was light. The white hulk of a refrigerator came into view. And a sink. A round table with four pearly vinyl seats trimmed in chrome.

"Ice is the last thing I need."

"What did your ax man look like?" Adam filled a mug with

milk and shut it inside a countertop microwave. He pushed a button. The oven window cast a pale glow. He took down a can of Hershey's cocoa mix from a cabinet.

"He was tall, over six feet at least. An older man with salt-and-pepper hair and a sad-looking face. He was wearing a black trench coat. He acted weird."

"Are we talking weird *other* than carrying an ax around?"

"It was like he was a robot. You know? Remote controlled."

The microwave dinged. Adam scooped two heaping spoonfuls of chocolate powder into the mug, stirred.

"I definitely did not see him," he said, handing her the cup. "We caught two creeps digging around the office. Looking at our computer to find somebody they thought was staying here . . ."

"So what? You think it's me?"

"Is it?"

"How the fuck would I know?"

"Sit here and warm up. I'm going downstairs to check things out. After what's been happening, I'm ready to believe anything."

"Wait a minute. Were they looking for a woman?"

"That's what they told my dad. Might be total bullshit, they could've been searching for cash in the office when he surprised them." He started to go.

"Hey! I'm not staying here alone," she said.

"You aren't alone."

Adam watched a shadow spread across the floor. His mother shuffled into the kitchen. She looked exhausted, feverish. Damp strands of hair stuck to her face. His father supported her, his arm snug around her slumping shoulders. Her lips were cracked. Eyes bloodshot, hooded. Skin white as paper. She lifted her head in Adam's direction. Then she rushed forward and squeezed him in her wiry arms. Tears fell. Adam felt them as she kissed his cheek. Her skin was hot. No human touch radiated so much heat.

"You're alive!" she cried.

"I told you that, honey," Wyatt said. "Adam is fine, and he's home. Home with us for Christmas. You had a bad nightmare. That's all."

His mother's pleading gaze leaped between them. "I saw Adam dead. It was no dream. I can't say whether I was seeing the past or the future. But I was there, the same way I'm standing here now. The things I saw were not a dream."

Adam said nothing.

His father nodded, slowly, once.

"We believe you."

That seemed to calm her.

Vera, who had sat silently drinking her cocoa during the brief family reunion, became her focus. The two women exchanged curious smiles.

"Who is this?" his mother asked.

Vera lowered the mug and held out her hand.

"I'm a guest here. My name is—"

Opal seized her.

Vera winced.

Chair tipping behind her, as she tried to stand . . .

"Let go! Shit! You're breaking my hand!" Vera cried.

The delicate bones of Opal's knuckles whitened, clamping down.

"You're the one they're looking for," she said.

The half-full mug fell to the floor.

Shattered.

CHAPTER 23

Palming the Ruger, with one half-frozen finger caressing its trig-ger, Max scanned the motel office. Frost haloed the glass, but he could see well enough. Empty. His lungs were blazing with spiked blue flames ignited in the howling storm. He'd run the length of the Rendezvous's back lot after seeing Vera disappear. The pain inside him stirred; a predator sensing a weak quarry's vulnerability, it began to hunt. Max had to slow to a deliberate walk. Around the corner, he passed vacant room after vacant room. The sense of desertion was undeniable. An Old West town shuttered against the coming gunfight.

I've read too many novels, he told himself.

Were people watching him? Without thinking he'd removed the gun from his belt. The sight of it in plain view shocked him. He pocketed it. He kept his hand down there, anticipating. The worst thing would never surprise him again. He had no magical protections out here in the open.

Inward, the pain lunged. Quick, breathless attack preceded an unhurried clawing and chewing at his guts.

He entered the building.

The warmth of the room flowed over him like bathwater.

The revolver held deep in his parka's pocket, he surveyed the check-in area. Yes, there were signs of a struggle. Pens scattered on the carpet. A calendar flung and displaying its ruffled months.

Overturned chairs and spilled coffee. No bloodstains. No bodies. An absence of ax gouges in the furniture.

He tried the door leading to the living quarters.

Locked.

Now what?

He could call out to Vera. What would that get him? Maybe she would come downstairs and open the door. Or maybe someone else would.

Max took the chalk stick from his pants pocket and drew an X on the door, and then he drew a circle around the doorknob and shaded it in. If it was the Pitch holding Vera captive, he hoped this was enough to keep them at bay. They shouldn't be able to open the door. Not without great effort. Though it was possible Whiteside could do it.

Max needed to get the stone from Vera's room.

He searched the pegboard behind the desk, until he found a second key that matched the number on her unit.

He took it.

His shoes squeaked on the freshly fallen snow. The sidewalk and parking lot were smoothed over by a Sahara of drifts. Under the drive-up awning, along the path that wasn't exposed directly to the sky and wind, he saw a single set of large footprints heading in the direction of the highway and slightly angled toward the center of town. It wasn't much to go on. But if Vera was correct, then that's where the man with the ax had gone.

Max pulled his hood tight and squinted into the chilled inferno of the storm. Like so many particles of ash floating up from Hell, he thought. He looked toward the dim lights at the town center. Dots of color played hide-and-seek in the murk.

He saw not a living soul.

And he was running out of time.

One hand on the room key and the other on his revolver, he marched off to find the Tartarus Stone.

Before it was too late.

CHAPTER 24

"Opal, you have to stop this." Wyatt placed his hand on his wife's shoulder. He steered her back into the bedroom. They made it as far as the hallway. She wouldn't go farther. Her steeliness never failed to impress him. It was one of the reasons he married her, though in this case he didn't need impressing. He needed cooperation. She felt like a railroad spike driven into the floor.

Unmovable.

"I didn't mean to hurt you," she called over Wyatt's shoulder.

"Whatever," Vera answered.

"My mother hasn't been well." Adam swept clinking shards of broken mug into a dustpan. "She doesn't realize how she sounds when she gets worked up—"

Opal stormed into the kitchen again. "I know how I sound . . . crazy."

Vera nodded.

"I'm sorry if I scared you," Opal said.

"You don't scare me that much. But those people you mentioned . . . the ones looking for me? I think they want to kill me."

Three pairs of eyes popped wide at her.

"What did you say?" Opal began to collapse to the floor. Wyatt caught her and helped her into a chair. Her limbs hung loose. But her gaze was expectant.

"I don't know if I can explain it."

"You'd better try," Adam said.

He set the dustpan on the counter and pulled up a seat.

Wyatt sat, too. Elbows anchored on the Formica. He couldn't remember the last time four people gathered around this table. It made the room shrink, as if the walls were compacting. He tented his fingers over his mouth and blew out a deep sigh. The elastic from his eye patch had gotten rearranged atop his head after the melee in the office and his hair crested into a rooster's comb.

"How can my wife know anything about people following you?"

"Beats me," Vera said.

As Adam filled up the coffeemaker, he said, "Mom thinks evil people are coming to our town. Demons, she calls them."

"Uh-huh."

Wyatt pointed to the window swamped with pale flakes.

"She says demons are across the street at the Totem. A couple of them are inside a mobile home in the woods conducting science-fictional experiments. Downstairs they're breaking in . . . but it makes absolutely no sense. How am I supposed to believe this? She claims they'll hurt my son."

"Sounds like demons to me."

"I'm not joking," Wyatt said. "Who's after you? What do they want?"

Vera stared at him.

"They call themselves the Pitch."

She told them everything. How she was running away. From Chan at first though now she thought the others were coming, too. How Chan told her he had been hired for an unusual theft by a group of freaks who followed occult rules, met at midnight, and stopped at nothing. She took them through the slaughter at the witches' house. The aftermath she had witnessed. Bodies ripped apart and presented in lewd mocking poses. Blood splashed everywhere. The box that wasn't a box and left scorch marks on wood and changed her boyfriend into a panicked coward who slapped her in the face; this stone that made her feel eyes glued to the back of her neck, and turned her room into a sauna, and killed the lights and even burned the Christmas strings above her door, and made the phone go dead, attracting the attention of that friendly strange old man who had a room here, too, and who drew chalk spirals and boxes on his door and she knew that he knew more about this than he was saying, she really couldn't put her finger on it, but Max had special knowledge . . .

"Max Caul?" Opal asked.

"He was outside with me when I came up the stairs. Oh my God, I forgot about him. We were worried about the man with the ax I saw coming out of the office and we came to check on you. Max was at the bottom of the steps."

Adam leaned over the sink, peering into the alleyway below.

"Well, he's gone now."

Vera was up and running for the back door.

"We have to look for him. That man with the ax could still be out there."

"This way," Adam said.

Their quick footsteps rumbled in the closed stairwell. Wyatt, behind them, at the top of the steps, asked, "What man with an ax?"

Adam answered, "She saw a tall man in a raincoat leaving the office. He was carrying an ax and acting—"

"Totally robotic," Vera finished.

Raincoat?

Wyatt didn't have a premonition. He didn't believe in demons. But he had vivid memories of a man in a raincoat and a bloodletting visited upon this town.

Adam tried the door, grasping the knob and shaking the panel in its frame. He twisted sideways and banged his shoulder into it. Once, twice.

"The stupid thing won't budge," he said.

"Don't go out there," Wyatt told them.

Opal slipped past her husband. Standing between Vera and Adam, she danced her fingers on the door's painted wood. The same door she had felt was unusually warm under her touch this morning. Now coldness lived there. Just on the other side. A hard block of ice or iron shoved against the door. They wouldn't be going out this way.

"We can't pass through here," she said.

"Down the back steps then," Vera said. And she was already moving around Wyatt. Adam followed on her heels.

Opal struggled into her snow boots. With her winter coat on, and a wool tasseled cap snugged down over her ears, she looked like a kid late for the school bus in her rush to make it outside.

Wyatt, dizzied, trapped in his own apartment, watched them. He was unable to put it into words, but felt that here and now was likely the safest it was ever going to be in American Rapids this Christmas Eve.

The eager three went out the back.

He chased after them.

CHAPTER 25

The key turned without resistance. The air in Vera's room was neither stuffy nor frigid. It felt cozy actually . . . if a bit gloomy. Max flicked the switch and was surprised when the lights came on. Much better—an occupied generic motel room like a thousand he'd seen in his lifetime: the rug worn, tread upon by numberless travelers' feet; a bedspread splashed with a parrot blue, orange, and yellow pattern, the bed itself neatly made; a red suitcase leaned open against a wall; and an extra pillow occupied the armchair. A standard television with a cable box angled toward the bed. He touched the power and a dot flashed on the screen, then an image of a newscaster sitting at a desk emerged. The woman's lips moved, but she was mute. The electricity worked. Max pressed a button and sent her away. The heater under the back window purred, circulating warmth that reached him where he paused at the threshold. Traces of floral air freshener and shampoo lingered. Max's heart pounded. Calmness descended upon him as well. He was like a sleeper having a deep but stimulating dream.

He stepped completely inside.

He engaged the deadbolt.

Attached the chain.

He placed the Ruger on the small writing desk where he could reach it. The parka came off. He dropped it on the bed. He rubbed his hands together, feeling the blood flow into his fingers.

Where was the stone?

That was exactly what Horus Whiteside wanted to know when he showed up on Max's doorstep years ago, when he imprisoned him in his own home, and converted it to a torture chamber. Whiteside was searching for the legendary onyx. Max, at the time, only knew the stone as a plot device. A MacGuffin. He'd borrowed it from earlier writers. An occult Holy Grail, a mere pulp contrivance to hang a short story or two on, a little voodoo to scare the kiddies at heart and turn a buck. It meant nothing to him.

Whiteside saw things differently.

He brought Max around to his point of view.

If only you could make yourself dream.

Dream on command was the way Whiteside had said it.

You'd live anything you could imagine. No limits. And do it all while you were awake. Your hand operated the controls. You were free of conventions, of man-made laws, of anything but your own set of rules.

That was one thing the stone offered.

Freedom.

I can help you do this now, Whiteside said. He smiled.

Max flinched. He had learned in short order that the smile meant pain was coming. The black lenses glided over him. Zooming downward.

He told Max not to be afraid. He petted his head. Max lying trussed like a pig on the floor of his home. Blood caked, sticky on his face. One eye battered. His chest exposed and scorched. The stink of singed hair and skin hung in the boxy rooms and narrow hallways of the ranch house, a homemade branding tool tilting at the fireplace mouth, forgotten for the moment, reheating in embers. The Egyptian eye seared into his flesh, over and over . . .

I am a doctor. A hypnotist. A magician.

Whiteside, a doctor.

I can make you relax. I can make you remember where the stone is. You will tell me. We will find it together.

"It's imaginary. A fiction," Max said. He spit out the words between hyperventilating breaths. He wanted to scream at the top of his lungs to his neighbors. But he knew that they probably would do nothing if they heard him. Yelling was too common here. It was that kind of L.A. neighborhood. Dropouts and fall-outs. Success stories in transit. An enclave of schemers, professional and amateur cons, and Hollywood heads inducing dreams by any method possible. People who yearned to live big and instead lived loudly. With all the parties came arguments, cries of passion, lust, hatred, surprise, disappointment. He knew that Whiteside saw screams as progress. They spurred him. They made him creative.

Max was trying to use logic.

He had yet to discover how fruitless that would be.

You can look, if you choose, at my glasses.

Where else was Max going to look?

It started as simple as this—you stared at him, and that meant at the glasses. The doctor educated Max.

We are accessing your mind. I am going to link my subconscious to yours. If hypnotism is light, then what we are about to do is a laser beam.

Flat reflective surfaces worked the best for some reason, better than cavities or bulges. The energy collected on the flat surface, organizing fields the same way a magnet used its invisible power to draw iron.

Your consciousness will soften like a pat of warm butter . . .

And the doctor sighed.

People do it all the time without knowing they are doing it. Call it daydreaming. Call it sleeping at the wheel. You go away a little. Take a mind stroll. Yet something always happens to break the spell. What if you harness this trance energy and guide it?

What happens then?

Max started to answer and Whiteside covered his mouth with a glove.

Typically, before you can tap the powers, the part of the brain that's kept our species alive for millennia, crawling on the jungle floor, kicks in. It draws us back inside our animalistic shell. For protective purposes, you see. You can't be off trancing when something might be trying to eat you. We haven't shed the habits of the hunted yet. Only a few of us have.

So you come back to earth in a snap.

Maybe you rub your neck, or give your head a shake. Clear the fog.

Wake yourself up.

But you never actually fell asleep. Did you?

Key to the process is: You had to have the right intention. The doctor insisted on that point. Said it was crucial. To demonstrate he brought the pincers down into Max's belly and pried a rubbery chunk of him loose. Blood drooled down Max's side and he felt it pooling under him. Max gritted his teeth.

Chewed his lips. Moaned. Flung beyond speech.

If you were able to trance at will, physical pain would be meaningless. You aren't going to tap the wellspring of this human power by accident. No, no.

A chuckle.

Focus was necessary. And discipline.

Stooping over Max like a bird of prey, Whiteside had the instant ability to terrify. The pincers in his hands had something to do with it. He exuded blunt arrogance, bone-deep narcissism on display with each stroke of knuckles against his smooth chin. Max guessed he'd recently shaved off a beard and was still getting used to the missing hairs. One hand rested against his shirt, the other fondled an absence. His skin was lustrous, pink as a birthday candle. He seemed to communicate approval with his gloved fingertips. He ceased touching himself. Now it was Max's turn. Max the whimperer, the dying.

There, there, my friend.

There, there.

Off came the glasses.

His eyes were holes. Max half expected something to crawl out at him.

He tried to shut down. He closed his eyes. But it didn't matter. Didn't matter because all he saw was the ragged holes. Open grave pits. Caves. Places where shadows crossed each other. Black ribbons tangled in the wind.

He wasn't certain what was real or not anymore.

He thought he might die there and then.

He *wanted* to die.

Instead there was a voice talking. Whiteside's. But the doctor's voice wasn't a harsh beast. It was as soft as a motherly squeeze. Except for one thing—mother had an awfully cold hand.

Be receptive.

Make yourself a vessel for whatever floats by.

Then it was simply a matter of patience.

Pick your spots, Max. Let's get started, shall we?

Max didn't remember anything after that.

Blackout.

Until the police arrived.

Whiteside and his bag of tricks were gone.

The stone wasn't in the suitcase. Or under the bed. Max found it though. In the armchair, behind the pillow Vera must have thrown to hide the thing, or to hide from it. A sharp-edged hunk of rock that would fit inside a bowling bag.

The Tartarus Stone.

So it existed.

Max lifted it.

It was heavy.

Max sat on the edge of the bed and straddled the octahedron

with its Byzantine markings, its hieroglyphs, and its odd spirals. He traced his finger along six columns of carvings, an alphabet of daggers. What did Vera make of these?

He didn't know what they were.

Amazing.

Romero's onyx, alive and well.

He wanted to be sure he was awake. Pinch yourself, pal. When Max did, the pain registered in the back of his hand. He winced. Okay . . . okay.

He had chased it for all these years because he had to know. Was Whiteside right? Was it possible?

To occupy two worlds at once, waking and dreaming. To have them both be real. To tap the power. To master the stone.

To live as you dream.

Now imagine dilation. The mad doctor's voice again, that snake charm rhythm notched up to full ooze. Max swore Whiteside was inside the motel room with him, talking. The words were too right. The sound of him. Max realized what was happening. He had blocked it out. Yet here it was again. Posttraumatic flashback, he guessed. Only this part must have come from the missing time. The blackout. Max was remembering the final pieces now . . .

Dilation.

Whiteside drew the last word out.

Diii-laaa-tion.

Max actually heard him despite the decades past. He was back in L.A., hog-tied and blinded by fear.

He glanced around Vera's room.

He was alone.

His forehead was damp. Trembling in his legs. Pulse racing in his neck and chest. But no pain erupting from his guts. No cancer. He needed to find out if the stone could save him. From what lay beyond the now. He was giddy with thoughts of deliverance. He needed to know if this goddamned thing was real.

The mind muscle, for years rigidly contracted into a knot, ex-pands.

Okay, mad doc, whatever you say. Just be gentle. It's my first time.

See it.

Damn if he didn't see it. His mind for eighty-odd years screwed tight like a middleweight's fist. It opened up. Just a little.

Then wider.

And wider still, in one quick burst, like a plant on the ocean floor, the kind that gulps fish as they swim by.

Infinity.

To grasp at infinity . . .

He'd done it. He had connected the world of reality to the world of dreams.

He might literally bring his dreams to life.

Be free of fear, save himself from death.

Now imagine the same scenario, only you've made a grave error. What if . . . ?

You're not the one in control.

Dilation.

Connection.

You occupy two worlds at once.

You're awake and dreaming.

"Wait a minute. Wait a damn minute," Max said.

He scrambled away from the stone, onto the bed.

His hands were gripping the sheets and blankets, tearing them loose from the mattress and flinging them at the stone, trying to cover it because . . .

Something was coming through.

CHAPTER 26

Nobody wanted to work at the Fuel 'N Snacks on Christmas Eve. Nobody. So naturally Erik Bronk got stuck doing it. They saddled him with every bad shift, every crap job. He learned to live with it. But he never learned to like it.

Luckily he didn't have any family. Or even a girlfriend to get mad at him.

That didn't mean he was any less of a person though.

He would've enjoyed kicking back and watching a few holiday movies. Maybe playing games on the Xbox while he cooked up a Tombstone pizza and chilled with his pet ferret. Take it easy for a change. Engage in serious lounging.

It wasn't meant to be.

As soon as the manager taped the schedule up on the door Erik knew it.

Toss in a snowstorm to top it off.

"Jingle Bells, this job smells, Erik's getting lit . . ."

He stopped singing and sucked on the joint. Toed the bucket he was using to keep the storeroom door cracked. Let the smoke trail out. The wind was fierce, greedy. Sleet and snow blowing every which way, making American Rapids look like a ghost town. Waste of time being open for business on a day like this. Everybody should've stayed home. When he heard the bell go off, he peeked back into the store. Shit.

Some dude. Strolling around leisurely. Shopping.

No rush.

Erik took another toke. He wet his fingertips and pinched the roach. Dropped it into the stupid green and red vest his manager made them wear. It *was* Christmas-y.

The man stopped in the candy aisle. Not facing any of the candy, but looking toward the coolers like he'd forgotten something. Or like he was waiting for assistance.

Erik hooked his thumbs in his front pockets and put on a smile that felt too big.

"Help you find something?"

"This is a thing I have to do."

The man was tall. His gray skin hung slack. He wore a raincoat, its thin belt trailing loose behind him like a tail.

"Last-minute shopping? I hear you. We have a few gift items, stuffed animals and such, on the back wall. Underneath the musical Mr. and Mrs. Snowman set?"

Erik noticed the ax resting against the man's leg. It looked new. They didn't sell axes at the Fuel 'N Snacks. The man must have brought it in with him. He hadn't moved an inch. He seemed lost. Maybe he'd gotten into the eggnog early.

"This is a thing I have to do," he said.

Do what? Chop down a Christmas tree?

"Looking for firewood? We sell it already cut up. In *bundles*?" Erik pointed to the pile of logs stacked beside the entrance. "They're on sale. Two for ten bucks."

The man wasn't even paying attention.

"This is a thing I have to do."

Erik's sense of time had gone jagged. It felt like he'd spent hours, days, standing in the candy aisle waiting for the man to tell him what he wanted. He was interested. But he was growing paranoid. What if telling him changed everything? He hoped it was nothing that big, only a side effect of the buzz he'd been working on. Damn. Here he wanted to mellow out and this guy comes in and nixes those plans, interrupts him, then starts talking weird, repeating the same words—it was annoying. If he said it again . . .

"This is a thing I have to—"

"Alright then, why don't you do it."

The ax went up.

Erik thought he saw the blade coming at him—fast, silvery, sideways.

But he wasn't sure.

The Fuel 'N Snacks spun around, and then turned on its side.

Erik couldn't move. He spied the world from floor level. His cheek, the one touching the floor, went numb. He was numb all over.

A hand gripped his hair. It didn't hurt. It lifted him.

He had no weight.

The ax guy was looking at him. Doing that head-cocking motion puppies do. Erik's vision fuzzed over. He blinked. Things got a little clearer. He felt dizzy. Floaty. He stared quietly at the ax guy.

He couldn't think of anything to say to him. Anything . . .

Henry put the head on the counter where the next customer would see it.

Then he went out into the storm.

CHAPTER 27

The office was empty. Wyatt and Adam checked the computer and the motel safe. Opal headed for the door to the apartment. No furniture obstructed it. There wasn't any way to lock the door from the office without breaking or somehow jamming the mechanism. She saw no evidence of damage. The hinges were on the other side. Nothing foreign lodged between the door and its frame.

Nothing . . . physical.

She stopped and stared at the chalk drawings. She touched the doorknob.

Turned it.

The door opened.

"Vera, could you get a few of those napkins?"

Vera grabbed a handful from the continental-breakfast spread. The paper squares were printed with holly sprigs and ornaments. "Max must have been in here. Those are the same kind of drawings he made inside his room. You want to clean them off?"

"I want to try something first."

Opal stepped inside the stairwell and closed the door behind her.

She tried to open the door from the locking side. She couldn't.

"Now go ahead and wipe the chalk off," she said, through the door.

Brush, brush. Vera was doing her best, probably feeling like she was spreading the chalk around more than taking it away. A thin fog of particles floated under the door.

Vera sneezed. "I really should use a little water."

"Rub off as much as you can. Erase the shapes. If I'm right, I don't think you need to make everything disappear completely."

More brushing. The click of her rings as they scraped along.

"Okay, that's pretty good," Vera said.

"Stand back."

Opal opened the door without resistance, not so much as a squeak.

The outside panel still looked as if it had a sprinkling of powder dulling its surface. She could see streaks made by the napkins. Otherwise it was clean.

"How did you do that?" Vera asked.

Opal didn't have a logical answer. Drawings can't lock doors. Can they?

"The extra key to Vera's room is missing," said Wyatt.

"Max must've taken it. He was the only one down here," Adam said.

"Not the only one," Vera said. "Don't forget the man with the ax."

"What's this?" Opal picked up a small cone of metal, mashed on one end, no bigger than a pebble, placed exactly in the center of the counter.

"Give it to me," Wyatt said.

She dropped it into his palm. "Is that what I think it is?"

"It's a slug from a bullet." Wyatt turned it in his palm. Moving it around like a hot cinder that would burn him if he didn't keep it in motion. "There's something on it . . . writing . . . letters. Somebody wrote on it with a permanent marker."

"Are they trying to scare us with this shit?" Adam asked.

"Yeah, well, this shit's working." Vera hugged her arms around her chest.

"It says S-O-R-R-Y." Wyatt spilled the slug back on the counter.

"Sorry?" Adam frowned. "Sorry for what?"

Opal watched her husband. The black eye patch he wore, from certain angles, was as good as a mask for hiding behind. His head didn't move. He was studying the slug, and then he raised his chin up from the counter and turned to the window and the orange lights down the highway. The glow was Henry's place.

"What did the man with the ax look like again?" he asked.

"He was tall. Salt-and-pepper hair. He had a sad face. He was wearing a long raincoat that looked too small on him."

"Too small?"

"Like it wasn't really his," Vera said.

"Or like he bought it years ago. Maybe an old coat that he'd outgrown. Did he get into a car?"

"He just walked away."

"Just walked away in his raincoat . . ."

"Wyatt, what are you thinking?" Opal asked.

"I don't want to admit what I'm thinking." Wyatt picked up the slug again and slipped it into his pocket. Shook his head. "If Max took the key, then he's after that stone. We'd better go and see."

"Do you think he's with the Pitch?" Vera asked.

"The two people I know who aren't with the Pitch are standing beside you."

Vera thought about that.

Wyatt pushed through the frost-starred glass, letting the wind chase around the office. "He hasn't driven out of the lot. There'd be tracks."

They found Max cowering under the writing desk inside Vera's room. He'd flipped a mattress over onto the stone. Adam and Wyatt lifted the mattress and tossed it against the wall. Max was mumbling. Indecipherable words flowed from his lips with a chantlike rhythm. He had taken the chalk from his pocket and crumbled it in his fists. Dust smeared beside him into the carpet—a moon shape. He didn't want to come out. He told them to take the stone away. It wasn't safe. He asked if anyone else was in the room.

Wyatt stood with his boot on one of the stone's points.

"Anyone else?"

"Did you see anyone other than me when you came in?" Max asked, his voice rising to the edge of panic.

"Like who?" Opal knelt close to him.

Max stared through his fingers at her. The childlike mischievousness had vanished from his eyes. He was a frightened old man. Spittle flecked his lips.

"Put the stone in the bathroom and I'll come out," he said finally.

Wyatt carried the stone over to the tub and closed the bathroom.

Max crawled out from under the desk. His collar was blotted with sweat. Fear, he smelled like fear. The Ruger dangled in his grip.

"Whoa," Adam said. "He's got a gun."

"Here, you take it. It'll do us no good." Max untwisted his spine and handed the revolver to Wyatt. "The women should go," he said.

"Why?"

"It's not goddamn safe, that's why. We'd all go if we were smart."

His eyes tracked to the bathroom. Narrowed.

"It can hear us talking."

Wyatt ignored the comment. He held Max's elbow, steered him to a seat in the armchair. Adam set the mattress back on the bed frame. The two women sat down with him. Wyatt bent over and looked Max in the eye.

"Who are you afraid of?"

"Everyone . . . no one . . . I want to check out. Draw up my bill, please."

"You're not going anywhere until you explain a few things," Wyatt said.

"I'm not your prisoner! You can't hold me here against my will!"

"Adam, get the stone."

Adam rose from the end of the bed. He walked across the carpet. He reached for the knob of the bathroom door.

"No, wait," Max said. "Let me, ah, think about this. . . ."

Adam opened the door and went into the bathroom.

Max shouted, *"Stop!"*

"Who are the Pitch?" Wyatt asked.

"Never heard of them . . . I don't know what you're . . . please. I'm a stupid old man. My mind . . . I get confused, you see. I should be in a hospital."

There was a loud screech as Adam tugged the shower curtain back. Then a thumping from the tub.

"Don't bring it out here!" Max faced Wyatt. "I'll tell you, okay? You win. Everything I know . . . just, please, I don't want to see it again."

"Leave the stone, Adam," Wyatt said. "Shut the door."

Max hung his head. He sighed in relief.

Wyatt perched on the corner of the bed.

"The Pitch, they're for real?"

Max nodded. "I've spent half my life studying them."

"Why go through all this for a rock?"

"It's no ordinary rock," Max began. "That's a fact. You see stones are technology. Old, *old* technology. The first tools humans made were stones. They elevated us above animals. Nearly all major religions incorporate the *stone* as a symbol of their foundation. '*The stone the builders rejected has become the cornerstone*' refers to Jesus. Go back pre-Christ. To Stonehenge. The Mayans carved stellae. Mystery spheres in Costa Rica. The Dome of the Rock. The Black Stone at Mecca. Jacob's Pillow that was said to cry out for rightful kings and queens. The Philosopher's Stone.

The Freemason's Ashlar. Druidic runes. Scrying stones and crystal balls. The Urim and Thummim. Worry stones and rosary beads. New Age healing crystals . . . it goes on and on."

"What does our stone do?"

"The Pitch religion is no different from its daylight counterparts. People yearn for rituals. Something they can see and touch. This stone is their central relic, at the very core, of their beliefs."

"Which are?"

"The dead aren't dead. They exist on a different axis. In death, we boil down to essentials. Good and evil. The two gravitate to opposite ends of the cosmos. Some call them Heaven and Hell. The Greeks had Hades. The lowest level of Hades was Tartarus. It was a dungeon for the Titans. The Romans thought there was room for sinners, too. The Abyss, as they pictured it—encircled with a river of flame, surrounded by adamantine gates and guarded by the Hydra—stretched vast. Christians say it's the pit where Satan fell, where Christ cast Legion. The Tartarus Stone acts as a compass pointing the way to Hell. It is also a key. In the right hands, it unlocks a doorway between our world and theirs. Satan will rise again at the time of Revelation. The man who leads the Pitch wants to open that door. He wants to let Evil in. The Orphics believed Tartarus was the first thing in existence. Nothing is older than darkness."

"What's the stone made of?"

"No one knows. Molten in origin. A tektite, a bit of natural glass made when a falling meteor slammed into the earth. It may have powerful magnetic properties which alter brain waves and cause vivid hallucinations. The Pitch believes the stone ejected from a volcano on the moon. They're moon worshippers. And have been as far back as the Egyptian pharaohs."

"You're claiming the Pitch cult is as old as the pharaohs?"

"Older, I'd say. There's no telling. Their leader today is a doctor. A former optometrist named Horus Whiteside—he's the only one who knows the secrets and the big picture. His group of followers will suit his current needs. They come and go. They die, or else he kills them off. To call *them* the Pitch is a misnomer. There's only one Pitch, and that's Whiteside."

"Why would they follow him?"

"He's offering power, riches, and everlasting life. People sacrifice themselves for much less. It's all lies, of course. Usually is with an offer that good." Max paused and rubbed his chest, scratching at the eye-shaped scars underneath. "Whiteside is a master mesmerist. He may have other powers. I can't speak to that impartially. He's dangerous. Forty years ago he tortured me for three days. Searching for the stone . . ."

Opal knew the name Whiteside, knew also that he was one of the men she witnessed in that trailer out in the woods. For the first time in months, years, she didn't think she was crazy. "What did you see here in the room with you?"

Max looked hard at the four of them seated on the bed.

Looked and said nothing.

CHAPTER 28

Henry was thinking. *Snow falls so slowly. Nothing else falls this slowly.* Not from the sky. He wasn't capable of feeling emotions anymore. He sensed things though. The way an instrument might, a machine that measures temperatures and pressures. His physical senses were heightened. The same sharpening happened when he went into the Pie Stop with his brother Jesse. While he watched Jesse picking the diners off. When he saw Wyatt Larkin hunched between the tables, then later when he shot Wyatt in the back. After the grenade went off, it was silence. Ears filled with white noise. A soft popping like Styrofoam kernels mashed together in a bag. He found his slug on the floor and took it. Like Whiteside had promised, no one seemed to see him. He was a ghost.

The grinding of gearings. Tires ripping up pavement. Lights.

Henry stepped out into the middle of the highway. He raised his arms above his head and waved. The headlights were fireballs.

Brakes hissed. The upper curve of the snowplow blade leveled with his chest.

His arms came down slowly like the snow.

He walked up to the driver's side. The guy sat close to the wheel. Gnomelike, bearded. A cigarette dipped from his mouth. The green felt cap he wore was melting off to one side. A bell glinted at its tip.

Santa's Helper was stitched into the band. The guy had the window rolled down. That would make it easier.

"You having a problem?"

"I found a bag of toys," Henry said.

"What?"

"I found a bag of toys. You drove right over it. It's under your front tire."

The driver chuckled, frowned. He plucked the cigarette away. Then he leaned out the window and looked.

Henry opened his coat. Tucked the shotgun under the driver's beard.

Pulled the trigger.

Henry wiped his face on his sleeve.

He popped the door handle.

The body sagged out. Cigarette still lit between the fingers.

Inside the cab, the heater was on High-High. The seat was warm. Henry adjusted it backward to accommodate his legs. The man who had been sitting there seconds ago sprawled across the highway's double yellow line. Henry shut the door and put the truck in gear. A strawberry spill fanned across the hood. The bell stuck in the middle of it.

He drove out to the edge of town.

The highway was the only passable route connecting American Rapids to destinations south. Windswept farm roads branched east and west. They'd be snowed under. After leaving the Fuel 'N Snacks, he punched a memorized number into the pay phone next to the air pump and called the border patrol. Said he'd be coming across with a bomb. That he'd blow it sky-high on the bridge. Vehicles trickling over from Canada this evening would be searched and slowed. Henry hammered south with the blade down. White orange sparks arced into the ditch. It was pretty.

A mile out.

No houses.

No business.

He increased speed. Steered right. The plow blade cut into the filthy ridge of snow. Throwing it back onto the highway. Cigarette butts, bottles, paper plastic glass rubber steel, the furred bones of excavated roadkill—all going back where it came from.

Gouging trash and leaving a black wound in the earth.

The cab rocked. The blade shuddering, jamming, kicking as it caught large stones and wedges of pavement banged loose from their sockets. He pulled harder to the right.

Off the road.

Running parallel. Killing the tires.

The plow snapped up a snow fence, spit the snarl of stakes and wire.

A stake—end over end, topping the blade—smacked a star into the windshield.

He knuckled down, hands tight.

The muscles in his shoulders burned.

Telephone poles—he chopped into them. The lines swooping like tentacles, slithering over the cab. The truck body lifting, dropping, as if he were driving over a field of boulders, no . . . grave markers. Horrible noises. Like the cry of beasts in the jungle. It came from the snowplow. The windshield buckling inward, giving, and finally it broke with a congestive cough. A shower of blue pebbled glass piled in his lap like jewels. He ignored them. His blade bent, cockeyed. Thrust forward like a great tusk. He was bleeding. His forehead cut—nothing serious—he thumbed the blood away.

He slowed to survey his work. Bringing the wheel around, reversing, nosing into his path of destruction. Stopping to bear witness. Yes. That's what he saw: destruction. No car or ordinary truck could pass this mountain of snow and ice. The felled wooden poles demanded chain saws and winches. He watched the blowing snow begin to hide them under blankets. It was like a monster sleeping in the road.

The highway out of town was blocked.

He tractored slowly through the torn field. He wasn't sure if the plow would make it. The ground was uneven, the plow damaged. He heard the shallow creek ice smashing under his wheels like mirrors.

Back on the highway, the side that was now trapped, the damned side—the home of American Rapids. Population 2,480. But not for long.

Henry idled.

Through the missing windshield the witch wind sprang on him fiercely. His face, stripped raw with pain, hardened into a mask of pinks and scarlet. He prayed for his death. Fully knowing he was a hell-bound sinner, he would have died, then and there . . . if he could have. He prayed from deep inside what Whiteside had made him. Prayed, but Death did not come.

He had more things he must do.

But first he had to wait.

CHAPTER 29

Max switched on the floor lamp. Velvet shadows scored his face. The skull loomed prominent beneath his skin. "The Pitch are not invincible," he said. He levered up from the chair and peeked through the curtains into the parking lot. Automatically, he went into his pocket for chalk, only to realize he'd crumbled his sticks. He extracted a cigarillo, snapping it lit with a golden lighter. Steel blue smoke hovered. "I may be the only man who knows how to defeat Whiteside." He didn't know if he believed that after looking into the stone. But he wanted to offer hope to these people. He *needed* their help.

"How do you stop a crazy man?" Adam asked.

"That depends on whether or not you think he's crazy." Max smiled around the cigarillo's plastic tip. Old, he felt so old. He stared at the back of his hand, the wormlike veins and fallen flesh. *I've become a reptile,* he thought with disgust. Time to shed this dead skin. "I need a drink. But I don't drink anymore, so I'm going to step outside and settle for a smoke. Can I have my revolver?"

Wyatt considered the request, and handed over the weapon. "If Whiteside really is coming, then we can wait for him. He shows up looking for the stone. We call the police. They'll arrest him."

Max shook his head. "Whiteside won't come."

"Why not?"

"He hasn't shown himself yet. Has he?"

"You've seen him," Adam answered.

"Four decades ago. And he didn't get the stone. The police nearly caught him. Since our encounter he's worked through his pawns. He's fulfilling a prophecy that dictates he can't personally take the stone. Whiteside must be *given* the stone by someone who doesn't believe in its powers. The Pitch hire out work to criminals. Half their membership is former forensic patients. They recruit the criminally insane. Automatons—each programmed with a mission."

"An army of brainwashed crazies? That's just great," Vera said.

"Whiteside worked with the U.S. Army. Details classified, of course. It involved mind control. Inductions. Out-of-body projection. When I read about the Pie Stop shooting in the papers, it drew me here. The killer was ex-Army. Wyatt's statement about a second shooter nobody else saw . . . that's one of the things Whiteside was trying to do. Use soldiers' telepathic abilities to confuse their enemies. Make them see things that aren't there."

"Or not see things that are," Wyatt said. He shook his head. "But why did *I* see the second shooter?"

"Nothing's perfect. Did you doubt yourself? Yes. That's good enough sometimes. Whiteside has occult talents. That's why the Pitch are in American Rapids. Everything happening today comes from tales Whiteside read in the past. He's convinced these stories foretell the future. That's how we'll trap him."

"Where are these stories?" Opal asked.

"Out of print."

"How do you know about them?"

"I wrote them." Max shrugged into his parka. "I'll be right outside." He rapped his knuckles against the door. "Give me five minutes. Think about what I told you. If you want to listen to my suggestions, let me know. Otherwise, storm or no storm . . . I'll pack my things, take my dog, and be gone."

Before Max quit the motel room, Wyatt told him about the Egyptian eye drawn in dog's blood on the wall at the Totem. The others listened.

"Wadjet," Max said.

"What?"

"Not a what, a wadjet." Max lifted his sweater and pulled out his thermal undershirt. He exposed his left hip. A raised scar, centipedal and shimmery—the shape was the same as the one on the wall—a crude, yet recognizable, eye. There were more scars. Max quickly bundled back up. He threw the parka hood over his head. "The stone . . . try not to touch it with your bare hands. Leave no one alone with it. Never sleep in the same room with the stone. *Never.*"

They nodded.

Max stepped out.

The cloud of smoke he left behind whirled in pursuit then dissolved.

CHAPTER 30

Bill Eppers had nightmares. His whole childhood it was bats, wolves, and a long-armed man who flicked knives at him and chased him through the park. When he turned fourteen, a girl showed up in his dreams. Slit-eyed, strawberry blonde. Ass like a rollercoaster he had to ride. She wore shimmery pink bikini bottoms and a Mötley Crüe tour shirt—a skull buried in roses. Her nipples bugged out like a pair of superballs. She grabbed the front of his jeans, slipped him some tongue. Her mouth tasted like a raspberry snow cone. She was that cold, too. Hairs started sprouting from her skin. Before he could do anything, she knocked him to the ground and sat on him, squeezing the air out of his lungs with her thighs. Stinking teeth pushed into his face. She had two tusks, like a boar's. She ripped him. Blood filled his eyes. She moved down his chest and stomach. He heard her chewing. He touched himself and felt a gummy hole between his legs.

Jesus, he'd wake up drenched with the sweats.

This was worse. A human head—plopped down on the bar-code scanner like a bag of circus peanuts.

He was going to be sick.

It just didn't look like something you should ever have to see.

Open fishy eyes . . .

The decapitated body oozing into the aisle . . .

Blood stinks. The smell gets into your throat. But he was a cop.

He didn't want the rest of the American Rapids cops laughing at him. They were all here, milling around the murder scene. He swallowed a mouthful of frothy bile. He hung tape across the doors of the Fuel 'N Snacks.

Down the highway, a truck horn blared.

His captain tapped'him on the shoulder.

"You're looking green, Bill."

"I'm fine."

"Maybe you should step out for a minute."

"I said I'm okay."

"Check around the perimeter. See if you spot any evidence."

"Oh, right. Good idea."

Eppers zipped up his winter jacket. They didn't want anyone touching the door. There might be prints on the glass. The door was propped open with a rubber wedge. He ducked under the tape into a gusting wind.

Four patrols blocked the two driveways. Eppers' was the fifth car. He had been the earliest on the scene. His patrol was the only one in a parking spot. The others kept their distance. Supposedly to preserve any tire tracks under the pump canopy. But didn't it make him look like a dumb-ass for pulling right up to the entrance? Who were they kidding?

The snow was knee-deep. There weren't any tracks.

The guy who called it in came on foot. Said he was thirsty. He wanted to buy a can of Monster to perk up. Unlucky bastard was wide awake now. Eppers glanced through the storefront at him. He was young, a gamey doper smell to him. Saggy pants and no jacket, only a hoodie with a Batman insignia stitched on the back. He didn't do this. Forever stupefied was what he was. Still they weren't finished talking to him yet. Bet he'd never buy another Monster in his life.

The horn again.

Closer. The driver laying into it. Toot—toot—tOOOOOOt.

Coming this way.

Eppers picked out the light: a yellow brassiness visible through the snow.

Growing.

Splitting into two distinct headlamps.

Stampeding horses. That's what it sounded like. The rumble of shredded rubber thumped like hoof beats. A snowplow. The blade mangled.

What the hell?

Eppers wandered out between the pumps.

Even in the cold, he could smell the gasoline fumes.

His shoes slipping, sliding . . . he had to be careful and not land on his ass.

TOOOOOOOOOOOOOOOOOOOT . . .

Was the driver drunk? Wouldn't be the first time . . .

Eppers took his Maglite off his belt. Switched it on as he hurried to the curb. He waved the light over his head.

How could the driver not be slowing down?

It looked like a damn roadblock with all their light bars—red, white, and blue—a regular Fourth of July. The plow was gaining speed. He was going to blow right past.

Dammit. Unbelievable.

All the cops inside pressed themselves up to the glass to see.

Well, Eppers wasn't about to step into the road and get killed.

But he did plan on spotting the plow's city number.

He stood there with his hands on his hips.

Unbelievable.

Eppers turned back to the Fuel 'N Snacks to see if the other guys knew what was coming. Crazy fucking day. The weird business at the Totem in the morning, now this. The captain stormed out. He was running toward Eppers. Shouting, but Eppers couldn't hear. Cap hit a patch of ice and skidded into the pumps. Fell to his knees. He looked like he might've dropped a loaf in his drawers. If he didn't watch out he'd have a heart attack. Eppers might end up captain yet. He shouldn't laugh. Cap was practically purple from yelling his head off, but it was like his volume went kaput. The stampede drowned out everything. The scraping blade and . . . how many tires had the plow lost?

Eppers shook his head.

Looked back at the highway.

The plow veered toward the Fuel 'N Snacks. The driver's door opened and something black and flapping fell onto the pavement. The plow kept coming.

"Oh fuck!"

Eppers dropped his Maglite and started running.

CHAPTER 31

Max took two puffs on his cigar and flung it into a snow bank. He double-timed it over to his room. After all these years, he'd finally seen the stone. Seen it . . . changing. He didn't want to witness that again. Maybe if he were younger. *I'm an old man who has lost his nerve,* he thought, *and I'm sorry, folks.* He fumbled with the key on its large plastic fob. Ann-Margret knew he was there. She could smell him. He heard her barking inside their room. It wasn't her happy bark. She was anxious. Yipping, whining. Her paws scratched at the bottom of the door.

"One minute, girl. My hands are shaking."

Absurd. Talking to a dog like she was a person. But he knew she loved him unconditionally. If he couldn't get the Larkins to help him kill Whiteside, then he would go. Forget packing. He'd take Annie and hit the road. Enjoy what precious time they might have together before the cancer ate him up.

He dropped his room key into the snow. "Shit."

Lights.

Flickering red beams slashed the parking lot.

Did Wyatt call the police?

Max couldn't spot a vehicle. The lights spun around dizzily. Hitting the iced pavement, the motel, tainting the few cars left buried in the lot.

They weren't moving on. Redness licked at the cold snow. He

walked to the corner of the Rendezvous. Shielded his gaze from the tumbling flakes. In time to watch the explosion. Flames bulged skyward. Hung there like a message from God. Burning tower—he couldn't spy the top. The boom, low and full, passed though his organs. Down the highway the treetops combusted. A half wall of bricks caved. The carcass of a plow truck sat in silky fire.

What was there before?

A gas station . . . gone.

Broken glass tinkled softly against the motel siding.

A second explosion. Deeper, like artillery. That would be the underground storage tanks. The earth shifted under Max. His cheeks smarted from the blast. Giant pillows of oily smoke stuffed the horizon. The blackened wrecks of police cruisers . . . Max saw them gutted in the firelight.

How many? He couldn't count. Flames. The poisoned air choked him.

"No," he said.

He wasn't looking at the fire.

It was the lights.

They came from an old ambulance parked in front of the motel.

The back doors were opening . . .

A man climbed out.

It wasn't Whiteside.

Max turned to flee.

Another man. And another who looked the same. Brothers? They'd crept up on him from behind. He tried to push past them. An arm barred his throat. A fist hit him in the stomach. Then hit him again. He couldn't breathe. Pain cramped his ribs and chest. The thickness of his parka did nothing to cushion the blows. It only made it harder for him to move. One son of a bitch throttled him while the other struck. The puncher wore steel across his knuckles. Like shark bites taken out of Max's torso. They added up quickly.

His legs went south.

The man from the ambulance said, "Put him in. Strap him down."

"Yes, Mr. Pinroth," said the puncher.

The two dragged him backward.

Max saw a knife scabbard hanging from the puncher's belt.

But he didn't need a knife.

The gunshot surprised everyone.

The puncher reeling. His face, not really there, anymore.

Max pointed his Ruger .357 at the second attacker.

Shot him. A grunt. A fall.

But Max was slow, hurting. He didn't turn fast enough to stop the man called Pinroth from whipping the back of his head with blunt force.

A gun—?

The thought never completed. Head-to-neck, the jolt traveled fast. Max's hands opened like a baby's. No pain this time. The Ruger released at his side. He didn't feel his consciousness slip. It was too quick. His window on the world slammed shut. He dropped. His chin smacked the ice.

Pinroth transferred Max onto a stretcher. Loaded him.

He strolled back into the parking lot. Two bodies down. Neither getting up again anytime soon.

Give the gray-haired writer some credit.

Pinroth picked up the eyeglasses the old man had lost in the struggle. He slipped them into his pocket. For the sake of thoroughness, he fired his Luger, pop-pop, into each of the brothers. He holstered his pistol, climbed behind the wheel of the ambulance, and drove off with their new patient.

CHAPTER 32

Eppers looked around inside the Fuel 'N Snacks. He saw the head of the clerk on the counter, undisturbed. There were no aisles now. An earthquake of food, cheap gifts, and auto supplies, a landslide of junk junked. The plow entered the store while he watched from across the highway, crouching behind a mailbox. His brothers in blue lay scattered, dead. The bodies were twisted around, broken and unnatural, limp as rag dolls. He saw faces in the rubble. Eppers looked away. The plow hit the pumps first. Momentum brought it inside. The blade stuck up through a hole in the ceiling; the hood buckled. Gallons of oil, antifreeze, and wiper fluid; paper towels, squeegees, trash; shattered glass and posters from the windows; tiles gouged from the floor—all pushed forward into a massive heap. He listened to the plow motor's dying hiss.

No driver behind the wheel.

He knew it! *The guy jumped.*

Someone was moaning inside the Fuel 'N Snacks.

Eppers didn't have his flashlight, but with the fire he didn't need any. Billows of boiling fluids, a cloud of poison hovered. Tainted heat touched his face. Eppers blinked and saw a hand lift from a pile of fallen shelves. In the burning, colors changed. Flesh roasted. Peach to red, bubbly brown, then black.

Eppers backed out of the ruin.

The hand was still there and still waving.

CHAPTER 33

They shouldn't be listening to Max's advice—Wyatt hadn't said that yet, but he was going to. Opal looked excited, her cheeks full of blood, which was preferable to zoned and spooky, or conked out in a sickbed. But this talk of occult visions only made her previous erratic behavior seem normal. He didn't want her encouraged into going off any new deep ends. Twenty years ago—the first time her visions started, right after she came home from the hospital with Adam—Wyatt didn't know what to make of them. The doctors said posttraumatic stress disorder. They said postpartum depression. But the way she talked didn't seem post-anything. It felt like a preamble of nightmares to come. Now nightmares landed on their doorstep. He wanted his familiar Opal back, the wife he cherished, the woman he'd fallen in love with and loved even more today.

He wanted everyone to be safe.

It was why he became a cop years ago—to keep others from harm.

He had to be the protector. Being the voice of reason was his job. Maintain the coolest head in the room. He wasn't about to suggest they dismiss Max outright. Just take his tale with a grain of salt, or a whole shaker for that matter. Apply logic to this mystic business about the powers of a moonstone and it unraveled into superstitious nonsense. It had to.

The Pitch? Murdered witches? A compass to Hell?

These things didn't belong in any world Wyatt knew.

Maybe he'd get his family to agree on that.

Bad vibes though. Cops, and ex-cops, believe in them. That slug in Wyatt's pocket hummed with enough ugly energy to make him twitch. Logic doesn't always work. That's an uncomfortable truth. He had the bad vibes *BAD*. He couldn't deny the gnawing he felt about Henry. Like a rat chewing its way from his gut to his brain. It was *Henry* who shot him at the Pie Stop. *Henry* was s-o-r-r-y. *Henry* was roaming around in a raincoat waving an ax. That's what the bad vibes were telling him.

It wasn't over, either.

He'd tussled with two real live dirtbags in the office. They triggered a vibe.

Like a tuning fork, he buzzed.

Normally he would put it down to ordinary weirdness. Coincidences can fool you into believing connections are there that really aren't. Storms make people strange. Holidays add to it. You have to roll along. Keep calm. Don't get swept under. But when enough weirdness stacks up, it gives you pause.

Instincts go fuzzy.

Then you're in danger.

Wyatt doubted himself and he didn't do that often.

Keeping things simple helped.

So . . . if Max wanted to leave the motel . . . fine. Bon voyage. Wyatt liked the man, but he wasn't going to stop him. The fewer burned-out California kooks running around this town the better.

It was Christmas Eve after all.

Shouldn't they go upstairs and have dinner? They might gain a better perspective after a home-cooked meal. Enjoy a little peace on Earth. Exchange gifts under a plastic tree. Why the hell not?

Opal asked, "What do you think we should do?"

He didn't have a chance to respond. The room rocked like a ship at sea. It was an earthquake. Or something sizable had blown up.

Wyatt avoided the window.

He put his ear to the door.

They all heard the gunshots.

Wyatt thought it was four. Spaced apart.

He told them to wait in the room.

But no one listened.

The others filed out behind him. Snow sliced diagonally, the sky churned battleship gray; tart smoke flavored the wind. Together they discovered the dead men in the parking lot. Max had vanished. When they opened his room it was empty, the dog leaping at them like a redheaded lord. Half the block to town was ablaze. Ash mixed with the falling snow.

Wyatt leaned over the dark-clad bodies. Same clothes. Similar builds. He took the knife from the faceless one's belt.

"These are the two guys from the office."

He had his Glock down at his side. The bad vibes were crawling on him. . . .

Adam had Ann-Margret by the collar. The Irish setter sniffed the ground, eyes rolling, seeming about to go mad. Fresh tracks mauled the snow. Footprints and tires. Blood congealed into nasty amoebic puddles.

"What'd we do now?" he asked.

"We go up to the apartment," Wyatt said. "Bring the pooch."

A siren wailed.

"Here comes a fire truck," Wyatt said. "At least that's positive."

The fire truck halted fifty yards from the conflagration.

More gunshots.

A fireman stumbled into the highway. A figure in black marched behind him and swung a farmer's scythe. The fireman screamed.

"Get inside," Wyatt said.

"Where's Vera?" Opal asked.

"What?"

"She was behind me when we left her room," Opal said.

The Camaro emerged around the corner of the motel, heading

for the highway, its tires spinning in the slush. The treads grabbed and it pulled away.

"That's her car," Adam said.

"I'll bet she took the stone," Opal said.

More armed figures gathered on the road.

"Inside now," Wyatt said. "Go!"

CHAPTER 34

She wasn't going to stay there and die. No way. Vera had come
this far and she had the stone, it was hers, not Max's or the Larkins'. It was her bargaining chip. She'd decide what to do with it.
If half of what Max said about the stone was true, then the thing
was money. She had to leave . . . she needed breathing room, sleep,
space to think . . . she'd figure out a way to peddle the stone.
Maybe she'd return to Chicago? Find Chan and hash out a deal.
She wasn't getting back together with him. She wasn't that stupid. But she might persuade him to sell the relic to somebody
other than the Pitch. They'd do business and go their separate
ways.

First, she had to get out of Dodge.

She pressed the gas pedal. Watched the speedometer needle
creep. Twenty. Twenty-five. At thirty, the rear end started to fish-
tail. She eased off.

Twenty-five.

Twenty.

The highway was empty. Traffic wasn't going to be the problem; snow was. But if she took her time, she'd put miles between
her and whatever the hell it was that exploded across from the
Rendezvous. And whoever Max shot dead in the parking lot.
She'd seen the two bodies lying there, blood staining the ice under
them like dirty oil. The Pitch, she was sure. If she sat tight, they'd

come for the stone and kill everyone in the room like they did in Chicago. She needed to take the offensive and go it alone. The Larkins seemed like good people. She didn't want them getting murdered. No expert in occult affairs, she'd heard and seen enough. She was leaving while she still had a chance.

Thunk.

Something hit the passenger door.

She turned to the sound. Outside the frosty side window, the last glow of the Totem Lodge's yellowy lights was vanishing. A dingy field came next. She checked her mirrors. Snow-blotched gusts; the totem pole leaned into the wind.

Thunk.

This time the sound of impact came from behind.

It was sharp *and* dull.

What could do that?

A thin dark shape flew over the roof of the Camaro. It landed a short distance ahead of her in the oncoming lane. It wasn't very big, because it disappeared completely under the layer of fallen snow on the pavement. Hoping to see what it was, she rolled down her window and sat up higher as she drove by.

A slit in the snow—that's all. Strange.

She closed the window and kept going. The ride was getting rough. Where the fuck were the snowplows? The Camaro bumped along as if she were following a rutted country road. But this was a county highway. She'd driven the other direction into American Rapids a few hours ago. Road conditions weren't this piss-poor.

She saw the shattered stumps along the roadside.

Toppled telephone poles.

Power lines writhed and spit sparks in the ditch. The frozen turf had been ripped apart, the ground scarred.

What the fuck happened?

She looked around in disbelief.

"Oh shit!"

She slammed her brakes.

Ahead, the road ended. A giant mound, higher than the roof of her car, blocked the way. For a second, she thought it was a snow-drift. But there were logs sticking out of it . . .

The car skidded, slowing down. She still had control.

Only something else was wrong.

It felt like she was driving into a series of deep potholes. The chassis rocked so hard she thought the doors might fly off. And that wall of timber and ice was getting closer. She clenched her teeth. Eyes shut tight.

The car stopped.

Engine running. Her front bumper kissed the roadblock. Over the Camaro's hood, the round top of a telephone pole pointed straight at her face. She could count the tree rings.

Jesus.

She was shaking.

She opened her door and climbed out. Her legs were like water. She hung onto the car for balance. She walked around the back to check for damage.

And saw an arrow sticking out of her trunk.

It was buried in the metal.

She touched the colorful vanes at the back. Neon orange and lime.

Circling the car, she gasped.

Her rear tire—most of it was gone. Shredded.

The wheel rim was damaged, too.

They'd shot her tire out with an *arrow*.

Another arrow had punched through the passenger door. Bright tail colors, the same as the trunk. She opened the door. Felt it sticking. She yanked and it came loose. A hole in the bucket seat spilled foam. She couldn't tug the arrow out of the door. Four razor blades joined at the point. A hunting tip . . .

In the distance, a motor growled.

She whirled around.

Her eyes searched in the veils of snow.

She raced around the car and got back inside. She reversed. Aimed the Camaro back toward town. She couldn't change a tire out here. She had to drive the way it was. Drive back to the motel before . . .

She saw a dark blot in the distance.

Moving low to the ground, getting bigger, but too small to be a car.

A snowmobile. One rider.

About twenty yards from the Camaro, the rider turned the snowmobile ninety degrees and stopped. He jumped off and ducked behind the machine. She watched him unsling something from over his shoulder: a form half-rifle, half-crucifix. A crossbow.

Before Vera could tap the gas pedal, an arrow was flying.

It penetrated between her headlights. The bladed tip clanged under the hood. She jerked involuntarily against her seatback.

She floored the gas. Tires spun. The damaged wheel shrieked. But she didn't go anywhere.

The windshield cracked. Out of the corner of her eye, she saw the deflected arrow bounce off into the fields.

"Oh my God, oh my God . . ."

She dropped into first gear. She forced herself to press the gas pedal slowly. The Camaro lurched, started rolling forward. She could feel the rear of the car hanging down over the missing tire. The steering wheel vibrated so much it hurt her hands. She shifted into second, heading straight for the snowmobile.

The rider's head popped up, surprised.

Vera shifted again, giving the engine more gas.

The rider scrambled onto his machine. His masked head swiveled to gauge her approach. She wasn't going very fast. She couldn't make much speed riding on a bent wheel. He hunkered low, his glove twisting the throttle and—

She hit him.

CHAPTER 35

"Henry! Henry, it's me, Bill Eppers."

Eppers had his Glock 22 drawn as he walked up the highway. All the businesses were closed for Christmas. The parking lots emptied. He found a couple of stray vehicles and checked their doors, shined his Maglite through the windows, looking for keys dangling in the ignition. He wanted to get lost. But he didn't want to do it on foot. He didn't want people seeing him, either. Walking like some dipshit who missed the bus. He didn't know exactly when it happened, but the freaks had come to town. The Fuel 'N Snacks blowup might've been the signal for it, like a starter's pistol going off. Because the highway was filling up fast with folks he'd never seen before. And they were armed and showing no mercy. He watched one of them take a machete to Pauline Hildebrand while she was complaining about the smoke drifting across her porch. Chopped her down—*Swack! Swack!*—standing there in her housecoat and pink hair rollers. Eppers thought about shooting him, but the chopper had friends. More friends than Eppers had at the moment. And he wasn't about to die for the shitty little salary the city paid him. Yet a man has his pride. Between dying and hiding there was running, and that was what he planned to do.

He met Henry coming out of the Ace Hardware.

"Henry!" he shouted again.

This time Henry looked at him.

Eppers drew up alongside him, dipping the Glock out of sight. Henry had his arms full, carrying a Poulan Pro gas chain saw and a ten-pound sledgehammer. Eppers glanced backward into the unlit Ace store, spotted the kicked-in entrance, the puddle of glass topping the snow. He'd never pegged Henry Genz for a looter, but you never knew what people were capable of under stress. He kept the Glock behind him, resting his finger on the trigger.

"What's going on, Henry?"

"I don't know."

They walked into the open lot. Eppers swept his eyes back and forth, searching for Henry's pickup truck, and marking the killers as they roamed the highway. They were oblivious to them for now. But he knew that might change.

He noticed Henry's torn filthy raincoat. His face looked raw and forlorn. Blood was dribbling from his scalp, around his ear, down his neck into his collar. He didn't seem to care. The sight of it clicked in Eppers's brain.

The craziness didn't start at the Fuel 'N Snacks.

It started at Henry's, at the Totem this morning, with the dead dog and the fire and the eye painted in blood.

Henry was in a state of shock.

"Are you injured or something?"

"Yes, I am."

"Okay, well, let's find your ride and I'll take you to the hospital."

"I can't go to the hospital. I have things to do."

"Where'd you park?"

Henry stopped walking.

Snowflakes fell on their shoulders. The two men squinted in smoky wind.

"We've got to get out of here," Eppers said. "Where's your damn truck?"

A thin grin creased Henry's lips.

"I parked it at the Fuel 'N Snacks."

"At the Fuel 'N Snacks—"

Eppers took a giant step back, swung the Glock up, and leveled it at Henry's right eye.

"Drop that shit! Do it now!"

Henry kept smiling.

He released the chain saw and hammer; his jacket billowed, and Eppers saw the shotgun hanging there in his armpit, its cut-down butt wrapped in blue grip tape like a kid's hockey stick.

"Son of a bitch," Eppers said quietly.

Henry raised his arms higher.

Eppers wanted to cap him. But he couldn't. He didn't want to draw the attention of citizens who might be watching from their homes. More importantly, the freaks on the road might zero in on him. He needed a ride.

"I'll dump your brains on the sidewalk. You got that, asshole?"

"Got it," Henry said.

"Slowly, with your *left* hand, lay the shotgun on the ground."

Henry reached under his arm. He grasped the sawed-off and pulled until the cord holding it snapped. He squatted. His knee-caps popped loudly.

"You ran away," he said.

"What?"

"That's why you didn't die."

"Shut the fuck up."

"I know what it's like to be a coward. The shame—"

"Put your weapon on the ice."

"Never passes."

Henry lowered the shotgun to the ground. His left hand stayed on it. He stared at Eppers. His right hand descended.

"Don't move!"

"I'm going to give you my keys."

His right hand disappeared in the pocket of the raincoat. Keys jingled.

"You can go now," Henry said.

Eppers watched the pocketed hand.

Henry pulled the trigger on the shotgun. The recoil sent the sawed-off skittering over the ice. Buckshot sprayed Eppers's shins and feet. He fell. He held on to the Glock though. Henry, still squatting, snatched the sledgehammer and rose up. Eppers fired, but Henry wasn't standing for long. He was coming down again. The bullet missed. The ten-pound sledgehammer mashed Eppers's wrist flat.

Eppers screamed.

Henry picked the Glock off the ice. He tucked it into his waist-band.

Eppers tried to crawl away on his back. But his legs burned. His feet burned. Snow slid over his belt and crammed into his ass crack. His right hand dragged along next to him like a dead dog on a leash. He was crying. Snow landed in his mouth.

A boot pinned his shirttail.

"You're going to dump my brains on the sidewalk," Henry said.

Eppers thrashed his head from side to side. He saw snow, fire, shadows crisscrossing the highway. He saw a red Camaro with a missing wheel rolling to a stop in front of a motel. He didn't want to see the sledgehammer rising. He closed his eyes and saw black. He smelled smoke and gasoline.

There was a flash.

And then the black got bigger and sucked him down.

CHAPTER 36

The room was white. It had nothing inside of it. Not a stick of furniture. No windows. No doors. Max realized that couldn't be right. He didn't have his glasses on. They fell off during the pummeling he took in the Rendezvous parking lot. Yet he should be seeing light and dark, the shapes of objects. He lifted his head and fell back against the pillow. Pain shot twin lasers through the orbits of his eyes. It felt like a crack had opened in the crown of his skull. Moving spread the edges, and more of the lasers leaked out. He'd been cold-cocked by the man from the ambulance, Pinroth. He had a head wound, probably a concussion. He tried lifting up again, slowly, his neck muscles bunched. He encountered resistance. Instinctively, he attempted to push up on his elbows, to slide his knees higher.

He couldn't move his arms or legs.

Panic flooded through him. They had him strapped to a bed. He felt pressure in the crook of his right elbow—an IV needle. The room reeked of alcohol preps and bleach. With his fingertips he brushed the cool metal tubes of a hospital bedrail. He wiggled his nose and the texture of the room shifted. There was a sheet pulled over his face; the corners tucked under the mattress as if he were wearing a giant blindfold.

"Where am I?"

"Are we awake?"

He hadn't expected that. The voice was close, but coming from above—someone standing at his bedside, watching him.

Cold-sweating, he fought the urge to struggle.

"It's no use trying to fool me, Max. I heard your breathing change."

He'd listened to that voice for three days in his L.A. bungalow. Listened to it questioning him and then telling him what punishments he would face when his answers failed to satisfy. The pincers . . . the branding iron . . .

Two fingers—Horus Whiteside's fingers—slipped under the sheet and gripped his wrist. Max could not speak. His chest rose and fell rapidly.

"Your pulse is racing, Maxwell. That's not good for a man in your condition. I'm administering a sedative. You'll start to relax in a moment."

Shoes walking on carpet. This was no hospital. Max knew as much. A crinkle of plastic, the squeak of an uncapped syringe, he felt a tug at his elbow—then warmth flowing into him. The sharp qualities of his perceptions blunted. A sensation of wetness like a damp rag lay at the center of his chest.

"No, don't—"

"Are you talking to me now?"

"Take this off my face. I can't breathe."

"You're breathing fine. Trust me. I only want us to have a conversation."

"I won't tell you a thing," Max said. His hands curled into fists.

"I disagree."

Max detected a smile behind the doctor's words.

The drug in his IV . . .

"You injected me with sodium pentothal?"

"Pure dose of ethanol, but I hope the outcome is the same. How are you feeling?"

Max didn't answer.

"We can sit here for a while, you and I . . . enjoy the moment together."

Max focused his hearing. What was out there besides White-side?

A beeping, at regular intervals—they had a heart monitor on him. Well, that meant this interrogation wasn't likely to kill him. Maybe Whiteside did want to talk to him. He hadn't hurt him. Not yet.

The beeping sounds calmed Max down. He also noticed a shushing, also coming at regular intervals but not the same intervals as the heartbeats. His lips were tingling, the way they felt after a sip of champagne.

"How's your dog?"

"She's great. I hope someone is taking care of her."

"I'm certain they are."

A hand massaged his shoulder. The drug was at work. His face seemed too large, the skin covering it too weighty, thick, and stiffening—a mud mask.

The shushing—it sounded like a ventilator. Max had listened to one for weeks while his wife was dying. He remembered it. But they obviously didn't have him on a ventilator. It made no sense.

"You looked into the stone."

"No . . . I didn't."

"Why lie to me?"

"I'm not lying. I started looking but couldn't go through with it."

"Failure of nerve or comprehension?"

"Nerve."

The beeping didn't really sound that nearby. It sounded across the room. He wondered if the drug distorted hearing. If he should trust himself.

The timing of the beeps. Max concentrated. He pushed his fingertip into the top of his groin and tried to find the femoral artery . . . there . . . his pulse, faint but true. The mattress under him changed. It got softer. He sank down into it. It didn't feel bad. He had to keep track of his pulse and the monitor noise. Part of his mind didn't care. Wanted the sinking . . .

He counted and listened to the beeps.

They didn't match up. His pulse and the monitor were different.

"I think we're ready to begin," Whiteside said.

That meant someone else was in the room, another patient. Max wondered who it was. "Who's here with me?"

"I'm here."

"No, the other patient. The one on the ventilator. Who's that?"

"That is someone I'm eager for you to meet, Max. But first things first. Are you feeling relaxed?"

"I feel like I need another drink. Make mine a rum and Coke."

"That's a beach bum's drink."

"Exactly what I said—"

His body encased in warm sand. Safe, drunk, hidden as treasure.

The blindfold loosened. Cotton collapsed against his cheeks. A stream of air touched his nostrils. The sheet pulled to the left. He saw vague canals, tension rippling in the underside of it—the pulling hand was almost ready to take it. The top of the sheet creased his eyebrows. His breaths came slow and even.

"Imagine your mind muscle expanding and contracting. Expanding. Contracting. You have a hole in your head, Max. See the hole stretching larger. See it growing. It gets bigger. Di*laaa*tion. The muscle is thin as a ribbon. It gives shape to the hole the hole is deep is inside of you but the hole leads outside of you and the muscle around the hole is so thin it floats away from the hole the hole in your head the hole belongs to me."

The sheet dropped.

CHAPTER 37

Ice shavings collected on the windowsill. Opal scraped a portal in the frost-blighted glass. Wyatt and Adam were downstairs with a Folgers coffee can of nails, hammering two-by-fours across the door. The pounding sounded more like a person furiously wanting in than anyone trying to keep people out. She was scared they might die tonight. She saw flashes in the sky, heard a rumble. These weren't man-made explosions. It was thunder. Lightning. More thunder boomed, a roll that went on forever and merged with the emptiness in the pit of her stomach. Snowflakes batted the window, tumbled away like dying moths.

Crazy weather.

Crazy people.

That's who she was seeing in the highway.

Groups of them, mostly men, scattered along the two-lane.

Some were dressed in normal winter coats, but others wore an assortment of quasi-military gear. Winter camouflage and fur-trimmed hats transformed them into inhuman shape-shifters. She counted at least forty.

They all carried weapons.

Old weapons that glinted in the firelight.

Spears. Axes. Pikes. She swore one of them hefted a sword.

Members at the front of each group had camping lanterns, the handles tucked in the crooks of their arms, or held aloft on poles, where they glowed like stars, molten light spilling on the ground, and also in their arsenal were powerful spotlights, which flashed with dreadful suddenness a cold white bolt into the doorways of silent houses. Opal imagined the people living in those houses. Moments ago perhaps they were sitting down to an early dinner or gathered around their Christmas trees. Maybe they were watching TV. Or maybe they'd been looking out the window the way she was. Hearing the explosions and seeing the fire unabated lick, lap, and slather flame from rooftop to rooftop and consume their town. Cinders dirtied the skyline.

Here and there, the curious moved outdoors.

Citizens stepped outside and wondered first at the inferno and next at the figures approaching down the road.

Figures walking in no great hurry . . . with hunting knives, hatchets, and lengths of chain clutched in their fists. Light floods a doorway. Sometimes it finds the eyes of those who live there. You see a face, a mouth stretched in fear or pure outrage.

Most fled back inside and turned their locks.

What little good that did.

The groups, or posses, attacked with wood-splitting clubs or battering rams made from heavy sections of pipe. One posse used a pointed log. Their arms swung in rhythm.

Doors broke, men went inside.

There were gunshots. No one had enough time to defend themselves.

People were dragged into the open. Young and old—the ambling figures did not discriminate. Man, woman, and child alike were welcomed to the road. Opal saw murder in the snowstorm. How could it be?

It didn't matter how.

It was.

Opal felt a shadow at her back.

"Lights won't come on. I think the explosion cut a power line. It'll start to get cold in here soon." Adam knelt next to her on the floor.

He swayed toward the floor. Horus pushed him gently backward against the wall.

The old man's eyes snapped open.

"You're so young," Max said, grabbing for his arm.

Horus shrugged loose.

A bib of blood stiffened Max's shirtfront. He was difficult to understand, slurring from the drugs. Black holes glared in his gums. Teeth were missing, but not far away; they were in a jar on the nightstand.

"How can I be so old and you're not?"

Horus had no time to explain.

The old man had proven to be a harder nut to crack than he'd anticipated.

The trance only took them so far.

Max hadn't told him anything he didn't already suspect.

Horus resorted to the pliers and started removing his teeth. But the ethanol muddied the pain. Max writhed. Max moaned. But he told him nothing more than the girl was inside the motel with the family who owned the place. They had the Tartarus Stone. They knew what it was because he'd told them and they recognized the threat against them. They had better or they'd wind up . . .

The old man stopped himself.

Good. So be it. The Pitch were out in the streets, putting on a show for the family. The threat *was* real. Horus needed the family to bear witness. Put the fear into them. They had to give him the stone. Do it freely.

Horus stopped when it looked like the old man might slip into shock. Throwing the pliers into a metal pan, mopping the sweat from his cheeks, and Max barely breathing under him, turning the color of candle wax—Horus shot adrenaline into him.

Placed ice, stuffed in a glove, on his forehead.

He tranced him again. Took away the pain.

Now here they were.

The old man asking him questions.

And wasn't that the way with old men? So much nagging . . . helpless one moment and prodding the next. Horus gave Max a cup of water.

"Drink this," he said.

Max drank.

Horus, standing, tore away his doctor's gown. Underneath he wore a white shirt, blotted with sweat, and a thin black leather tie. Black pants, black boots. He unbuttoned his cuffs. The buttons were mother-of-pearl. He rolled back his sleeves to reveal forearms as hairless as if they'd been shaved.

"Pinroth!"

The motel room door opened.

"Sir."

"Prepare the patient."

"A transfusion?"

Horus nodded.

Max sat stupefied. "You were my age . . . back in L.A. Forty years." He shook his head, as a dog would, as if to clear it. Blinking, he rubbed his face. "How can you look the same? Not a day older?"

"I've never met you before. Now shut up."

Max slumped back into the chair. His legs were like a corpse's legs sewn to his body. He pounded his thighs. Tried to bring the feeling back. He had to get out of there.

Horus walked over to the second hospital bed.

The occupied bed.

Around it was an Oriental screen of red lacquered wood. It was heavily, intricately carved. Dragons lived there. And people's faces. Disfigured faces—each missing some vital sense organ— nose, ears, eyes, tongue. The dragons feasted on them.

Horus collapsed the screen. He moved over the patient. The ventilator changed its sound. Horus stepped to the side and held the hose in his hand. Air blew from it.

In the bed, a swaddling of bandages shifted, crackling like paper in a fire.

The sticklike man, if it was a man, lying on the bed, lifted his head and turned to Max. It couldn't look at him because it had no eyes.

The bandages—the Stick Man was unraveling them.

More bandages than flesh.

"Don't do that," Horus said. But he made no attempt to halt the man's actions. Instead, he stripped the bloody sheets from the bed where Max had been tortured, and climbed in. Pinroth was there with a fresh wet needle, a roost of bags hanging on poles like transparent bats. He put the needle into Horus's arm. Then he went to the Stick Man's bed. He took hold of the Stick Man's limb. Another needle splintered light, before it vanished into the bandages. The Stick Man had no reaction. His focus was Max. The breath coming out of his mouth slit was like no thing Max had ever smelled. As it pointed its snout at Max, spidery streams of grit sifted from the bandage creases.

The thing—he decided it must be a thing, not a man—croaked dusty words.

It sounded like "Ax, Ax."

"Oood to theeeee youuu, Ax."

Good to see you, Max.

Max rose from the chair and fell crashing to the floor.

CHAPTER 39

Adam shut the door to his bedroom. The stone lay on his bed. He had taken it from Vera after they'd rushed her inside the office, his father locking the doors, a lot of good glass walls would do when the assault came, but they saw a group of the Pitch eerily keeping their distance, not storming the motel, only making silent gestures in the direction of Vera, or likely at the stone she'd hidden in her jacket.

Somehow the Pitch knew what she'd taken with her inside.

They retreated to the stairwell; the two Larkin men nailing braces across the doorway, while Vera sat on the steps behind them, breathlessly telling of her failed escape, the blocked highway, a snowmobiler shooting her Camaro full of arrows, and how they were *really* goddamned trapped now.

"That's enough."

It was his mother speaking from the top of the stairs.

"You want to live? You'd better start helping us. We need to barricade the back door." She came right down to where Vera rested and took away her pistol.

Vera looked more afraid than angry.

Adam brought the stone into his room, deposited it on the bed, dead center of his Mossy Oak camouflage comforter, not knowing what else to do. He made a point of not looking at it. He didn't think twice about that.

Not at first.

He still had the hammer in his hand. Nails clamped between his lips. He quickly decided his bedroom window was too high and too small to worry about intruders. They'd need a ladder to reach it. The window slid sideways, instead of up-and-down, and at its widest was about eighteen inches across. He gazed out, and saw thick fingers of ice knuckling around the edges. He made sure to check the lock anyway.

At the street level, the crazies howled for more blood. Adam thought he heard someone calling his name. He drew nearer to the window.

Smoke, clouds, and snow. Shades of gray. In the distance, a man was climbing the town's water tank. His apelike silhouette advanced hand over hand up the curve, clinging to unseen icy rungs. Adam watched him reach the summit.

He's cutting the cell phone tower.

A transformer exploded across the highway. Sparks gushed. The streetlights blowing out like birthday candles—*whoosh*. The town slipped into electrical blackness.

Everything tinged Halloween orange because of the fires.

Below him, in the parking lot, one of the Pitch twirled a steely hook attached to a long chain coiled between his legs. He was letting out a few more links with every revolution. The chain blurred. The creep doing the spinning moved from shadow to shadow in his dark coat. He was tall. A lantern passed behind him. Snow glazed his hair, turning pink with his, or somebody's, blood.

Adam pressed his cheek to the glass. The guy's hands looked freezer-burned. He must have noticed Adam, because he shuffled closer, wading into the turbid haze beneath the bedroom window. His head hung down, chin buried in the collar of his coat like a man hurrying through the weather to meet a train.

Adam couldn't see a face.

The hook went flying.

The pink-haired, freezer-burned guy—he'd let go of the chain.

The metal claw slammed into the motel facade under Adam's window.

Adam jumped back.

He listened to the hook scrabbling along.

The guy hauled on the chain and pulled loose a panel of siding with a horrible splitting screech.

The hook dropped.

Clanged.

The panel hit the ground and the wind dragged it out of sight.

Pink Freezer guy went back to twirling.

Adam looped the hammer on his jeans. He brushed his sweating palms against his legs but couldn't seem to dry them. Looking away, avoiding the window, his eyes fell to the stone. Jagged silver-black points flickered at him. It seemed bigger than it had back in Vera's bathroom. Trick of light? His thumb glided along a hard slippery edge. It surprised him. Oily, lubricated. He looked at his fingertip. Saw no residue. Touched the stone again . . . it was warm.

He held it up. It didn't seem as heavy as when he carried it upstairs. He set it down again on the bed.

Two pyramids glued together. If he wanted to, he could spin the thing like a top. Eight triangles, eight flat panes for gazing into—four sides tilted up and four slanted underneath.

He couldn't say why, but he locked his bedroom door.

Adam stared down at the stone. The triangular pane facing him was clear. Why hadn't he noticed this before? He looked in.

The stone was hollow.

He was able to see the entire inner chamber.

It was empty.

He pried his fingernail along the edge of the clear pane. Like a trapdoor, it swung open. Sticking out at him like a stiff, pointed tongue.

Shadows lay along the cracks diving to the bottom, which looked deep as an air shaft, and wider than the limits of the stone's outer surface. A coppery light illuminated the chamber, but he could see no bulb or flame. The stone's inner sides swirled rich with colors, not black at all, but honeys, caramels, toffees. He could smell something now that he'd opened it—a woody forest smell, pleasant and clean. The smell changed. Sweetness followed, not the scent of wildflowers—the candied sweetness of sugar cooking, melting in a pan. He let his eyes soft-focus. He emptied his thoughts. He stared into the bottom of the stone.

And he waited.

Crystals.

There was a thin layer of what appeared to be raw sugar crystals at the bottom. Adam tried measuring the level against the outside of the box. Maybe not so thin. How could he even tell? Was it rising?

An optical illusion, he knew.

It had to be.

Max had said he saw things in the stone.

This wasn't exactly what Adam expected. But when Max told his story, Adam had to admit he wanted to see something, too.

Now it was happening.

A slow lick of sugar curled around inside the stone enclosure; it traced the edges, bulging like a wave, or as if a living thing were burrowing beneath the surface.

Testing.

The sugar level rose higher. No. Something had begun to rise out of it. A bubble, perfectly round, was growing and quickly filling the space. As the bubble expanded, the crystals spilled away like sand running off a smooth oval rock.

He could see skin now.

Tan in color, but authentic human skin, taking shape.

He saw the top of a skull.

Man or woman—he did not know. But the skull floated up slowly inside the stone. Enlarging, inflating like a balloon, it spread outward in all directions at once. More than half the inner space was now occupied.

The shadows reddened around the emerging head.

It was a birth.

Like all births, great expectations preceded it. Adam angled to the left and then right, trying to glimpse more features, a nose, ears . . .

The sugar disappeared, funneled to the bottom, past the chin, out of sight.

It was only this one thing now—a shaven head.

Adam leaned in. He could see pores in the taut skin, a light beading of sweat beginning to pop, and the twitch-twitch of living nerves underneath.

Still he could smell the sweetness. It seemed heavier. Cloying.

He could hear . . . yes, there was no mistake . . . he could hear breathing. Slow, steady, rhythmic—like the pattern of a person asleep. He watched his own chest rise and fall. The same beat. But he wasn't asleep. With each exhalation Adam smelled more of the sweetness that was coming, he realized, from the hidden mouth.

The head stopped rising an inch from the trapdoor.

It stayed perfectly still.

Adam stretched his hand out.

And quickly drew it back.

It was amazing how real the thing seemed. There were faint freckles and bumps and grooves where the cranial bones fused. Adam could see the tiny divot of an old scar. It was easy to believe this head was real and not . . .

Adam screamed.

He slammed the trapdoor closed. He pinned it with his knee. He fumbled as the head pressed against the clear pane, forcing its way out, pushing.

Pushing.

Adam hugged the stone and kept his knee against the pane. He wondered if it might crack. Shatter. And he screamed again, as frustration and a second wave of fear swept over him.

The pushing stopped.

It took real bravery to lift his knee off the trapdoor lid. He slid backward on the seat of his jeans, never taking his eyes off the stone, until his tailbone hit the wall. The sides of the stone were opaque. Solid rock and black as a pit.

He sat there.

What had he just seen?

He was asking himself this question. He wasn't having much luck coming up with answers. The facts were plain: The head in the stone had moved, turning slightly to the left, then back to center and off to the right, like something a person on a strange street corner might do to get their bearings. Adam felt his own head mimicking the movements as he watched.

What the . . . ?

The head in the stone snapped back. Flesh hit against rock. There was just enough room for the head to look up.

That's exactly what it did.

Liquid pupils peered at him like sacs of jellied darkness. The nose—nothing was there but a ragged hole. Thin lips parted, breathing out sweetness.

Adam's face was inches away.

Eye to eye.

He had a good long look.

But that wasn't what made him scream.

The face he saw was immediately recognizable as male, yet unblinking and hideously rigid, like a mask. Gradually, the features unfroze, softened. Skin crinkled around the eyes. The lips curved into a familiar human expression. Under normal circumstances Adam's response would have been to smile back.

Instead, he shuddered.

His pulse raced. Neck hairs stood on end. Time ground to a halt. But that didn't make him scream. Viewing didn't push him over the edge. A thought did. He realized the thing emerging from the stone was also taking a good long look at *him*.

And, Adam knew, it liked what it saw.

Pounding at the door . . .

His mother and father were calling for him. The door shook in its frame as his father rammed it with his shoulder. Wood crunched with each hollow thud.

"Adam! Unlock the door!" His mother's shouts mingled with the voices of the Pitch and the people dying outside.

Words rebounded. Distorted, far away, calling up to him. He had the sensation of standing on a precipice over profound windy depths. Vertigo trilled through his bones. He didn't get up to let his parents in.

Despite his terror, he wanted most of all to flip open the trap-door again.

Yes. That was what he should do.

The stone cleared and the head bobbed inside, nodding, agreeing.

He reached for it.

CHAPTER 40

Vera heard Adam's screams. But she couldn't leave her position. Opal was already treating her like a criminal. It wasn't fair. She hadn't stolen from them. Hadn't hurt anyone, either. But it wasn't worth arguing. Opal wouldn't see things from her point of view because she only wanted to protect her family. Vera needed shelter. And they *were* trapped. Opal knew it, too.

They had to work together.

Opal unplugged the industrial-sized dryer and disconnected the flex pipe to the natural gas line; then she and Vera frog-walked the front-loader over to the rear exit. But they had no time to move the washer before Adam cried out. Opal told her to stay there, keep working. If the Pitch broke down the door, they could dislodge the dryer and force their way to the second door, the one leading to the kitchen. The idea of them getting in the same room nauseated Vera.

She unhooked the washer hoses for the clean water and the drain, but she couldn't get the machine to budge. It was heavy and wide, awkward to grab. She tried bracing her feet against the wall and shoving hard with her backside.

It moved a few inches. The utility room wasn't insulated. Cold drafts swam around her. Her perspiration chilled.

Wyatt and Opal were yelling. They sounded panicked. And that frightened her. She heard someone slamming into a door inside.

Again and again. The entire motel seemed to quake. Were the Pitch breaking in? Is that why Adam screamed? Was he dead? Would Wyatt and Opal be next?

How long until the Pitch came for her through the dark?

A rapping on the storm door glass startled her.

She was crouched between the washing machine and the wall. If anyone saw her, all they saw were her feet. She tried to keep still. To breathe.

The rapping continued. Steady as raindrops.

She peeked around the corner of the machine. One quick look. Whoever was knocking stood on the snowy deck. She'd been out there herself. Not much room. No more than two adults could fit. She didn't hear any talking. They weren't bashing the door. So it was probably a lone person. What if it wasn't the Pitch? What if it was someone who'd come to Wyatt and Opal for help?

Vera couldn't leave them to die.

And what if it was Max? They didn't know where he was. Only that it looked bad in the parking lot—the bodies, the blood—when he disappeared. He might've been hiding. He could be wounded. That might be him knocking.

She looked.

A shadow ghosted behind the frosty glass.

She ducked.

It wasn't Max. Too tall, too much shoulder. It was a man, though. She didn't notice any weapons. But she could only see him from the waist up. With the frost it was hard to tell much.

She studied the glass again.

The man had a hoodie over his head. Leather jacket, zipped. He hunched forward, one hand deep in his pocket. He dragged open the storm door. Wasn't it locked? She paused, thinking. Bare knuckles drummed the frosty glass of the second door. Fingers scratched.

She hid.

Looked.

The man put his lips against the door crack, whispering.

"Vera? Is that you?"

She knew the whisperer.

"Chan?"

"Oh my God, it is you! Let me in, babe."

Vera stood up. But she stayed behind the two machines.

"What are you doing here?"

"I came to save you. Let me in."

"How did you know I was here?"

"We don't have time for this, babe. The Pitch are going to burn the town. Burn it to the ground. We have to leave."

"Leave how?"

He jiggled the door handle.

"I've got a four-wheel drive. We can go over the border."

Vera came around the washer. Chan sounded funny, like he did after a visit to the dentist. Words thickened in his mouth.

"There are other people in here with me. Three of them," she said.

"We'll take them, too. I promise."

He was right against the glass. His breath smudged the single pane. He wiped it. Oh God. They'd beaten him. His face was lumpy purple. A shallow incision grinned across his throat. One eye puffed shut—a flaming velvet slit—but apparently he was able to see her.

"Are you helping the Pitch?" she asked.

An eyeball darted inside the slit. "Open up."

"Chan . . . I . . . I don't think I should."

Vera glanced back. The apartment was quiet. That silence made her feel even worse. She called out, "I need help here!"

"What're you doing?" Chan elbowed the glass. It spidered with cracks. "How . . . *(glass breaking)* . . . hard is it . . . *(shards tinkling on the floor)* . . . to open a fucking door?"

"Hurry up! He's getting in!"

He grabbed the handle with both hands and shook it furiously. He tried to rip it loose. He smashed his fist through the broken window. Glass flew at Vera.

Chan's arm came through to the shoulder.

He grabbed her wrist.

"You little fucking bitch! I'm going to cut your head off. Give it to the Pitch on a silver fucking platter."

He dragged her toward the hole in the window. His fingers were cut, bleeding. He lifted her. She kicked air. He hauled her over the top of the dryer.

"Give me the stone."

She slithered out of his bloody grip. Ready to bolt.

He fastened onto her hair. Digging his fingers into a handful. Jerking her off her feet. It felt like he was scalping her.

"Shit! Let me go!"

"Tear you up, bitch."

The apartment door burst open.

Opal, wide-eyed, looking frail and exhausted, lost in her bundled layers of clothes. No Wyatt or Adam with her.

She wrapped her arms around Vera's waist, and the tug-of-war began.

Chan grunted and tightened his fist at the back of Vera's head. Vera locked her legs onto Opal. Opal leaned toward the safety of the apartment.

The women were winning. But Vera's hair was ripping out. She could hear it. Feel the strands yanked by their roots. The skin on her cheekbones pulled taut. She couldn't even blink.

Chan thrashed Vera's head wildly, side to side. Her neck twisted and hot rapid tears spilled from her eyes. She unlocked her legs. She tried to pry Chan's fingers loose. She scratched him.

He pulled harder.

Opal slipped from Vera's waist to her thighs, knees. Ankles. She dropped low, used her body weight to anchor Vera.

Chan changed tactics. He was no longer attempting to extract Vera through the door. He was coming inside.

"Kill you both," he snarled. His bruised face contorted.

He cracked away the last hanging corners of glass.

His neck wound—from the torture Whiteside administered in the abandoned house—wept. A blood-soaked *V* spread down the front of his hoodie. He lunged and clamped a second hand around Vera's throat. His thumb buried into the underside of her jaw. He worked his fingers around her windpipe.

She choked.

Using both his arms, Chan had the advantage. He outmuscled the women.

Opal let go of Vera.

Chan lost his balance. But only for a second. He gathered Vera into his arms, barred his right forearm under her chin and squeezed.

Vera's face went scarlet. She couldn't breathe.

Chan was whispering vile obscenities in her ear.

Opal leveled the Bobcat she'd taken from Vera in the stairwell. She aimed the revolver at Chan and fired.

The blast was deafening in the small room.

Chan's leather jacket turned slick and red.

He released Vera. Pawed at his injured shoulder. His fury increased. He scrambled in one final charge through the broken door. Oblivious to the glass shards puncturing his knees. To the gun pointed at him. His bloody open arms closing like a pair of enormous claws.

Opal fired.

Two. Three.

Four shots.

Chest. Head. Chest. Chan stopped struggling. He slumped halfway through the gap. Wind and ice chattered around him. Stained red, teeth bared, he looked less like Chan than a wolf fresh from slaughtering his winter kill.

Opal climbed on top of the dryer and planted her boot squarely on his forehead. She kicked his body onto the porch. The others—who were waiting below, out of sight, preparing for the ambush that would never come—scattered into the night.

Vera knelt on the utility-room floor. Breathing shallow. Touching her mauled throat. Listening to the thunderous rush of blood returning in her ears. Thanking God that she was alive.

"Let's go inside," Opal said, helping her to her feet.

"Thank you," she tried to say. But her words were tiny croaks lost in the spiral of wind tunneling through the door.

CHAPTER 41

Father and son, Max thought, rising up on his haunches. Two Horus Whitesides. The older man, massed in bandages, a bag of bones lying on the sheets exuding the sweet corruption of rot—*he was the man who tortured me years ago. The other is his son.* That was certain from his looks alone. Legacies. A succession of monsters. Madness passed on like heirlooms. And power. Linkage with the underworld.

"The transfusions give him headaches," Horus the Younger said from his hospital bed. A purr as it lowered him prone. "Without them he would be dead." He looked over at the husk of his father. "More dead than he is," he added.

Max sat up between the beds, dragging himself away.

Pinroth guarded the door.

"My father believes in immersion in the world of thought, extreme denial of the flesh. He is a literalist. Over the years, he performed many of the procedures on himself, under local anesthetic. *Distractions must go,* he said. Ever seen a human tongue severed? It takes two hands to do the job right. Tongs and a blade. I held the tongs. We perforated both eardrums repeatedly until he met the goal of silence. Using a mirror, he eviscerated his left eye. That was a real breakthrough. Amazing control displayed. His visions increased a hundredfold. The dead appeared to us. They spoke. My initial reluctance faded along with my doubts. Pinroth and I kept him from bleeding to death. From dying of shock at each maiming. Manhood, the year I took the right eye. As his body weakened, his mind grew stronger. Pain and pleasure reversed beautifully. He stopped eating and drinking a decade ago. We use a feeding tube. Vaseline his mouth. I am the caretaker. It is tedious business keeping a human body on the brink of death for years and years. From that precipice, though, he sees everything. The transfusions help to stabilize him. We are a perfect blood match. He speaks directly to my mind. He is the master of the Pitch. We serve him."

"Does he see me?"

The Stick Man cackled. "I see you on your knees," the Elder said.

Strange laughter hissed again.

Max was getting better at understanding him. The decaying man's lips weren't moving. The voice, he realized, spoke right into his head. It made his stomach convulse.

"Dad hasn't lost his humor," Horus said.

The transfusion catheter connecting him to his father flooded red. The dead thing drank life through its arm. Max imagined he could hear blood squelching as the cadaverous veins sucked nourishment.

"Max is dying, too," the corpse Whiteside said. Its shrunken head bobbed like a voodoo doll's brainless stuffed sack.

"Not fast enough," Max said.

Bandaged hands clapped. Dust motes floated in the medicinal stuffy air.

"Stop it before you pull out your needle," the son said.

"What if I do? My time is come to be born."

Max rose to his feet. Unsteady, dizzy, claustrophobic. His balancing stride brought him closer to the exit. He pulled up short. Pinroth's hawk face and the black zero of the Luger trained on him.

"What does he mean?" Max shifted toward the beds. "To be born?"

The younger Whiteside rested a pale arm across his forehead. "The stone is the key to his freedom. He will depart this house once and for all. The Tartarus Stone is more than you realize, Max."

"It points the way to Hell," Max said.

"It is Hell," the skeleton replied.

The thought sobered Max. If Hell was real, couldn't it be inside a rock? Why should Hell have to be a place far away? What size is a soul?

"Why do you need it?"

The Stick Man held up his twig fingers. He mimed an old child's finger-game.

Here is the Church. And here is the Steeple.

Open the Door. See all the People.

"And set them free." He wiggled his twig people. The light in the room dimmed.

Then it went out.

"Fuck it." Horus yanked the needle from his arm. "Pinroth, get Father into the ambulance. There's a bag of blood in the mini-fridge. We'll do the full transfusion later. I can't have him dying on us now. There's no time for this."

"Time is not important," the Stick Man said.

Pinroth handed a bandage to his boss standing next to Max. *Son of Horus,* Max thought. The younger man put his lips to Max's ear. "Time isn't important to him. But I have to live in this world. Chained to his side from the moment I first saw him. Better off in the asylum? Don't think I never considered it."

"Stop t-t-talking about me," said the voice, like ash collapsing in a fireplace.

"Pinroth." Horus pointed to the bed. "Ambulance."

Pinroth rolled the hospital bed with the Elder out into the hall.

"Why don't you let him die?" Max asked.

"Let him die! I won't *permit* him to die until I have what's mine. He wants to reign in the spirit world. I want power on earth. To be king to his pagan lord is good enough for me. He promised it would happen. I've paid with my blood. I need him alive. When the wasteland comes, I want a skybox seat."

"You're both insane."

"Insane? God is a lie. We stomped on His face for two generations. Yet we experience not the slightest retribution. Evil, on the other hand, is infinite. No matter how far I push inside, there's always more room, another turn, another crevice to squirm into. It accommodates. I've spent my life's work on this project. Evil alone exists. When I'm down in the very thick of it—the greasy, stomach-churning, shocking pit that is, indeed, bottomless—I am not myself. Nor am I by myself. I have company in the shadows. Some pretty big fish are swimming the depths with me. The unnamable. They've always been there, under the surface of things. Haven't you sensed them? Whispering and waiting. Ancients. Man-eaters. Devourers. They're hungry for sacrifice. To abandon their realm of unseen influence, take form, and inhabit the earth. The bad news for most of humanity isn't that there's no God watching us. But there's no *nothing,* either. The old man taught me well. What's waiting in the stone is actively evil. Father will free it soon. And it owes me big-time."

He stuck his finger under the bandage in the crook of his arm. A red smear from the needle puncture—he wiped a crimson eye on Max's forehead.

"I'm not going to kill you, Max. Do you remember what I told you to do? When I had you relaxed on the bed?"

"No . . . I don't remember anything."

"Good. Then sleep."

He pinched Max's shoulder and Max's head dropped to his chest.

"Wyatt, Opal, Adam, and Vera are your enemies. They secretly wish to kill you. Bring me the stone or return soaked in their blood. That is the path of your survival. The stone will cure you of your pain. It's the only chance you have. Awake and go to the motel. No one will stop you."

Horus slipped the Ruger under Max's belt, at the small of his back. He helped him into his parka.

"Wake up, friend," he said, escorting Max from the room, along the carpeted hallway, and out the front door. Putting his hands on Max's shoulders, he pointed him through the jerking fiery darkness from the Totem Lodge to the highway beyond.

CHAPTER 42

Wyatt wrestled Adam to the floor and finally snapped an old pair of handcuffs behind his son's back. Adam wanted up off his stomach. His chest heaved. He breathed audibly through his mouth. Sweat ringed his shirt. Wyatt sat on him.

"I want to see it," Adam said.

"I told you, no."

"Let me fucking see it! Or I swear I'll kill you and Mom!"

"You don't mean that."

Adam attempted to lift off the ground. Wyatt grabbed his ankle, yanked, and they both fell flat again.

"You're suffocating me."

"Stop fighting."

Adam growled and strained to glimpse the stone on the bed. He couldn't.

"Please, Dad, we should all take a closer look. You and Mom, too."

"No."

"*I hate you! I hate you!*"

"I love you. So does your mother."

Adam calmed for a moment. Wyatt felt his son's lungs filling and deflating. Filling slowly. Deflating. In through the mouth, out through the nose. When he spoke, the words were level. "I'm better now. Let me up, okay?"

"Not yet."

Adam gritted his teeth. "I'm going to let them in, you prick."

Wyatt didn't ask who. He had the Glock 27 in his right hand. If Opal didn't come back in sixty seconds, he would go. He'd take the stone, too. Lock Adam in the closet. It wouldn't hold him for long. But he didn't have many choices. He heard them struggling with somebody, or a gang of somebodies, in the utility room. Four gunshots. The most difficult thing was to sit here on his son's back and wait.

He hoped the change in Adam was temporary. Passing delirium. A spell.

Adam banged his head into the floor.

With his left hand, Wyatt forced the boy's head down. Pinned it there, giving him no room to hurt himself.

Adam cried.

"Please, please, *please* . . ."

Footsteps in the hall. Lightweight, moving quickly. Wyatt couldn't see around the corner from his spot next to the bed. The room was dark. A black and orange tree grew from the shadows on the ceiling. He fingered the trigger.

Waited.

Opal. In the doorway. Candle flame guttered in her hand. Behind her was Vera.

He took his finger off the trigger.

Icicles dripped in his guts.

"The stone . . . it's doing something to Adam. Take it away."

Opal grabbed the stone and left the bedroom.

"Anything I can do?" Vera asked.

"Who was out back?"

"My boyfriend Chan; he tried to get me to let him in and when I wouldn't he broke the glass and grabbed me and started pulling my hair and . . ."

"Where's he now?"

"Opal shot him."

"Dead?"

"Yes, he's dead."

"Are you injured?"

Vera shook her head.

"You did the right thing. Opal did the right thing. You know that?"

"Yes."

"Give me a hand. Let's put him on the bed."

Wyatt shifted off Adam's back. Adam didn't move. He appeared to be asleep.

"Maybe whatever happened to him . . . maybe it was like a seizure. His brain misfired and now it's shut down for a little while." Vera knelt and brushed her fingers through Adam's damp hair. Adam's mouth was slack. All the tension in him had vanished. His eyelids fluttered. His eyes were moving under them like he was deep in a dream.

Wyatt set the Glock on the nightstand. He straddled Adam. He flipped him face up. Asleep. Snoring. The damnedest thing. Like a knockout dart.

Wyatt lifted Adam's torso and Opal returned in time to help Vera with his legs. They left the handcuffs on him. Rolled him on his side.

Opal put an icepack on Adam's neck.

She threw a blanket over him. Kissed his cheek. Shut his door, partway.

They went into the kitchen.

"Where's the stone?" Wyatt asked.

Opal nodded at the oven.

"I'd like to broil the thing," she said.

Vera went into the bathroom. They heard water running. She was blowing her nose. Sobbing, trying to do it quietly. Opal looked at Wyatt.

He put his arm around his wife.

"I killed Vera's boyfriend," Opal said.

"She told me."

"I had to."

"And you did. You okay with it?"

"No. But I will be."

Wyatt hugged her close. "So let's keep busy. You get the back door secured?"

She shook her head no. "Is Adam going to be better?"

"I think so. He did what Max said we shouldn't. The rock . . . it's like it drugged him. I think it affects the brain. Vera said something about seizures—"

"We keep away from it. All of us," she said. She let go of her husband. Took the coffeepot off the stovetop and poured three cups. "What if we give it to them?"

"Are you serious?"

"I don't know. No, I guess not. They're killing everyone outside, Wyatt. We're sitting here on our hands. How's that supposed to make me feel?"

"I know."

"My sister's out there. Ruby and her family. Our friends."

"It's not our fault."

"We have to do something. How many bullets do we have?"

"Not enough."

CHAPTER 43

Wyatt pounded the last of the nails into the door between the kitchen and the utility room. The washer and dryer were on the other side, wedged against the back door. He didn't think they'd try coming in that way again. Not after Chan's killing. They could only march up the back steps one at a time, not a great option for attack. No, they'd try another approach. He wasn't sure what was coming next. But he had an idea he wanted to explore first.

Opal exited Adam's room.

"He's awake," she said. "He doesn't remember anything that happened. Says he went into his room to check the window. Looked outside. Then he started inspecting the stone. After that, he's drawing a blank."

"Probably better if he can't remember."

"He asked me to take the cuffs off."

"Did you?"

"You have the key."

"Oh, right." Wyatt slipped the key into Opal's hand. "He tried to trick me before when I had him pinned. He wasn't very convincing. You believe him?"

Opal nodded.

"I'm going up on the roof," Wyatt said.

"Why?"

"I'll be able to see the whole town. Get a better idea of what's out there."

"The darkness and the storm . . ."

"The Pitch are carrying lanterns and spotlights. They're in tight groups. I can find them easily enough. I'll get an idea of their numbers . . . how they're moving. The fires are blowing south to southeast. We're not in their path right now. Winds can change. And if they do, so will our chances. I'd like to assess the damage. Plan an escape route . . . if we have to run for it on foot."

"What about our trucks?"

"They'll have trashed them for sure. If not, they might be lying in wait nearby. It's too risky."

"We won't make it far running."

"Not all four of us together. We need to create a diversion."

"We're not splitting up, Wyatt."

"I didn't say that. I want a look around. Figure out our options. Right now I think it's best to stay put. But I don't want to be heading into the night without a plan. I can get out to the rooftop through the attic."

"I'll come with you."

"No. If Adam's awake, he can go."

"Why can't I?"

"It's safer in here."

"I just killed somebody *in here*."

"If Adam goes off on that stone again, I'm the only one who can handle him safely. He's coming with me," Wyatt said. "Agreed?"

Opal nodded.

"Time for a little scouting of my own," she said.

"I don't follow you."

"I'll make myself have a vision."

"What? You can do that?"

Opal shrugged. "I don't know. Never tried it before."

"Sounds like a bad idea. You shouldn't be taking any chances."

"Look, I had a vision of this Whiteside before *without* trying.

Maybe it's not so much of a curse. I could figure out where he is. What he's up to. We'd gain the advantage."

"You think you have a psychic link to this bastard?"

"You tell me."

"If you can get in his head, I pity him." Wyatt smiled.

Opal smiled back and said, "He can't hurt me, not physically. He's out there and I'm barricaded in here, right?" She didn't sound too confident.

"I don't see how he could harm you," Wyatt said. "But to be safe, have Vera stand watch. She stays at your side the entire time. Monitors your behavior, any reactions you might have to the encounter. You're in trouble, she pulls the plug."

"Okay, let's do it."

"Okay."

Wyatt kissed her.

Opal wanted the night to be over. To have Christmas dinner and return to their normal life of daily ups and downs. Live their small-town lives in peace.

Tonight was going to be far from peaceful.

Wyatt collected the flashlights in the apartment. They had a heavy-duty policeman's Maglite, a Snake Light for handyman jobs, and two LED pocket-sized lights they used for camping. Wyatt was obsessive about keeping the batteries fresh. Each flash snapped on to full brightness. Their beams shined on the wall.

Four moons.

He clicked them off, one by one.

Adam stood in his doorway, silent. Hands still manacled behind his back. His tousled hair fell over deep-set eyes circled with tiredness. Shoulders slumping forward, a yoke of muscles bunched around his neck. He tipped his head to one side, squinting, as if even the dimness hurt his bloodshot eyes.

"I need some water." His voice crackled like dry leaves.

Opal unlocked the handcuffs.

Adam shuffled to the sink. He bent and drank, guzzling from the faucet, taking long, deep swallows that slurped loudly in the basin. He cupped water in his hands and poured it over his head. Water trickled off his elbows onto the floor. He straightened up and slicked down his hair. In the candlelight glow, his face appeared badly sunburned, peeling. Stubble blackened his chin.

Vera came out of the hallway and joined him at the sink.

Adam slid along the counter to make room for her. He didn't glance her way. Arms hanging down, his fingers drummed the oven door.

Oven door.

Wyatt wondered if he'd overheard them, knew the stone was shut inside.

He shifted gradually to the balls of his feet. Body tightened for a launch.

Adam gripped the door's handle and began rocking it open a few inches and then closing it. Over and over again. It was an unconscious act, a nervous fumbling, which reflected inner unrest. He didn't know he was doing it. The hinges squeaked. The door thudded shut. *Squeak. Bang.*

He opened it up again. Wider this time. *Squeak.* Candlelight wasn't sufficient to penetrate the dark hollow of the oven's compartment. *Bang.*

Squeak.

Through the reappearing crack, Wyatt glimpsed something. Movement? Changes in the dark—a greater depth gaped at him: the vertical sliver of a colorless eye. It blinked. The oven door slammed.

Wyatt wasn't certain he'd seen anything there at all. It was too unbelievable. But he *had* seen it. He couldn't deny his own observations. And his physical reactions—his whole body trembled. Adrenaline flooded his bloodstream.

Adam wasn't acting out consciously. The stone still had talons buried into his mind. It was in control.

Squeeeeeeak. BANG!

Vera picked up a coffee cup. She glanced sidelong at Adam, prepared to duck away if things went suddenly violent and Wyatt had to tackle him again. Adam seemed oblivious to them both. His stare had locked on the wall above and to the left of Wyatt. The wall was blank. A sight beyond the wall intrigued and terrified him. His mouth hung slack, a trickle of saliva ran down his chin.

Vera tapped his shoulder.

He jumped like a person roused from a troubled sleep. Brushed his knuckles against the spittle on his face and frowned.

She offered Adam the steaming cup. Smiling at him, though her hands betrayed her. She was shaking. Coffee sloshed over the cup's rim.

Wyatt admired her guts.

Adam registered his surroundings. He surveyed the room. Confusion and struggle marked his every move. As if he were struggling to stay awake. He nodded his thanks to Vera, sniffed at the cup, and tentatively drank.

"How're you feeling?" Vera asked.

He coughed. Shook his head to clear the cobwebs.

"I've got a massive headache."

"Welcome to the club," she said.

She dragged a chair away from the kitchen table and sat down.

Adam moved stiffly, watching his hands and feet, willing them into action and unsure if they would obey. But he sat, too, joining her, more than an arm's length from the oven. He sighed as he sank into the chair. Relief.

Smart girl, Wyatt thought.

Wyatt passed the two mini-lights to Opal. "We'll take the Mag and the Snake. You and Vera can use the LEDs if you need to." He turned his attention to Vera. "Help Opal. Do whatever she asks. Keep her comfortable. She's going to induce a vision. She'll be vulnerable. You need to sit with her and pay attention. Any sign of danger, snap her out of it. We don't even know if it's going to work. But it's worth a try. Adam and I won't be gone long, I hope."

Adam rubbed his wrists.

"Where are we going?" he asked.

"The roof," Wyatt said. "You ready for that?"

"Yeah, I'll get the ladder." He stood up too quickly and swayed. Faltered. He leaned on Vera. She helped him back into his chair. "Guess I'm a little dizzy. As long as I don't have to climb out there, I'll be fine."

He pressed the heels of his palms to his forehead. His eyes clamped shut. His hands slipped down his face. He sat there, elbows on the table, face hidden behind his closed fingers, as if he were playing a game of peek-a-boo with them.

"Adam?" Opal asked. "Honey, are you sure you're feeling—?"

"Where's the stone?" he asked, not taking his hands away. He didn't show them his face. His voice sounded miles off and yet it resonated. Wyatt felt a thrumming in his breastbone. *Could that be Adam's voice?* It had to be. Yet it sounded so alien.

The room filled with the smell of burned matches.

Vera gasped.

The candles sputtered as if tiny mouths whispered into them. In unison, the flames shot up, dancing high over the pools of rapidly melting wax. The wicks burned tall and golden white. Liquefied wax bubbled, flowing off the table's edge until every candle burned out with a hiss.

"We hid it," Opal said. "And we think it's best that we keep the hiding place a secret. That way you won't be . . . bothered by it."

Adam cocked his head, considering.

"How very clever you are," he said. He hadn't moved his hands. But the grin behind them was so large it showed, ear to ear. "Maybe I already know where it is, ever think of that, Mommy?"

"If you knew, you wouldn't ask," Opal said.

"Don't presume."

It wasn't Adam talking. Wyatt knew that now. They all did.

"I want to talk to Adam," Opal said.

Adam's body contorted. He shoved the table away.

The violent thrust knocked Vera backward. She landed hard on the floor.

Slapping at the air, Adam flailed against invisible attackers swarming at him from all directions. His quick breaths came juiced with panic. He punched his chest. He swung his arms in wild roundhouses that cut the air and kept his parents at a distance. He pulled his hair and raked his fingernails down his face.

Wyatt and Opal tried to restrain him.

He cast them off. Poised for greater self-torture.

As quickly as the assault came, it ended. Blood and skin stuck under his nails. Scratches furrowed his forehead and cheeks. When he dropped his hands, he looked like Adam again, wholly unaware of what he had done.

Vera stood watching him.

Adam's bleeding face, more haggard than before, gave her pause.

Wyatt read her thoughts because they were his own.

While they worried about securing the motel, the Pitch had found another way inside. *Through them.* Had the malevolence possessing Adam cleared out for good, or did it simply lie low and bide its time?

Adam coughed and drank his coffee.

CHAPTER 44

Hell on earth, Max thought as he moved among the Pitch. Here along the edge of town he was seeing the infernal as fact. Men dressed for the outdoors wielded instruments of warfare and the hunt. He watched a man in a motorcycle helmet club a woman in her front-yard nativity scene while blood-speckled wise men looked on. He didn't turn to see what the man was doing with the body. He walked. Face forward. Negotiating a path through the mob. The screams. Chaos. Everything happening too fast. He couldn't process it. Didn't want to. He drifted like a specter on a battlefield. More surreal than any LSD or mushroom trip he took in his L.A. magical mystery days. Pure terror powered him. His heart boomed. Alive, in revolt, the organ wanted to escape the cage of his chest. If Max could have spoken a word, he would have said he was dying.

He walked instead.

Placed foot in front of foot. He had no choice and he didn't quite know why. Only he had to go to the motel. He had to do something there. He couldn't remember what. But he knew it would be awful. They were killing people for no reason. Flames tongued skyward. No, they had reasons. *The windmills are burning,* Max thought. *My mind is on fire. Fear chokes me.* It was the old Frankenstein movie finale in reverse. The monsters had the torches and pitchforks, and they were destroying the village.

Though the villagers weren't going down without a fight.

Shotgun blasts ripped the night.

Trucks and cars roared down the highway, scattering the marauders.

It was only a matter of time before those vehicles had to stop. Snowbound, forced to turn back on a midnight road, or surrender up their passengers to wind-whipped fields strangled with ice. The hunched figures were waiting for them.

He saw the ambulance drive up and keep pace with him.

No siren blared.

The cherry light swirled red loops around him.

He did not turn to look at the driver.

Eyes on him, he felt their scalpel chill.

The ambulance picked up speed. Passed. The tires threw a fan-tail of gray slush across his path. Through the rear windows, a faceless face peered back.

Horrid, mummified. Jolly.

Bound to a stretcher, with a bag of ebony blood swaying from a hook above, the Elder wagged its fingers at him. The voice ice-picked his brain.

The church.

The Steeple.

All the people . . .

Max walked on to the motel.

CHAPTER 45

Opal settled back into the recliner. The room was unlit. Chinks between the boards in the windows glowed faintly like trails of dying embers. But the den was so familiar, she wasn't afraid to be there. Vera was with her. She could almost pretend they were about to pop a movie in the DVD player and settle down to share a big bowl of buttered popcorn. Only the widescreen television stood as dark as the windows had been before they boarded them up. She told Vera to put a candle on the foldable TV tray beside her.

"I'll concentrate on the flame. Maybe that will help."

Vera set the candle down. She went off into the corner and found a purple beanbag chair, which she plopped down near Opal's feet. She curled into the chair and the foam beads inside crunched like a pile of autumn leaves.

"Are you ready?" she asked.

"I guess so. I spent the last few years trying to stop my visions. I've never invited them in."

"If it looks like you're in danger, I'll break the trance . . . bring you out."

Opal nodded. She reclined back as far as the chair would go. *Napping position,* Wyatt called it. And, as her legs came up and her head went down, her body's blood flow changed, and she felt the weariness of the unbelievable day running off her like pounds and pounds of loosened sand.

She *was* exhausted.

Her arms tucked into the armrests.

"Slip my boots off, would you?" Opal said.

"Sure."

Vera unlaced the boots and slipped them off. She fetched a knitted afghan blanket from atop the cedar chest against the wall and draped it over Opal's legs and socked feet.

"How is that? Cozy?"

"I might end up falling asleep."

"You start snoring, I'll know."

Opal's eyelids drooped. She focused on the candle's flame. Her chin rested against her chest and she took deep breaths through her mouth and let them go slowly. Through the walls she could hear Wyatt and Adam opening their ladder and fitting it into the closet. She told herself not to listen to them. They would take care of each other. She needed to do this experiment for them.

Vera settled into her beanbag.

She was on the edge of Opal's field of vision. Silent now.

Around Opal domed the candlelight—low and gemlike, the flaming wick bent and danced around its pool of shimmering wax.

She closed her eyes.

After five minutes, she was on the brink of sleep.

Ten minutes later, she felt herself rousing. Impatient, irritated. It was any insomniac's nightly ritual. The more she tried to relax and think about having the dream vision, the less capable she felt of doing it. The altered state of consciousness evaded her, almost as if it were a willful opponent. An enemy.

Could Whiteside prevent her from seeing him on this other plane?

She didn't know the answer. It was all such new territory. She didn't have time to explore it at her leisure. Her muscles were tensing. She could feel her abdomen hardening with stress. And her jaw clamped down, tooth on tooth.

She opened her eyes wide.

Dark room. Candle. Vera sat a few feet away, staring at her intently.

"Is everything alright?"

Opal sighed. "We're wasting our time here. I think we'd be better off helping Wyatt and Adam in the attic. Actually doing something? Or maybe we should check the back entrance again and make sure . . ."

Opal started to get up. But Vera laid a hand on her leg.

"Try again," she said. "Empty your mind."

"It's too hard with what's happening. I can't tune it out."

"Think about, I don't know, a long grassy meadow where you're walking and walking, or maybe you're in a sailboat on a calm lake or floating in outer space. See your body going out into the unknown and being safe but searching."

Opal leaned her head against the padded cushion. She shut her eyes.

"Here I go. Countdown to takeoff: ten, nine, eight, seven . . . six . . ."

Vera took over for her with a silky whisper.

"Five . . . four . . . three . . ."

Opal's eyelids felt like black paint over her eyes.

I'm holding on to a rope and lowering myself into a cave.

Lower and lower. I feel the air cooling. Hear the trickle of moisture dripping down the walls. The air is clean, fresh. The light above is getting smaller and the cave is opening up like a cathedral underneath me. . . .

But seriously. This wasn't working. She wasn't in a cave or on her way to outer space or anywhere but here in her apartment in American Rapids.

"Two," Vera said.

Opal thought her voice sounded so small.

The wind keened.

She snuggled down into the plush recliner and drew the blanket tight around her. Vera's voice had gone from uttering soft syllables to absolute quiet. Opal couldn't even detect her breathing.

"Aren't you going to finish? You know, one and . . . blast off?"

Vera didn't answer.

"Vera?"

Opal bolted up like a blind woman startled by an intruder. But she wasn't blind. She opened her eyes.

Vera wasn't there. Had she run off on them again? That little sneaky—

The candle was blown out. A string of smoke tangled in mid-air. Even the lights peeking between the boards were extinguished. It would have been a perfect dark. Except the TV swirled with electrical snow. And out of the snow, a shape formed. Opal's fingers tightened on the blanket.

It was a head.

Filling the entire screen, it grew huge. A man's head, she decided, though it was difficult to tell much because of its condition.

Without ears or a nose, it was very oval.

Like an Egyptian king whose mummy she saw once in a museum.

It looked at her with a sly, knowing dirtiness.

It began to unwind its bandages.

CHAPTER 46

The trapdoor leading to the attic hung on upward swinging hinges like a submarine hatch. Wyatt lifted his arms over his head and pushed. Slow creaking. A sifting of gray dust sprinkled down. He felt it on his face; his eyes tearing up. He sneezed. Itchiness burrowed down under his collar. His scalp prickled. He gripped the unpainted wooden supports. Brown-eyed plywood knotholes stared at him. The area around them rotted with shadows. Chill air cascaded down like an invisible waterfall. He climbed through it.

The ladder wobbled slightly as he pivoted off into the rafters.

"Okay, come up," Wyatt called down to Adam. "You'd better . . ."

His voice trailed off.

Had something shifted away from him, or was it the unfamiliar pressure of his weight making the boards moan?

Below, Adam's Snake Light clicked on. The beam dazzled him.

Wyatt moved away from the opening.

The attic wasn't used for storage. It was dead space. There were no internal walls, only wooden beams—the exposed skeleton of the motel—and metal piping for electricity and ventilation. Instead of a floor, he saw the heads of two-by-sixes, row after row of candy-pink insulation. The external cinderblock walls. It smelled like a tomb. Despite the ladder, Wyatt had the strangest sensation of descent. The inversion made him dizzy. His eyes were adjusting to the mix of strong directed light and heavy shadows. An underground quality persisted.

It's the low ceiling that makes it feel like a cave.

That, and no windows.

Claustrophobia squirmed against his logic. Fear of entrapment lit circuitry in a jungle remnant of his brain. He planted his feet apart on a beam. His thigh muscles tensed as he balanced. Off to his left, the ladder wiggled and squeaked.

Adam's grinning face pierced the square hole. He braced his elbows on either side of the cutout and leveled his light.

"I can't seeeeee you. . . ."

Was it exertion that made him appear that way? Or pain? The blood smeared his face like ghoulish makeup. His eyes were wet. Did dust or emotion make his son cry? Was it Adam who scampered half-in, half-out of the hole?

Wyatt put up a hand to shield his blinking eyes.

"That's better," Adam said.

Wyatt turned away from the glare.

A bulky figure cloaked in white loomed in front of him.

Adam clicked off his light.

Wyatt startled. Nothing more than an involuntary jump back from the large irregular shape. But it was enough movement to disrupt his balance. One boot sole pressed down, one kicked air. Arms wheeling. He slammed his elbows out, wedging between two roof supports. His Maglite sliced a crazed arc across the rafters. Then it was gone from his hand. He fought for a handhold. Layers of dust, thick as fur, made slippery contact. Rough wood bit his palms.

What had he seen?

There and gone in an instant. So close.

He looked again. But the resealed darkness gave no answers.

Silence.

He waited for a deathblow.

Held his breath.

Waited.

The trip-hammer of his heart pounded. A strong forearm wrapped around his chest. He struggled as someone hauled him backward into the attic loft.

"Easy," said a whisper in his ear.

Then, "Keep quiet."

The arm released him. He wanted to dive back down through the trapdoor. To retreat. Escape. But he didn't. A faint glow to his left. There, in a nest of insulation beside the trapdoor, was his Maglite. He reached for it. Came up short by a few inches. He crawled to the edge of the trapdoor. Stretched and retrieved the light. Ready to strike with it. But a hand quickly covered his beam. The fingers cupping the lens turned blood-red.

It was his son's hand.

Adam guided the hooded Maglite, subtly illuminating the looming figure before them. Milky plastic sheeting, partially torn away from staples in the ceiling, hung like a man-sized spider-web. Or a white cloak.

Reflected light bounced back at them. Wyatt squinted. He saw the plastic shroud shiver as a frigid breeze passed behind it. His son thumbed the switch. The shroud disappeared. The dark pressed in. Phantoms leapt at Wyatt as his eyes fought to readjust. Adam whispered in his ear again.

"Somebody removed the vent panel. We may not be alone up here."

Down below, inside the closet, Ann-Margret circled and barked up into the echoing blackness. Adam closed the trapdoor. The barking muted.

Wyatt thought he heard Vera calling, but the sound was lost in the walls. The wind made a dry sharpening noise. The plastic sheet crackled. Even in this state of near blindness, he sensed it was trembling gently, less than six feet away. He said, "When I count to three, scan ahead with your light. I have the Glock. If you see anyone, shout location and stay down."

"Don't worry about me, Dad."

"One . . . two . . ."

Wyatt thought he heard shuffling. A soft grunt followed by a squeaky *crunch, crunch*. The rhythmic dragging sound of metal scraping against wood.

A chain?

"Three."

Lights on.

Crossing his wrists, Wyatt aimed the Glock and Maglite together. He swept from the peak of the roof to the narrowest corners. The plastic sheet blocked out a portion of his view. Dodging to one side, he shined around it. He found the gap where the vent panel was missing. His light cast a silhouette against the wall. When it reached the gap, the night sucked it in. He retracted the beam and scanned the attic once more, slowly this time, half-expecting an intruder to burst up from the insulation.

Nothing. No one.

He looked over his shoulder at his son, who tried to suppress his giggling.

The attic was empty.

CHAPTER 47

Vera's father told her when she was a little girl she used to sleep with her eyes open. Some nights he'd be down in the living room watching the end of the late-late movie, cops and robbers, a cowboy gunfight, or maybe the final innings of a White Sox game out on the West coast; he'd dial the TV sound low, a cold one in his hand and he'd sip, sip—sleep crouching over him like a shadow. His angel would glide up behind him and stand there, quiet as a whisper. He'd feel something in the room. Turn his head. And she'd scare the hell out of him. Sleepwalking with her eyes peeled wide, hair hanging damp in her face. White shins poking out under her nightdress, barefoot on the carpet—she'd sway as he took her gently by the shoulder. Those eyes looked out, not at him, but at the shrunken after-hours world, the moony glare of TV. She was looking, yes, but really seeing the dreams she was having. What dreams? He never knew. Leading her back to bed, he'd feel his heart galloping in his chest. A grown man spooked by his daughter. Like being in a room with a ghost, he said. The stories always made Vera laugh.

Now she understood.

Opal sat up. She clutched the afghan to her chest. Her mouth dropped. Lips quivered. Her gaze locked on the widescreen television. The power hadn't come on. The screen was dead gray, slippery-looking. Vera stared at it and saw their reflections and the tiny blade of the candle flame poised behind them.

"What do you want?" Opal asked.

She wasn't talking to Vera. She addressed the TV. She saw something there that terrified her. The apparition must have convinced her it wasn't caged inside this box of glass, plastic, and circuitry. It found a doorway. Yet she was standing up to it, using every ounce of courage to hold her ground.

And because she *couldn't* see it, Vera felt terrified, too. She lifted her Bobcat from where Opal had set it on a bookshelf. She tucked the pistol inside her jeans at the small of her back; the metal sent a chill up her spine.

"We won't give it to you," Opal said.

The stone, Vera thought.

The spirit in the television wanted them to fork over the stone.

She watched Opal's reactions, could tell that Opal was listening carefully to every word the spirit said. Vera tried hard to hear it. But that was impossible, she realized. Nothing in this room was making any noise. It would be like eavesdropping on someone else's nightmare. Still she couldn't help but strain to pick up any shred of sound. The silence throbbed in her ears.

"Don't hurt him," Opal said. Then quickly she added, "I don't want to see. I won't look. If you show me, I won't . . ."

Opal's voice caught in her throat. She lied. Whether she wanted to or not, she *had* to look. She covered her mouth with her hands. She bit down on the knuckle of her middle finger; drew blood. She rocked back and forth in her seat. A moan started in her lungs and moved into her head, getting louder and higher, higher and louder, until it became like the shriek of a drill.

"No, no, no, n*ooooooooooo* . . ."

Vera had to stop this.

Loud knock on the wall. Scraping on the other side, curved from high to low; vibrations traveled as something clattered to the floor. Vera spun around. The disturbance came from the bedroom closet where Adam and Wyatt were. The ladder had fallen. Annie barked. Wood creaked in the attic.

Were Adam and Wyatt rushing back down?

Or were the Pitch breaking inside?

"Stop it!" Opal yelled. "Stop! Stop! You can take the stone. I don't care what happens but stop . . ."

Opal collapsed onto the floor. She was weeping, her arms outstretched to the blank glass screen. She slapped at the television. She got to her feet and grabbed the top of the widescreen in an effort to topple it.

Vera rushed to shake her awake when she heard her mumbling— hoarse, jagged, in a voice of utter defeat. "Take her. She's the one who stole the stone. We didn't know. We only tried to protect ourselves. She's the one you want."

She's talking about me. Vera wanted to touch her, to bring her back. Yet her hand paused in the air as she listened.

"Kill her," Opal said.

"Don't say that!" Vera screamed. "Wake up! Don't tell them that!"

She shook Opal as hard as she could.

"Kill her! Kill her!"

CHAPTER 48

Wyatt faced the gap left by the missing panel and heard the sounds of the Pitch savagery carrying on outside—he approached with caution. Glock first, finger snug on the trigger. Stepping carefully, finding the joists hidden between pink rolls of fiberglass. A false step would put him through the drywall ceiling and into the apartment. He ripped down the plastic hanging from the underside of the roof. It was up there to keep drafts from seeping into the living area. Someone had torn it loose. Left it drooping like shed skin. Wyatt figured the intruder didn't have the forethought to bring a light. So he had walked along these same joists, touching the roof, hand over hand, to keep from bumping his head. Then, probably, he made a misstep. Wound up clawing at the plastic to keep from falling, and it worked. Wyatt knew the plastic shouldn't be there and the vent cover should. Instead, he had this new window in his attic.

Adam had stopped giggling. Had he ever been? Wyatt couldn't say.

The snow was letting up. Maybe it was only a lull. Or a wind shift. The apartment reached one story higher than the motel rooms. The rooftop was split-level. There was the roof above the attic, which was unreachable in this weather, and the roof below, that ran the length of the motel and was wider than the apartment. They had a view of half of it. Moonlight transformed the lower rooftop into molten silver. Lightning cracked a fault line in the horizon. Thunder roared. The *tick-tick* of freezing rain began hitting the motel siding, an incessant rattle that set Wyatt's teeth on edge. Icy droplets flew past the opening. Soon it would be too slick to venture out for a look-see.

Wyatt paused.

Two clumps of dirty gray-black snow rested just inside the attic. Scrapings. After the intruder broke inside, he cleaned his boots off.

Wyatt crept closer.

Footprints in the rooftop snow. One man. In and out. He was long-limbed. The trail led from the rain gutter, stopped under the vent, then curved out of sight. A second set of markings marred the snow. Thin, serpentine. He'd been dragging something behind him. Wyatt couldn't decide what it was. Rope?

Adam leaned toward the opening. "I saw this guy in the lot before. He had a steel hook on a chain."

Wyatt craned for a better angle.

"Look. There's the vent cover," Adam said, pointing. "See the hole in it?"

It made sense. So where did the Hook Man go? The retreating footprints rounded the corner of the apartment level. Did he jump off? Or was he at the other end of the apartment prying his way inside?

Wyatt poked his head out.

Icicles and moonlight. Clouds harassed the moon. The sheen vanished from the snow. The freezing rain increased its tempo.

"I'm going to drop down and take a look," Wyatt said.

Adam chewed his lips.

Wyatt said, "I'll come back. Five minutes."

"Not if he finds you first, you won't."

Wyatt zipped the Glock into his front pocket and started lowering himself through the open vent.

Adam grabbed his hand.

"Five minutes," Wyatt said.

Then he let himself drop.

CHAPTER 49

Wyatt fell into a crouch and, without rising to his full height, advanced to the corner of the apartment edifice. His eyes flicked from the footprints to the space immediately ahead of him, waiting for the Hook Man to appear, a point of steel glinting in the night. Ice pellets pattered against his chest. The rain was falling harder, glazing the rooftop and all of American Rapids.

Trapping them in an ice rink.

The snow crust snapped into shards underfoot. Soon the ice layer would be thick enough to send him sliding and tumbling. Bracing his gun hand, he swung around the corner. Ready to fire at anything.

The footprints loped away, disappearing into the darkness on the other side of the motel. Wyatt changed direction. He lay on his belly and scooted over to the roof's edge.

It was worse than he imagined.

A river of firelight spilled onto the highway.

Fire and ice.

He saw the Pitch parading from the Totem Lodge. Silhouettes, a small army of them, materialized out of the gloom. Their stark homemade weaponry triggered a primal fear—hunting knives mounted on wooden handles, circular saw discs welded to barbells, hedge shears repurposed for battle, one ambitious straggler even duct-taped his fists around two lawn-mower blades.

Nearest the motel was a teen in a red ski mask. Scrawny, androgynous. Identified as male only because he was shirtless; dressed in a pair of jeans and, hanging off his shoulders, a woman's floral robe. The back of the robe was shredded. Blood-soaked. The kid was wearing flip-flops, swinging a Worth baseball bat studded with sixteen-penny nails, fashioned into a mace. He slammed it into the tire of a car abandoned in the highway, its doors hanging open, drag marks and bloodstains leading around the trunk and off to . . .

Wyatt couldn't tell where.

There was an explosive hiss. The front end of the car kneeled. All the vehicles parked in the vicinity had flats: the kid's work. He planted a flip-flop on the fender and wrenched the bat up and down until the nails tore loose. His head bobbed to unheard music. He began to dance. Unfazed by the rain. Gyrating in ecstasy, he capered, oblivious to Wyatt observing from a few feet above.

Wyatt backed away.

Zigzagging from end to end along the rooftop, he scouted. When the darkness clotting around him felt thick enough—though never completely safe—he lifted up on his knees, his feet, and then tiptoes, to peer over the town.

Hopelessness struck a blow in the pit of his stomach.

There were too many of them. A hundred or more, he estimated by their lantern clusters and the amount of mayhem. Surprise gave them every advantage. Surprise and viciousness. Attacking on Christmas Eve, the Pitch caught the town with its guard down. They'd killed the police and firemen. Cut off contact with the world at large. Confusion reigned. The blaze spreading out from the demolished gas station was their greatest ally. That and the night.

In the morning things would change.

Their initial energies spent, the Pitch would be getting tired. They had no reinforcements coming. Wyatt was almost certain of that. This operation was quick and crazed. By morning light, the citizens would move away from their defenses, climbing out of their bunkers with their own mad assortment of fighting tools. Plenty of hunters lived in town. And once they emerged from their homes, they'd mobilize. Taking back their turf. Well-armed state police and local lawmen from the vicinity would arrive on the scene, too.

The roads would open.

Chaos would end.

If they could hold out until then . . .

How much of American Rapids would be standing?

What was the purpose of destroying the town?

Except for the progress of the fires, the most intense destruction was taking place within sight of the motel. The logic of it became immediately apparent to Wyatt. They didn't plan to destroy the whole town. It was, in its own sickeningly violent way, a performance. The Pitch didn't care if American Rapids stood or fell by morning. Their goal was singular: to possess the stone. The town was collateral damage. A staging area for psychological warfare aimed at the audience inside the Rendezvous. Max told them the Pitch believed they could not take the stone directly. It had to be procured by a surrogate thief, or *given over to them freely.* Wyatt understood now.

They're hoping to break us.

Red emergency lights flashed below. They weren't the tricolored light bars used by the PD. Wyatt wondered if a lone law enforcement vehicle had crossed the border from Canada, someone off-duty who was passing through and, by chance, found Hell. The flickering moved slowly. Vivid scarlet rays stabbed between houses. They were about to merge with the highway. Even before he saw their source, Wyatt felt a terrible sinking in his belly and for the first time since he lowered himself outside, he shivered uncontrollably.

The old ambulance turned the corner.

A scratchy loudspeaker voice called out.

"No more need to die. What we ask for is easy. Give us the stone. We will go away. No more need to die. . . ."

The announcement repeated.

In front of the motel, the ambulance stopped.

Wyatt flattened himself.

The microphone on the loudspeaker clicked open. A rhythmic rushing of air filled the channel like surf rolling up a beach. In his mind's eye, Wyatt saw the oily iridescent waves. He smelled the night's dead haul of the sea and the ripe putrid tang of a garbage dump. He swore he heard the rubber-on-glass cries of seagulls. Their hungry insistence swooped down on him, the sharp beaks drawing closer and closer as if he were a bit of meat quivering inside a cracked, immobile shell.

It's someone breathing, he realized. *The ambulance talker knows I'm up here. It's Whiteside. He's laughing at us.*

Wyatt resisted the desire to stand up and empty the Glock into the ambulance. He sensed that was exactly what Whiteside wanted him to do. To lose control. To give in to his anger and frustration and show himself.

He refused.

Adam whispered through the chattering rain.

"I can't see you. Are you there?"

Wyatt didn't want to answer despite the impossibility of anyone inside the ambulance hearing him. He had the terrible sense that Adam was the Pitch's puppet. If he could see Wyatt, then the Pitch could, too. They would use him, pull his strings, and control him. And there was nothing Wyatt could do to stop them. A hot wave of shame washed over him. Whiteside's presence was as real as any hunter's, waiting for him to move so he could proceed to the kill.

Adam leaned out of the vent hole.

Wyatt rolled onto his side. He waved Adam back inside.

Adam hesitated for a moment then retreated into the shadows.

When Wyatt returned his attention to the highway, he saw the ambulance pulling away. The parade of silhouettes from the Totem parted, allowing the vehicle to pass. They bowed their heads and touched their hands to the ambulance body. The red lights flashed over them. The bronze glow of the fires continued. It was as though the town were now made of flames, the fuel to keep them burning, and nothing else.

Wyatt picked his way carefully over the rooftop.

He slipped and fell to his knees. The hard landing sent pain up his thighs.

He crawled until he was under the attic opening.

Adam's arm reached down to him. They locked hands. Wyatt's boots scraped along the motel siding. He heard Adam straining to hoist him higher. Wyatt tapped his free hand along the wall. He found the edge of the gap. His fingers clawed at the threshold and he maneuvered himself into the hole. Iciness trickled along the naked skin at the back of his neck. He startled, thinking of the Hook Man. And he almost teetered backward out the gap.

An icicle fell from the peak of the eaves above him.

The cold spike of it broke across his head.

He heard a glassy clinking.

A thicker rattle followed.

More icicles dropped.

A windy slicing . . .

The sound moved left to right. It wasn't falling ice.

Wyatt looked into Adam's eyes and saw terror. Adam stared at a spot behind and above Wyatt's head. Wyatt was doing all he could to push forward into the attic. But he couldn't move fast enough.

He felt a rough tug. It was taking him backward.

Next came the tightening, like a muscle spasm in his shoulder.

Finally, the pain seared through him. He never felt the hook penetrate. Only now it grabbed him from a place inside. Lodging. Twisting.

He looked down at his chest. He expected to see the bloody steel tip poking through. He didn't see anything but the zipper of his jacket.

He craned his head back to look up toward the eaves.

The taut chain stopped him, frigid links brushed his ear. Another tug. Stronger. The man on the attic rooftop grunted with satisfaction.

Pain kicked loose every thought. Wyatt fell out of the gap. The hook was buried deep under his left arm. He was suspended there.

Swaying.

The hook dug into bone.

Wyatt screamed.

His good arm flailed out at his side. Flapping absurdly as the Hook Man anchored his chain around a chimney pipe and raised him up.

One foot. Two.

Three.

Wyatt looked down at Adam in the cutout. Adam leaned, reached, groping for his legs. He wrapped his arms around Wyatt's ankles. Hugged them.

"No, no . . . please don't take him."

The steady pulling from above drove the hook deeper. Wyatt didn't want to look at it now. He was too afraid. He saw the snow underneath the attic opening turning liquid black and knew that it was his blood. He snatched at the chain. His free arm wouldn't stretch far enough. Pain stole his breath.

The chain creaked. Chunks of snow rafted off the roof above. Wyatt was lifted higher against his will, the hook point gnawing, an excruciating torment; his left arm slowly being ripped from its socket. Agony exploded across his body. He trembled uncontrollably. Red-black spots filled his vision.

"Let go," he said to Adam.

Adam shook his head.

"You have to . . . he's killing me."

Adam released him.

The chain moved quickly.

In a few seconds, his father was gone.

CHAPTER 50

The freezing rain stopped as if someone had switched it off. Clouds rent apart. Max looked for stars in a patch of blackest sky. Void. Smoke tatters closed the gap, hiding the heavens once more. But he knew what was there above him—a nothingness shaped like a great jet eyeball.

To his left, a midnight cellblock concealed its threats.

The motel.

His low chuckle escaped at the name painted on a sign in the dark.

THE RENDEZVOUS . . . WHERE VISITORS ARE ALWAYS WELCOME!

He couldn't trust his eyes.

He trudged through the snowy lot. A block of ice on wheels was parked in the rear. *That's my camper.* It phosphoresced greenly as if it were made of glow-in-the-dark plastic. He was drawn to it, first his eyes, then his footsteps. *I have to get inside the camper.* The marauders hadn't touched it. Why not? The tires were full, half buried but full. Snow gathered like the sands of time. He unlocked the driver's door. Ice crackled as he broke the shell. He climbed in.

Quiet as a crypt.

He drummed his hands on the steering wheel. What now?

He watched as his hands took a set of keys from his pocket. *I'm not doing that,* he thought, amazed. In an absolute sense, of course, he was doing it. What he meant was, *I may be doing it alright, I'm just not willing it.* He tried to stop his fingers from moving around and found he couldn't. It wasn't as if he couldn't feel them. He could. The nerves were working fine—so, too, the muscles, tendons, and bones. The mechanics of him were being set in motion. But his conscious thoughts weren't at the controls.

The fingers inserted the correct key into the ignition.

They didn't start the motor. Instead, they fluttered above the dashboard. Rising upward, afloat. Like a schoolboy nervous to ask his question.

Waiting for the next command.

He had to think.

I know I'm not leaving this place. I'm going inside the Rendezvous. I have to make them believe me, convince them to follow me. But what is it I have to tell them and why . . . ?

The fingers were moving again.

They turned the key.

His foot pressed the gas pedal. The motor coughed and came to life, chugging, shaking. He gave her a little more gas. *His foot* did. She settled down.

He put the camper in gear, tried to rock her out of her icy boots. The tires spun. They sounded like sawmill blades whirring. He smelled burned rubber.

"C'mon, c'mon . . ."

Into reverse. Then first gear. Reverse. Drive forward. Find pavement.

Yes. That's it. She bumped clear of her rut.

He eased her into the lot, feeling proud. The compacted snow squeaked.

Where to?

Idling outside the motel lobby door, he stared in at the locked apartment door behind the counter. He squinted.

At the Fuel 'N Snacks across the highway, a police cruiser's gas tank exploded.

A plume of fire, tall as a lodgepole pine, lit the sky.

Peering inside the office, Max saw spikes poking through the drywall around the doorway. Nails. *They're barricaded in.*

He pulled the front end around and positioned the VW camper perpendicular to the glassed entrance. Straight ahead of him was the highway. He used the side-view mirrors to line the camper up. Backing until his trailer hitch nudged the doors. Satisfied, he pulled forward allowing for the necessary space to run up, building the momentum he'd need. If the gas tank on the camper ignited, then he'd fry . . .

Act. Don't think. That was the message he heard in his head. In taking action, he thought less about what he was doing. Forget why.

He became preoccupied with simple execution.

He meant to do this thing right.

Reverse.

His foot clamped down on the brake. He took a deep breath. Checked his seat belt. In his mirrors, he found the glass doors and behind them the apartment entry. *Okay, let's do it.*

He lifted his foot off the brake and stomped on the gas.

No trouble finding traction this time. His maneuvering had eaten away a path. The camper lurched backward. He watched the glass doors getting bigger. Then he saw them webbed with whitish cracks. But only for an instant because the glass shattered, flying, and the rear end of the camper lifted, dropped, the counter buckled in two; the motel enveloped his RV, the rooftop peeling off like a can of kippers, ceiling tiles and wires falling, the drawers opening in his tiny kitchenette and dumping knives, forks, spoons, and playing cards, ballpoint pens, a Ziploc bag of chalk, scraps of paper, campsite brochures, maps, bins of food tossed, his spare clothes jumped out of the closet; Max gazed into the mirrors, distracted for a microsecond by his own bloodshot eyes— *who am I?*—with a final jolt, the apartment door smashed to splinters.

He jammed on the brake.

He was standing outside the camper. Disoriented. His forehead hurt. He touched it and his fingertips came away tacky with blood.

Must've hit my head on the steering wheel.

He limped to the rear of the camper. The hole caved into the wall. He could see carpeted stairs. He leaned into the hole.

"Vera! Opal! Guys! It's Max!"

The camper's motor was still running. Exhaust fumes filled the lobby. His eyes burned. He felt around the small of his back for the Ruger. It was there.

"Can you hear me?" he shouted.

Voices? Were people talking upstairs?

CHAPTER 51

Vera slapped Opal across the face. The blow knocked the petite older woman backward into the recliner. Vera climbed on top, raised her fists, ready to do some real damage. Opal's insistent urging—*Kill her! Kill her!*—had pushed her beyond her limits. Yes, she'd run over the crossbow attacker on the snowmobile. He was probably dead, certainly gravely wounded; but that was her car crashing into him, not her flesh and bone. She never even saw his face. He was more an abstract threat than a human being. Here was someone who had saved her life and Vera looked down at Opal and wanted to hurt her. Waves of guilt, shame, and fear converged. *I'm no better than Chan.* Trying to resist the riptide of emotions and not let them drag her out to sea, she stumbled dizzily off Opal, banged her shoulder into the vending machine standing sentinel in the corner; her knees gave out. She hugged herself and slid to the carpet.

The candle on the TV tray was still burning.

Opal blinked at the weaving flame. The trance fog burned away. She seemed to be fighting with its afterimages. Ghosts in the room—she avoided them. She threw off the afghan.

Vera didn't want to look at her.

How could she?

Opal perched on the arm of the recliner. Coldness crept between them. But it had little to do with temperature. Vera peeked between strands of hair. She caught sight of Opal's faraway eyes. A blank expression of grief hung there. Were scenes from the vision scorched into her retinas? What had she seen?

Vera lifted her head. Her voice was almost imperceptible.

"You back with us?"

Opal nodded. "What happened? Did I—?"

"You said horrible things. Vile, horrible things . . ."

"Whiteside talked to me. He looked . . . spindly, his skin, mouth . . . it was like seeing a spider jump out of its hole."

"He appeared inside the television?"

Nodding, Opal said, "I guess you could tell from the way I reacted. I must have been looking at it."

"And that's when you bargained with him?"

Opal scowled. "He asked for the stone. I said no. He showed me the punishment for not cooperating with his wishes. We didn't exactly negotiate."

"You told him to murder me."

"What are you talking about? I never said that."

"I know what I heard. I'm not the liar here. You said everything was my fault. So you must believe that. I wish I could leave this place. But I can't. If you know what's good for you, you'll stay away from me."

"Vera, don't you see? He put words in my mouth to divide us—"

The apartment shook.

CHAPTER 52

A boom echoed in their ears. A cacophony of cracking wood, pulverized drywall boards, harsh metal shrieks. In the silence that followed came the intermittent jangle of falling glass and the steady thrum of machinery—an engine running.

"It's them," Vera said.

"Quiet . . . I think someone's calling," Opal said.

"Can you hear me?"

Opal took the flashlight from her pocket. She aimed it into the kitchen.

Ann-Margret barked at the hall door. She danced, tail wagging, thumping madly on the floor. She barked and whined. Her nails scratched the door.

Footsteps mounted the stairs.

The dog stuck her nose under the door. Huffing and blowing. Her whine growing shriller, she pawed the carpet.

"I'm coming up. Don't shoot." The footsteps quickened. "Annie, girl, oh, I missed you, too."

More footsteps. Louder.

"It's Max," Vera said. She was on her feet again. She stood behind Opal, her chest pressing into Opal's back. She urged her forward. "Let him in."

"Wait."

"Why? We know who it is."

"We should wait."

The knob on the hall door turned.

Vera stepped around Opal. "I'm going . . ."

The door opened slowly. Bony white fingers petted Ann-Margret's head.

"There's my girl. Max isn't going to leave without his Annie."

Vera rushed to the muddy shadow emerging at the top of the stairs.

Opal shined her light on Max.

Vera stopped.

His eyes were bruised. He smiled at them. Dried blood, crusted in the corners of his mouth. His tongue filled the gap where his front teeth should've been.

Vera held his arm.

"What did they do to you?"

Max looked confused. He touched his face with his fingers. He'd forgotten. How had he forgotten . . . ?

A fresh rivulet of blood ran from his hairline.

"I hit my head . . . steering wheel . . . I came to make . . . to rescue you."

He swayed. He didn't seem to know quite where he was.

Or why he'd come.

Opal watched from the den.

Ann-Margret licked Max's face. He rubbed her sides. Then he was sobbing as he buried his face into her furry bronze neck.

"Where were you?" Opal asked.

Max wiped away the fresh blood with his sleeve. "They grabbed me when I went outside for my cigar . . . I shot two of the bastards dead but another one hit me from behind . . . listen, we have to go. Now. The Pitch don't have control of the town yet. We can get out in the RV. There's no time to talk."

"Wyatt and Adam went on the roof. I'm not going anywhere until they come down," Opal said. She hadn't moved any closer.

"I think we should leave," Vera said.

Max said, "Every second we wait is wasted. We'll get out and go for help. Over the border bridge, that's the best way. Wyatt can take care—"

"No," Opal said.

Vera stood beside Max. "Hey, she can stay if she wants. I'm going with you and Annie." Her fingers pulled the edge of the door, opened it wider.

Max considered it. "Sure, that'll work. We'll take the stone and draw them away from the motel . . ."

"Take the stone?" Opal asked.

"It's in the oven," Vera said. "I'll get it."

Max shrugged a strap off his shoulder. He passed a weathered, saddle-brown leather satchel to Vera. "Here. Put it inside this."

"You're not taking the stone." Opal came nearer.

"I'm afraid it's the only choice," Max said.

Vera opened the oven, took the stone out, and dropped it inside the satchel. She cinched the buckles and looped the strap over her head. The strap lay taut between her breasts.

"All set," she said.

Fumes from the camper's tailpipe drifted into the apartment. The gasoline smell made Opal sick to her stomach. She wasn't going to allow them to leave with the stone. The Pitch couldn't take it from the apartment. A nonbeliever had to give it freely or steal it. Without the stone they had no protection.

"You're not taking it!"

Max aimed the revolver at her.

"Please don't. If you won't join us, then we have no choice. The stone can't stay here. We can't, either."

"He's right."

Adam materialized from his bedroom doorway. The darkness behind him stitched itself together. "It isn't safe here. We have to leave with the stone."

Opal watched the dark for signs of Wyatt.

"See? Adam knows what's right. The boy knows!" Max lowered the barrel of the revolver to the floor. "Time's against us. We've got to move."

"Where's your father?" Opal asked.

Adam walked to the head of the stairs and pulled the door back. He nodded in the direction of the camper. Max went down the stairs first. Vera followed. The dog chased after them. Adam put his arm around Opal and steered her to the threshold.

She resisted.

"Mom, please . . ."

"What happened on the roof? Where's Wyatt?"

Opal stared into her son's eyes. He said nothing.

Then he looked away.

She struck his chest with her fists.

"Adam? Oh my God . . . where is your *father!*"

CHAPTER 53

Henry pulled on the chain. He peered over the edge of the roof. Wyatt was almost to the top. He'd stopped struggling. Passed out or in shock; it didn't matter. He was dead weight but easier to handle this way. Henry pulled.

When Wyatt was under the eave, Henry squatted and seized him by the collar. He lifted his old friend up onto the slanted rooftop. He supposed he could throw him over the side. Bash his body on the icy parking lot below.

He'd shoot him in the head first with Eppers's Glock.

To be sure there were no mistakes this time.

No survivors.

Henry withdrew the hook from Wyatt's armpit. The chain coil glinted in the snow; he added the hook to it. *Clang.* Wet red steel steamed. He thought he heard Wyatt moan. But the wind was strong. And his ears were frostbitten. He grabbed Wyatt by the ankles and dragged him to the front of the motel. He'd throw him from here. Then he was finished. He could eat the Glock. It would end.

That was all he wanted.

He wondered what would be next.

Hell or nothing?

He was hoping for nothing.

His frozen grasp on Wyatt's ankles released. *I'll shoot him in the eyes. One, two. Over and done with.* He slipped the Glock from his pants, turned.

The hook caught him under the jaw.

Knocked him off balance. And when he righted himself, he choked on blood, bit down and couldn't, because the hook wedged between his teeth. He grunted. Where was Wyatt? Gone . . .

Not gone.

Looping the chain around his throat and Henry fallen to his knees tried reaching back but his tight raincoat pulled tighter and he raised the Glock fired *fired* fired it, no use, into the air shooting the moon the stars . . .

. . . the barrel of a gun pressed into his spine . . . but how? . . . he still saw the Glock swimming in his hand the bark of it drowned out by . . . the links squeezing on his neck the balloon of blood about to burst *bursting* in his head . . .

Blood running from his mouth.

Exploded from his chest.

And he didn't care. He didn't care about Whiteside or the Pitch or Jesse. Dead. Because this was what he wanted. This.

No more than this.

Wyatt laid Henry facedown in the snow. His lungs refilled, emptied. Go slow. Think. His gun hand trembled. Don't faint. Got to get off the roof. Stop the bleeding. He clamped his arm down and stifled a shout. Think.

CHAPTER 54

From the back of the ambulance issued a stream of mumbles and the grainy rustle of what constituted laughter. A thought wormed through a borehole into Pinroth's submissive mind. He knew it was not his own. He welcomed the alien presence, recognized it as his Master's telepathic communiqué. They must begin the final preparations. The delivery of the stone was on its way; their journey had, after decades, culminated. Pinroth understood. He did not show it—his visage remained blank as a slab—but he was experiencing joy.

The son of his Master appeared feverish with anticipation. A stethoscope pinched at the younger Whiteside's neck. His fingers clutched emptied blood bags as though he were attempting to squeeze out their very last drops. His pale sweaty face filled the rearview mirror.

"Our time has arrived, Pinroth. Though I'm worried he isn't strong enough to carry it out. Heartbeat's erratic. Blood pressure dropping."

"He's always been the strongest among us," Pinroth said.

"Agreed, agreed."

Distracted, the son refitted the eartips of his stethoscope and pumped the black rubber bulb of the blood pressure cuff attached to his father's branchlike upper arm. Shaking his head as the needle bounced feebly inside its gauge.

"I'll take us back to the lodge now?" Pinroth knew the answer. He'd been told what to do. Nothing could stop him once the Master had commanded. But the Master's son needed to feel in control of the smallest matters. The Master had warned Pinroth of this weakness and how, if mishandled, the servant son could turn poisonous against them. The antidote was acquiescence—the illusion of servitude. If the antidote failed . . . without removing his eyes from the road, Pinroth reached into his jacket and closed his cool grip around the Luger.

"Yes. I want him in a bed. Stationary. He needs to be hooked to the monitors. To lose him at this stage is not an option." The black goggles slipped crookedly on the junior Whiteside's nose. He pressed his face downward and whispered to the unseen elder on the stretcher. "Your lust for Death won't fuck me over. I'll make certain you give me my due."

Pinroth gritted his teeth. Outside the ambulance, filling the road, the Pitch were bowing and pushing past each other to see into the windows, to graze their fingers along the slow-gliding chassis.

A latex-gloved finger pointed at Pinroth in the mirror. "Get us back there in one piece, or I'll have you gutted like a carp. They'll drag your entrails out on a rope if I tell them. Speedy now, run over bodies if you have to. Do it."

"As you say," Pinroth answered.

He released the pistol and switched on the siren.

Its call was a shout of elation. The Pitch would hear and know their Master's chariot thundered to the finish line. The crowd parted.

Pinroth glanced into the rearview mirror. The servant son bent over the bundled figure on the stretcher. Pinroth did not make it a habit to anticipate commands. This was not his nature. He did not make wishes, either. Though a single wish tempted him, and in his fantasy of its fulfillment, the Luger jumped and the back of Young Whiteside's head sprayed a fine dark mist.

Pinroth obeyed but one Master.

CHAPTER 55

The wreckage of the lobby took them by surprise. They couldn't help gawking as they piled into the damaged VW. The camper's top had sheared off and the rear end was crushed, leaving a tight space inside. Cracks veined the windows. A strong odor of gasoline tainted the air. Max insisted it was fumes and the Westy would run and get them where they needed to go.

"Where are we going?" Vera asked.

"Away from here . . . you have the stone?"

She patted the satchel. Ann-Margret was sandwiched between her legs. Max reached over to scratch the setter's head, as if for luck. Adam tried to clear a seat for his mother. He passed a Ziploc bag of chalk to Max.

"Want these up front?"

Max grabbed the bag and tossed it on the dash.

Opal gazed backward over her shoulder at the vacant stairs. Her eyes glistened, though she wasn't crying. That worried Adam. Cheeks gaunt, she took on the pallor of wet clay. She moved like a person submerged. Her fingers felt wooden inside Adam's hand. He feared she was slipping into shock.

A slender figure in a red ski mask lurked at the far end of the lobby. He sprung up, holding a club of nails, the end of the club engulfed in flames. His torch ignited the lobby couch, the wide-backed chairs, and the curtains.

"Close your eyes," Adam told his mother.

She didn't. Her mouth gaped in horror.

Their motel. Destroyed. Their home. Invaded.

Wyatt gone.

How could it all happen in a night?

A ceiling of filthy smoke lowered. Heat from the roasting furniture penetrated the camper, palpable, suffocating.

"Get us out of here," Vera said.

Max released the brake. They rolled into the lot.

Adam glanced through the demolished doors. The red-masked intruder climbed into the apartment access, ducking under a pair of shattered two-by-fours. Fire writhed like a serpent at the end of his club. He ascended the stairs nimbly, tapping the steps, scorching the carpet, dragging the tip of his club along the walls. Paint bubbled, charred.

Adam expected others would attack the camper. They'd rush the vehicle from every direction at once. Defeated by numbers. It would be over soon. He didn't even have a gun.

But that didn't happen.

The town looked desolate.

A siren wailed.

Then abruptly fell silent.

As they slid into the unplowed drive, he noticed the lights were back on inside the motel. Lamps blazed at every window. Only it was the fire. The boards they'd hammered over the windows were burning. Smoke boiled out from under the eaves.

Max turned onto the highway.

Most of the Pitch had disappeared. Where had they gone?

From the side view of the motel, Adam saw the torch pinwheeling out of the attic vent. Next came the red-masked arsonist. He hit the snow and seized his still fiery club before skidding off the roof and out of sight.

Adam wasn't watching him anymore.

He saw the chain.

A body swayed from it. A man's body, stripped down to only

underwear, was hanging from the peak of the roof. Firelight and shadow played over the stained flesh—darker because of all the blood. Smoke seeped from every cranny of the building. He lost sight of him. The wind gusted and back he came: a smudged face turned aside as if in embarrassment, neck broken, clearly dead.

Dad?

It had to be.

The Hook Man killed him.

He'd left him hanging there for everyone to see. Adam raged. Death didn't satisfy the Pitch. They needed desecration. To take what was good and shit on it. Defilement. There was no reason. No balance. That's what made it worse. The absence of logic, the insanity. Evil for evil's sake.

Killing his father over a rock? Or was it what Max said?

Did Vera carry a compass to Hell inside her satchel?

Opal screamed.

She was looking up there. Following her son's attention, through the gauze of blowing flakes, the coal dark night, she'd seen it, too: the hanging corpse. Beneath it—columns of smoke, a rising red dome—the motel reduced to a roaring funeral pyre.

Adam yelled at Max and slammed the back of his seat.

"Drive! Drive!"

CHAPTER 56

Headlights.

The road was a black-and-white photograph, mottled at the corners, streaked with lines, everything fuzzy. Falling snow made the whole picture dissolve, erasing it inch by inch, until all was lost inside a white inferno. If they drove off the edge of the world, it wouldn't surprise her.

Vera concentrated on what lay ahead.

She didn't react to Opal's scream or Adam's panic-laced cries.

If I don't look back, then I won't see it.

Whatever's there, whatever might be coming—I won't know until it's too late, and then—well, it'll be too late.

She hugged the satchel without thinking. It wasn't heavy or hard. *It's almost like a baby in a sling,* she thought. *I have to protect the baby. I have to make certain the baby gets home safely. Max will take us there.*

Adam kicked at the driver's seat. He shouted in Max's right ear.

"You're heading the wrong way!"

"Where would you like me to go?"

"Off this highway . . . look for a farm road. If we can't get out of town, maybe we can find a better place to fight them."

"All the roads are blocked," Max said.

"How can you know that?"

Blood wept from Max's head wound. He swiped at it with his knuckles but only managed to smear a rouge crescent on his cheek. He squinted at the road. They were crawling along. Vera checked the speedometer.

Five miles per hour.

"Maybe you should jump out," Max said.

"What are you talking about?" Adam asked, growing louder, exasperated.

"You and your mom take a hike. Find a place to hide. The dawn is coming. A new day rising. It's almost over. Vera and I can handle the rest. We'll bring the stone in."

"Pull over. I'm driving."

"It doesn't matter who drives. Nothing matters," Max said.

Adam started climbing into the front. Something he saw through the windshield made him pause. In the obscurity, Vera detected bulky shadows. Tall barriers had been installed along both sides of the highway.

"I don't remember seeing those before," Vera whispered.

The headlights perforated the wall of snow. The barriers were moving.

"They're men," Opal said. "He's bringing us to the Totem Motor Lodge. Whiteside's waiting. He's been there all along. Max is delivering us to him."

The Pitch appeared out of the murk. Standing shoulder to shoulder, they formed a living chute that curved off to the right, dipping into a low spot in the landscape. Vera couldn't see any faces. Hats, upturned collars, blankness. Then she realized they were facing away with their backs to them.

A larger form towered over the camper.

Vera looked up through the hole in the roof.

The totem pole.

Gargoyle faces stacked up. The top head stuck out its beak. Sharp-edged, curved like a knife. Tapered fangs crowded the mouth.

Icicles. They're only icicles.

A sudden terror seized her. She was convinced that the second

- 276 -

they drove underneath the beak, it would strike, plucking her out of her seat.

They had no choice. The only route led between the rows of men.

It's just wood. The faces aren't real.

Why was she imagining them suddenly animated? The carved tree lips mouthing words in silent unison. Glittering eyes, sentient, malevolent. No, that wasn't possible. The men must have put glass in them. Or it was ice like the fangs. That sparkling had to be a reflection of their headlights. That was it.

Wasn't it?

She shut her eyes.

Beneath the beak was exhaled heat. She gagged on the stench.

Bird shit and fish guts.

Breathe through your mouth.

A coppery saltiness coated her tongue.

She startled. The satchel—something inside it shifted around like an animal growing suddenly alert.

The camper drawing forward: a toy pulled on a string.

As they descended through the turn, the lodge came into view. Lanterns suspended from upraised hands. Tiki torches liberated from the lodge's storeroom were rammed in the snow. The log structure bathed in firelight.

Outside the main entrance, the ambulance sat parked; its rear door hung wide open. The vehicle was empty. They'd left it in a hurry; the keys were still in the ignition. Interior lamps shined a cobalt wedge into the lot, illuminating the lodge entry. Max steered toward it.

"We aren't going in there," Adam said.

"We have to," Opal said. "It's the only way."

Max stopped the camper. He put the emergency brake on. "Listen to your mother. She's a smart lady."

Vera held up the satchel.

"If we give it to them, will they let us go?"

Max didn't answer. He didn't look at her. His body sagged.

Tears trickled down his cheeks. Snowflakes were catching in his hair. His skin turned sapphire under the cold artificial light.

"I can't help you," he said.

"It isn't your fault, Max." Opal patted his arm.

"Something's here with me. It's making me do these things."

The dog, sensing her owner's distress, came to him. Max gathered her into his arms and she licked his grizzled chin. Opal leaned into the front seat, grabbed the bag of chalk off the dashboard, and dropped it into Max's lap. Before pulling back she kissed him lightly on the cheek. She opened her door.

He pointed at the lodge. "There are two of them."

"Two?"

"You only need to worry about the dead man. He's lost in dreams. If he sees what awaits him, you have a chance. Make him see it. Send him to hell."

"What does he mean?" Adam asked.

Opal shook her head.

Vera joined them outside the camper.

The men hadn't moved. Snow padded their shoulders.

The Totem Lodge. It was like standing at the mouth of a cave. The front doors were missing. Removed. Vera saw the bare hinges; the doors were stacked one on top of another, discarded in the bushes. Torches smoked along the walls. Patterns of dark and light alternated down an endless hallway.

Vera froze in her tracks.

"I can't do it," she said. She passed the satchel strap over her head and offered it to Adam. "Here, you take it."

"No."

"Give it to me," Opal said.

"Mom, listen, okay? Let's just leave it by the door."

"That won't work. I'll take it to them."

"Dad wouldn't let you do that, and I won't, either." He blocked her path.

"Adam, you mean more to me than anyone in the world. I'm

asking you to step aside. Not because you want to, or because you think it's a good idea. Do it because I asked you." Opal held out her hand to Vera.

Vera passed the satchel to her.

Opal slid the strap around her wrist and tucked the satchel under her arm.

Adam stepped up to protest.

His mother hugged him. "I love you," Opal said.

"I love you, too."

She pushed him back and motioned to the men guarding the lodge.

A half-dozen of them advanced on Adam and Vera. Vera tried to call out, but a cold damp glove muffled her scream. They surrounded Adam, four against one. He dropped an attacker with a right hook. They wrestled him to the pavement. "Don't go in there!" he shouted.

They tore a roll of duct tape. Slapped a gag over his lips.

Vera bit the man who tried gagging her.

The men bound their wrists and ankles. The last thing Vera saw: Adam's wide eyes as they stuffed his head into a leather sack. Cinched it tight with a cord. Her hood was next. She stopped fighting. Her head inside the bag: It smelled like a shoe. She couldn't see anything. They picked her up, by the sounds of effort they were taking Adam, too, carrying them through deep, soft drifts to the back of the lodge. Everything was over in less than a minute.

Opal didn't watch the struggle. She might've quit if she did. And quitting wasn't an option. She took the LED flashlight from her pocket. It had worked at the apartment, throwing a bright purple-white beam on the wall. Now nothing happened when she clicked the button. She shook the batteries. Tried again. Same result. Dead. She cursed and hurled it into the lot. Opal walked past the torches, disappearing deeper and deeper into the hallway, alone in the darkness.

Knowing she would not be alone for long.

Inside the camper, Max crawled in shadows on the floor. He kicked debris away, clearing a space, putting himself at the center. He sat curled up with his knees to his chest. He took a stick of chalk from the bag.

He started to draw a circle.

CHAPTER 57

Scents of pine and citronella oil swirled in the drafty hallway. Opal peered into empty guest rooms as she walked by. A maintenance supply closest. The humid soapy aroma of the laundry facilities. All the doors were missing. The Pitch had been busy inside the Totem Lodge. Hinge pins lay scattered on the floor.

Why would they take down the doors?

A gust of wind nudged Opal along.

She came to the hallway's end. The wings of the Totem lodge split.

Left or right?

To the right was total blackness.

Left were more torches, terminating in a bright wash of electric light coming from the last room.

Left, then.

She turned and kept walking. Her boots thumped on the carpet. She shifted the satchel higher up her shoulder, tightened her grip on the strap. She didn't want anyone popping out of a doorway on either side of her and snatching away the stone. She stopped peering into the rooms. They were too dark. Her mind played tricks on her. She saw heavier shadows shifting in the black voids. Red lines flickered and disappeared. They were like the streaks she saw on the inside of her eyelids when she closed them on a sunny day. Her heart pounded. She forced herself to take deep breaths. Despite the cold, she was sweating.

Taking the doors off didn't make the Pitch any safer. It was just the opposite; if they were preparing to make the lodge their stronghold, they'd want to keep the doors closed and locked, just as she, Wyatt, and the kids had done back at the Rendezvous. But the Pitch weren't worried about defending themselves from attack. Not tonight they weren't. They didn't need doors to protect them from outside threats. So why take them down?

She clamped her arm on the satchel.

A stony point jabbed her ribs.

The stone.

It had something to do with the stone.

Max said they believed the stone was a compass pointing to hell.

If the Pitch weren't worried about keeping people out, maybe what they wanted was to let something in.

The final torch shed an orange pool on the carpet.

She waded through.

Grazing her fingertips along the log wall as she went, she noticed rough marks engraved into the wood. The logs were cold, their touch like cemetery stone. The carved lines felt warmer, as if they pulsed with some feeble yet undeniable circulatory life. She inspected them more closely. Spirals and slashes—a pictography of amoebic creature shapes. A number of the wood cuttings displayed greater detail. High and low, the walls resembled an alien fossil bed—mollusks, trilobites, sea spiders, cone-headed squids, and worm casts. With her thumb Opal traced the outline of a two-headed fish, its body an arrowhead of bones, the gaping mouths prickled with spiny, needlelike teeth. She glanced backward down the hallway. The strange carvings were everywhere.

How had she missed seeing them?

She drew her hand back.

Her ears were filling with a watery silence. She experienced a plunging moment of panic, imagining herself to be the last woman on earth. Wyatt was dead. She was absolutely alone. Exposed to anything lurking in the hushed dark.

"She's here."

The sand-choked, slithery voice—she recognized it immediately as belonging to the man from her visions. The rotted face from her television.

Whiteside.

She should have been terrified.

But a muscular slowness invaded her body, and at the same time, a relaxing detachment overtook her mind. She wandered forward, drugged by the occult strangeness surrounding her, drunk perhaps on too much fear; yet there was more to it. She lost any sense of control over her body, mind, and emotions. She felt untethered. A pleasant gush of euphoria pumped into her veins.

She entered the room.

Unable to specify what she expected to find, she could at least say this was not it. The bright electric lights were precisely that: Battery-powered lanterns of various sizes and models lined the interior perimeter of the lodge suite. Tables and dressers supported more. An insectile humming vibrated the air.

In the center of the room were two beds elevated on cinder blocks.

Their height and flatness reminded Opal of altars.

Hospital monitors crowded the bedsides. One bed was empty, a mess of twisted sheets and a cheap foam pillow.

Whiteside occupied the other bed.

She recognized him instantly.

How she knew it was Whiteside was harder to explain.

Because he did not appear now as he did in her visions. For one, his bandages were intact; although they were soiled, stained rusty yellow around the edges, and in obvious need of changing. The body cocooned inside the bandages barely made a swell under the sheets. Wasted, atrophied, inert. She could not fathom how this dying man could rise, speak, and threaten her in the vilest terms. His fragile head looked like a white wasp's nest. Oxygen tubes were taped to the tip of his nose. He slept soundlessly. Only the scrolling, jagged, lime-green peaks on the heart monitor gave any evidence he was alive.

The scrape of leather on carpet . . .

The silence drained away. Opal turned to see a man standing inside the doorway, his back aligned straight against the wall. He said nothing. His eyes staring ahead like a military sentry.

He was the nurse from her vision inside the trailer.

She saw the German pistol holstered under his arm.

Nurse and *bodyguard*.

She did not appreciate the danger. Still curiosity piqued her. An eagerness to witness a predestined event. But mostly she felt enveloped, wrapped in cotton, cushioned from the reality of her situation, comfortably numbed.

In the background, from around the corner of a half wall, came the rushing sound of water falling into a sink bowl.

A third man emerged.

He did not seem surprised to find her there.

"Pinroth, get the lady a chair."

He wore black lenses. His eyes were a secret. He had been there in the trailer, too—the man she thought of as a patient. He had his shirtsleeves rolled up. More doctor than patient. He smiled at her.

"You've brought the artifact."

"I . . ."

The bodyguard, Pinroth, placed a chair behind her. She sat.

"Excellent," said the doctor with the secret eyes. His lenses reflected the lanterns, changing from black to glaring white. "We should get started."

CHAPTER 58

Filthy roaches.

The Pitch mob poured into the Totem.

Max watched from his chalk circle. He drew white beetles marching on every surface he could reach without vacating his protections. He remembered all he had done. The details of his betrayal came back starkly. He thought if they did not butcher him before the dawn, then he would kill himself. Tilt the Ruger up under his chin, pull the trigger without thinking twice, and see what the next world would bring. Though he suspected the next world might be worse, or his place in it severely degraded. He'd never been one to indulge self-pity. Tonight was different. He didn't have any strength left. He was small, weak, scuttling.

Maybe I'm a roach, too.

A face appeared at the cracked camper window.

Red, woolen. A mask.

"Leave me alone!" Max shouted.

Knuckles rapped on the glass.

Max turned to his harasser. Or was it his soon-to-be killer?

Red ski mask. A baseball bat-cum-mace balanced on the knuckle rapper's shoulder. The nail points jammed up with gore. Long raincoat. He looked at the mask again. Only one of the eye sockets had an eye in it.

"Wyatt?"

The mask nodded.

"Where is my family?"

Max narrowed his eyes. He crawled out of the circle. He opened the camper to a charred smelling wind. He touched the raincoat to make certain it was real, that the man wearing it was no figment of his imagination. The red mask appeared full in Max's face.

"Where's Opal? Where's Adam?"

Max said, "They've taken them inside. Vera, too. He'll kill them all."

Wyatt's lone gray eye closed.

When it opened again, it looked into the lodge.

Max raised his chalk and began drawing on the raincoat. "This may help you pass through the crowd unnoticed. But I can't be confident . . ."

A hand grabbed his wrist.

"Opal has the stone?"

"She does," Max said. "Tell your wife to let him have it."

"What?"

"He'll influence her. Cloud her mind. You need to help her. Scream if you have to. She must act swiftly."

Wyatt let go of his wrist. The long coat snapped behind him as he vanished into the Totem Lodge.

Max rested his hand on the window to keep from toppling over into a snow bank. His fingers were sticky. He had touched Wyatt on the back while he marked up the raincoat. Now the glass showed a handprint.

In blood.

CHAPTER 59

The man with the secret eyes hoisted an old-fashioned doctor's bag onto the empty bed. Flap of leather sliding though brass buckles. He began removing instruments, holding them up for a brief examination before dropping them noisily into a metal pan.

Scalpel.

Scissors.

Clamps. Miniature steel hammer. A hacksaw.

"This invalid is my father." He aimed the saw. "We share a name and a mission. I take it Max explained the significance of the artifact to you?"

The saw clattered into the pan.

Opal blinked. "He said it was a kind of compass."

Other less recognizable tools: clacking mineral orbs resembling eggs; a cruciform latticework of peeled sticks; a gold wire star; and a wicker doll bound together with what looked like three colors of human hair.

Horus shook his head.

He placed the cruciform, inverted, on his father's pillow; secured the golden star to his forehead of soiled bandages.

Primitive knives badly corroded with age; tongs with fanglike arms; a long polished bone grooved along each side and barbed like a harpoon; an iron twisted at one end into a pupil-less eye.

Horus unpacked a pair of thick liver-brown rubber gloves.

He put them on.

"The Tartarus Stone, also known as Romero's Onyx or the Damnation Stone, is *not* a compass. It is the seat of Hell. Prophecy dictates our present options. We cannot take the stone but it must be given to us freely by an innocent who does not believe in its powers. This we accept to be true. So, I must ask you. Do you believe you hold Hell in your lap?"

Opal considered the question carefully before answering.

"I don't know," she said finally.

"Doubt is all I need from you. Let's proceed. My father is going to die before sunrise. Will you give the stone to him?"

The body on the bed did not smell clean. Opal thought she heard the rustle of cloth. Then a sound like paper catching fire. The sheets remained still. She didn't know where the sounds were coming from.

Horus repeated the question.

"Will you give the stone to him?"

"I want something in return."

"You aren't entitled to any requests."

Opal removed the stone from the satchel. Like two pyramids glued bottom to bottom, an octahedron, Max had called it.

"Let my son go free, and I'll give you the stone."

Horus nodded, smiled.

"Pinroth, bring me the boy."

Opal could feel the heat of their sweating bodies as they neared; their breathing was like one beast, filling and emptying itself of air. The four men were bearing a hooded, hog-tied, and horizontal Adam. They brought him in headfirst, as if they might, at their whim, ram him into a wall just to see what was inside his skull.

They stood him up. Sat him forcibly down in a chair.

One of his captors cut the cinched cord around his throat. They tore the bag off. The lights were such a harsh change Adam was temporarily blinded.

His eyelids fluttered.

Horus sorted through a metal pan. He turned around. Opal was shocked to see the long-handled tongs in his enormous gloves. She felt a scream building in her lungs, but before it could escape, a hand covered her mouth.

Adam couldn't see his mother because the men held him.

He pleaded, "No, wait, wait . . ."

But Horus did not wait.

Expressionless and determined, he ripped aside Adam's jacket then his shirt, exposing his bare chest. Without hesitation he closed the pincers on Adam's left nipple. Blood spurted like flames. Adam was the one screaming now; no one quieted him. Opal saw the pincers rock side to side, stripping away pink meat in their claws. She was sick. Acid dribbled down her chin. The world shrunk to a fuzzy gray tube. Through the tube she watched Horus drop the tongs heavily on the bed. She felt her heart beating in time with the blood leaking from her son's cut flesh.

She cried out as the smothering hand came away.

"Stop it!"

"Give my father the stone," Horus said.

She was sobbing.

Horus picked up the tongs again.

CHAPTER 60

"Don't hurt him any more."

Opal rose from the chair. Color drained from her skin. Her legs were trembling. She held the stone in two hands. The satchel slipped from her lap. She kicked it away. She took small steps, as if anchors weighed down her feet.

One step closer.

Then another.

Vera knelt on the floor. They'd brought her in the room, too, threw her to the carpet, and snatched the bag off her head.

She saw what Horus did to Adam.

The pitter-patter of blood dripping into a wet patch under his chair.

She knew they were all going to die.

The man guarding her began searching through her pockets. He patted her down, paused, and slipped the Bobcat from her jeans.

He showed the handgun to Horus.

"I found this on the girl."

"Really, Pinroth, what's next?"

Horus smirked in her direction, a hint of admiration on his lips. He took the Bobcat in his glove and stepped closer. He pointed it at her head.

Vera shut her eyes. She waited for the explosion. Would she hear it?

Or would her world go blank?

"Don't," Opal said. "I'm doing what you asked."

Horus caressed Vera's cheek with the barrel.

The icy scratching metal went away.

Vera looked.

He tucked the Bobcat into his belt.

"Fair enough," he said.

Men crowded the doorway. Bloodlust excreted in the air. *It's about the killing,* she thought. Better than sex. Brute power. Extremity explored. About doing whatever they desired without consequence. She thought of the witches slaughtered back at the greystone in Chicago. That's how this ends. Her fear pushed through to a deeper level. Paralyzed her. She wanted it over. Let it be quick. *It won't be.* Not a gunshot to the head. They were saving her for something worse, something she couldn't imagine. They'd make her pain last.

One man in the doorway inched closer.

He wore a red ski mask.

Watching Opal.

His fists clenched. Leaning forward on the balls of his feet.

He can't wait for it to start.

Adam slumped forward.

He'd fainted, or maybe he couldn't watch.

Vera had to watch. Her eyelids felt stapled open.

Opal approached the bedside.

There was a person in the bed, swathed in bandages. Crossed sticks shared the pillow with an oblong mummy head. A gilded wire ornament contorted above his eyes, the place where the eyes should have been; because Vera didn't see eyes, or even slits for them. Opal was talking to herself in a low voice. Or was she talking to the body in the bed? The body remained still. Vera wondered, for a moment, if they had dug it up from underground. Dirt, fungus, and clayey moisture—their commingled incense soured the room. Invisible fires burned with invisible smoke. A decayed moldy finger burrowed down her throat. Her stomach convulsed in protest. It wasn't the earthy perfume of pulled roots, not the sulfurous taste of water, either, that filled her nose and mouth and made her feel as if she were drowning in soil. But a cloying sweetness insisted something was both burning and drowning. The sweetness spelled Death.

The thing in the bed was dead.

The monitors said it was alive.

Opal raised the stone up in her hands.

She had the same look as she did in the apartment above the Rendezvous, when she fell into her trance. That sleepwalking fixed stare.

The monitor alarms sounded.

Vera looked at the array of screens. Numbers falling. The jagged scrolls dissolving into a uniform smoothness.

"He's flatlining," Horus said in total disbelief.

A growl gurgled in his throat. His rage wasn't directed at Opal. He yanked the Bobcat from his belt.

"Fucker! You promised me. Lies! Do you hear me? Keep your promise, or I will stop this myself. We'll both have nothing."

Pinroth grabbed Vera's shoulder. He shoved her down flat.

Opal raised the stone high over her head.

Horus aimed at Opal. "Stop."

His gaze flicked to the monitors.

The alarms buzzed.

Straight lines filled the screens.

"You will not abandon me," Horus said.

He pulled the trigger.

The bullet smacked harmlessly into the wall. Point-blank range. How could he have missed? Horus stared at his hand. Vera did, too. He only had two fingers left. He tried to squeeze them. The gun dangled, dropped. The useless muscles twitched. Blood poured its dark syrup from the ruined stump of his palm. He'd given so much of his blood to the old man over the years.

The boom of the gunshot echoed in Vera's ears.

Pinroth shot Horus a second time.

Horus staggered into the monitors. He'd kill the bitch with one hand if he had to.

Pinroth fired again.

Again and again. So many gunshots. Vera tried covering her ears. The shots came in such rapid succession she couldn't count them. Exploding from behind her—the multiplying shots overlapped. Horus Whiteside Jr.'s body twitched in a mad dance. Red blooms covered his chest. Blood sprayed the wall.

The man in the red ski mask.

He was shooting Horus, too.

He and Pinroth were both assassins.

The gunfire ceased. Noise of the blasts reverberated. A dying Horus stared with hatred at his father. He crumpled to his knees, smearing the bedclothes with his blood; yet he clung to the bed frame and attempted to rise once more to his feet, concentrating, squeezing his eyes tight. His skin crimsoned, and the veins in his neck stood out thick as worms. He failed. His body slumped against the wall between the monitor carts. His legs jerked spasmodically, then not at all.

The thing in the bed shifted.

Its shell of bandages cracked open and a face emerged.

Vera witnessed it with both horror and fascination.

A human face.

Fully fleshed.

The profile of a pharaoh, olive-skinned and regal, with eyes of pure ebony.

CHAPTER 61

Wyatt wouldn't be able to recall the sequence of events following the killing of the son of Horus Whiteside. They obeyed nightmare logic, causing him to question his sanity in the moment. Stress. Blood loss. Desperation. Any of these could have been responsible for his brain's aborted attempt to sort and understand the unexplainable. He knew this much: The ambulance driver and bodyguard, Pinroth, pivoted toward him. Little more than an arm's length away, his impassive face altered with astonishment. He started to swing the Luger pistol up at Wyatt. There would be time for one shot. One bullet exchanged between two men. Vera sprawled underneath Pinroth. Bound but not helpless, she kicked his knees. Her assault wasn't enough to bring the large man down. Their legs entangled and he lurched backward—his gun hand flying out for balance.

Wyatt had a double advantage. He wanted to save his family more than anything on earth. And he had a better angle of fire.

He shot first.

Pinroth clasped his hands over the fountaining wound in his throat. The impassive stare slid back into place. He let his arms fall to his sides. His puppet strings were cut; he collapsed on a flailing Vera who screamed and screamed as his blood-soaked, dead weight pinned her.

Opal ignored the chaos.

Sweat beaded on her cheeks, plastered her hair wildly to her face.

If she doesn't move, I can take him out.

Wyatt pointed the Glock.

The trigger clicked.

Empty.

What he saw then couldn't have happened. He would never speak of it. Never admit what he had witnessed. Under the blankets, limbs bent. Too many limbs were stretching out, blindly testing their too many joints. Stiff pale hairs punctured through the sheets. Whiteside's bony chest lifted. Inflating and deflating. His bandaged head reshaped, bulged. Gauze ripped. But it wasn't a human face emerging. Horned spidery mouthparts chewed away the bandages.

Wyatt tore off his ski mask.

The Pitch stayed back. Frozen in awe.

Their god was being born.

Wyatt remembered what Max told him outside.

"Let him have it!" he shouted.

Opal looked at him.

With all her strength she drove the stone into Whiteside's head.

It was her husband who dragged her away from the pile of filthy bandages. She released the stone. Her fingers sticking together. The spike of the stone nestled in what remained of a ruined skull.

"Don't look," he said.

And she could see him averting his gaze, his bleary eye searching the empty doorway. The Pitch fled. Their running footsteps rumbled in the hall.

The lodge suite revolved around her. Lanterns spun.

Wyatt groaned when she hugged him tighter.

She couldn't tell which one of them needed support more. Together they limped over to their son. Adam sighed raggedly and lifted his head. Opal brushed his cheek. His skin had paled to a milky blue, clammy and cool as if he had just surfaced after a long swim in the sea. A thick glistening clot of blood filled the gash across his chest. He hovered between states of consciousness.

But he was breathing.

"He needs a doctor. You all do." Max was there with them. Cutting the bindings around Adam's feet and wrists. He helped Vera to stand; freed her so she could assist him in walking the other three out of the Totem Lodge.

"Get them into the ambulance," Max said.

He went back inside the lodge.

Here and there, through the flickering snow, the slowest followers of Horus Whiteside scattered. The fastest were already blending into the blue twilight of dawn. They wouldn't get far.

In the middle distance, rifles boomed. Hunters preferred first light.

Vera pulled the ambulance doors shut.

Max climbed into the driver's seat. Stuffing something into the hollow under the dashboard. He had his dog at his side. He started the motor.

"Hold tight," he said.

He found the clinic with Opal's directions. The windows were dark. No electricity. Unlit strands of holiday lights trimmed the roof edge. Tinsel fluttered. A plastic tree darkened a corner. But people were milling in the waiting room. Victims of the night's attack. A doctor. Nurses.

She heard Max talking with them. He pointed at the ambulance.

"They're in shock," he said.

Familiar faces appeared, framed in the ambulance windows. Gentle hands led them to the exam offices. Opal pushed Adam in a foldable wheelchair.

Max tapped her shoulder.

"Please take care of Annie. I tied her leash to a fence near the entrance."

She asked where he was going.

He was out through the doors.

He didn't hear her question, or he'd chosen not to answer.

She saw the ambulance leaving the clinic lot.

Max ditched the ambulance in front of a pizza parlor. He left his Ruger under the driver's seat and locked the doors. He drew the zipper on his parka tight under his chin, and covered his head with the hood. He walked three blocks, following tire ruts in the highway. Splats of snow obscured the sign posted on his right. He already knew what it said. He crossed the border on foot. His steps rang out on the steel bridge. The powerful spotlights transformed the landscape into a bed of embers. Molten river waters flowed under him. At the guard station, he was terse. They were watching him. Their scrutiny made his skin itch. He slid them his passport. "I'm taking a vacation," he said. "Visiting friends to ring in the New Year." No tobacco. No liquor. No firearms.

"When will you be returning?"

"One week," he lied.

A guard scooted back his office chair. He approached the inspection window. He was fat, fifty, mustached.

"What's going on over there?"

He didn't need to ask where. American Rapids was burning in the semidarkness two miles out. Max's parka carried a patina of soot.

"I was only passing through," he said.

"You must've seen something."

"A gas station blew up. I think a truck hit the pumps."

The guard nodded. He handed back his documents.

"Enjoy your trip."

"Which way is the bus station?"

The guard pointed to a streetlight.

"Turn there. You'll see the building on your left."

Max thanked him. He didn't feel safe until he bought his

ticket, climbed aboard the idling bus, and sank into his seat. A handful of other passengers. No one looked up as he went down the aisle.

Nobody asked about the satchel slung over Max's shoulder.

Nobody asked to see what was inside.

When the appointed time came, the driver took the wheel, closed the doors, and drove off. The coach cabin was warm. To the riders sealed within, the only detectable sounds were the hum of the engine, whirring tires, and the timed thump of the wipers as they cleared away a little snow. The sunlit air glittered.

Arms around the satchel, Max was already asleep.

CHAPTER 62

In late July, the northern border of Minnesota cooked under a heat wave for twenty-one days straight. Daytime highs flirted with triple digits. Nights were muggy, and even the mosquitoes, which were plentiful, seemed lethargic, having grown obese on the blood of slow-moving people whose relief-seeking efforts ended disappointingly around lukewarm backyard pools, sun-baked patios, or lawns that crackled like needles when you walked across them barefoot. On the twenty-second day, things changed. A cold front dipped its big blue toe down from Canada and churned up the skies with thunderstorms. Squadrons of anvil clouds shot forked lightning from their underbellies, dropped buckets of rain, hailstones, and at their southernmost edge—the counterclockwise rotating vortex of a tornado.

Adam sat in the doorway and watched the heart of the afternoon go dark, as if a bowl flipped over—*bam!*—trapping everything in sight. The wind carried the mineral smell of coming rain. It tested the repaired screens of the cabin and slapped a loose piece of paper off the table. Adam retrieved the paper and pulled his camp chair a little closer to the open door; he kicked it a few inches wider, the better to see the storm. He wiped ice chips off a can of Pepsi he'd taken from a red Coleman cooler, popped the tab, and took a long satisfyingly oversweet sip.

He never wanted this summer to end.

After the Pitch had laid siege to his town, burned down his family's motel, and nearly killed every person he loved in this world, he decided to take a semester off. He had a month left until his break was over. He'd be back in school. Life would return, pretty much, to normal. It was about time to take another shot at being a college student, and he was determined to be a decent one this time.

He booted up his laptop.

It hadn't exactly been a long lazy vacation.

After his parents collected the insurance money from the Rendezvous fire, they agreed not to rebuild and instead put the highway lot up for sale. The future demanded a new setting. They did not have to go far. Lakefront property on stained river-fed water interrupted by a cluster of uninhabitable rock islands: Along the western shore ran a string of cabins badly in need of refurbishing and an old bait shop complete with its miniature armada of sun-faded Lund fishing boats and 40 HP Mercury outboards. Now that his wounds had healed, his father had enough work to keep him busy for a decade. Or two.

Kalypso Kottages.

Adam could see the signpost if he leaned forward far enough.

There it was . . . right off the gravel road, stuck on a hilltop above a staggered arrangement of knotty-pine A-frame chalets with spinach green roofs. What any of it had to do with "Kalypso" he couldn't figure. He heard the whine of a circular saw and guessed his dad was in cabin number 4, fixing the ladder that led up to the sleeping loft.

Adam had other plans for the weekend.

He smelled coconuts.

She was so quiet climbing down from above.

Vera bent over, her hair falling in his eyes, as she kissed his neck. He felt the sunny touch of tight bronze skin. Her warm, wet lips. Coconuts and limes.

"Nice nap?" he asked.

"Wonderful. I could get used to this weekends off thing. I've got so many splinters, my blisters are feeling jealous."

"Where else can you work on your tan, spend day and night with your new boyfriend, and get paid?"

"A hard-labor prison camp?"

"Ha ha."

Vera hopped her bottom up on the table. She was wearing a bikini, unbuttoned denim cut-offs, flip-flops. She noticed the piece of paper next to Adam's laptop. She picked it up. It was a postcard. She'd seen it before. Max sent it to them from Death Valley a couple of weeks ago. She'd read the thing so many times she knew it by heart:

> *Max, here. I can't wait to see you guys. I have something to tell you, and I think it will put your minds at ease. At least, that's what I'm hoping. Tell Annie her daddy's coming to get her!*
> —M

There was a date for the visit scribbled underneath.

Today's date.

"Think he'll show?"

Adam shrugged.

Vera flipped the postcard over. The photo might've come from another planet. No extra moons on the horizon; it was enameled blue, not a cloud in the sky, but the ground was covered with what looked like dirty icicles growing upward. The fine print said the place was called the Devil's Golf Course. It was a salt pan. The icicles were crystals. Vera thought it was creepy. Why would anybody go there? It looked like where people got lost and died of thirst.

"He knows where we are," Adam said. "My parents put the info about the cabins up at the Rendezvous Web site. It says we won't reopen until the fall. But Max can find us if he needs to."

At the mention of her owner's name, Annie began to thump her tail against the floor under the table. Vera twitched off a flip-flop and ran her foot through Annie's thick silky coat. "He'll come back for her," Vera said. "She's all he's got."

"He has the stone."

"I thought you didn't want to talk about that."

"My mother hasn't had a vision since Max took it. She's happy. My dad's happy. I'm . . . we're happy. I don't want to risk that."

"Max isn't a bad guy," she said.

"But he attracts them."

"Maybe he's figured out a way to neutralize the . . . artifact. Maybe that's what he wants to tell us. So we don't have to worry."

"I notice you didn't say *destroy* it." Adam tapped keys. He checked his e-mail, and then he checked the in-box of the Rendezvous Motel.

One new message.

With an attachment.

From Max.

The e-mail was blank. The attachment was the message. Max sent a video clip. It took forever to load, and the virus and spyware scans took even longer. When it started to play, the resolution was poor. Max was sitting at his computer in the back of a new camper. He looked . . . healthy. He was eating a tuna salad sandwich and beaming into his Webcam.

"Hey guys, I sure miss my old Westy, but I put satellite Internet in the Winnebago! All I need is Annie and I'm ready to hit the road again. (He looked at his watch.) I'm about two hours from American Rapids. The sky's turned to shit and I was hungry, so I stopped for a bite to eat and a bottle of Dew. I'm working on a book, you know? It's kind of a dream log. Dark fantasy, of course. (Laughter.) First novel I've written in twenty-five years. Let's hope I haven't forgotten how to do it. I know you were probably pissed at me for taking off like I did when you were at the clinic.

I had no choice. That's how it felt to me at the time, and that's how it feels now. I hope you understand. I want you to know I'm in control. My body . . . inside . . . I feel like a kid again. The pain disappeared overnight. I don't need a doctor to tell me the cancer's gone. And I don't think you kids need to ask why, either. That satchel hasn't left my side since Christmas. We got it wrong before. Our perspective was prejudiced. (His hand moved as if he were erasing a chalkboard.) *It's a miracle, really. What I learned is that Whiteside was the problem, not the Stone. Well, I'll explain it all to you in a couple hours. Annie better get her kisses ready.* (The sound of rain drummed on the RV.) *See you soon . . . if I don't drown first."*

The clip ended.

Midnight. Max hadn't shown. They received no more messages. No calls. Adam and Vera decided to go out looking for him. First, they watched the video again.

"Definitely looks like he's at a rest stop," Vera said.

Adam found the Mn/DOT Web site, clicked on a map of the state's rest areas and waysides. "If he really was two hours away, then he was here." He pointed to the screen.

"Okay, we drive there and see if he broke down, or something."

"Right," Adam said. *"Or something."*

"What if we see—"

He touched her. "We call the cops and leave."

They drove in his pickup. They didn't tell Opal or Wyatt where they were going. Annie sat between them, staring through the windshield. The rain had stopped, but the highway glistened. Trickles of water branched out over the glass. Adam drove fast. He didn't expect to find Max pulled over on the shoulder with a flat tire or bad hose. He expected much worse.

They didn't talk.

They didn't play the radio.

Ninety minutes.

"There's the rest stop," Vera said. She pointed to a wash of brightness across the highway. Adam took the next exit ramp. He reentered the highway traveling in the opposite direction. He pulled off at the rest area, followed the sign for CARS, and saw nothing. The place was deserted. Light poles shined down on the wet walkways, grass, trash barrels, and an empty parking lot.

"We'll go around the back," Adam said.

He reversed to the sign, this time going in the direction of the sign that read TRUCKS.

In the second to the last extended parking spot . . .

"Oh my god," Vera said.

A Winnebago.

It was the only vehicle other than theirs.

Adam pulled up behind it.

He saw the satellite dish on the rooftop. "That's got to be him."

The RV's interior lights were on. The front seats were unoccupied. They didn't see anybody, or any movement, through the rear or side windows.

"I don't like this," Vera said.

Adam popped his door.

Annie whimpered.

Vera said, "I thought we were going to call the cops?"

"We will."

"When?"

"When we have something to tell them."

He slid out of his seat.

Vera climbed behind the wheel. She handed him the dog's leash. Before she let go she said, "One quick look and you come back."

"One quick look," he said.

Adam walked up to the passenger door. He peered in. Tried the handle.

It was unlocked.

He opened it.

The interior smelled like leather upholstery and new carpets. He pressed a button on the door control panel. The side doors to the coach slid open.

To Adam's left and coming closer, Vera said, "There's his computer."

She couldn't stay in the pickup.

Adam wasn't about to argue with her.

He stepped into the Winnebago. "And here's his sandwich."

Half-eaten.

Set down between bites?

"Let's look for it," Vera said.

For ten minutes they did.

Found nothing.

No stone.

No Max.

Adam sat in one of the coach's leather swivel seats.

"He said it hasn't left his side since Christmas."

Vera turned in the other seat until their knees made contact. Anything.

"So?"

"So if somebody knew that . . . and they lured him . . ."

Adam scanned the parking lot. Black trees shaking in the wind. Wet grass. Rainbow puddles on the asphalt. There at the edge of the lot, where the wooded nature preserve buzzed with insects: a bottle.

He went for it.

Annie sniffed the ground.

It was a Mountain Dew, Code Red.

Ann-Margret stopped and lifted her head in the moonlight to make the saddest sound Adam had ever heard.

"What is it?" Vera yelled.

"Nothing," he said. "Go back."

It's nothing. No one.

The darkness.